"Thanks for the carnation. It's pretty."

"You're welcome," Jamie says with that slight smile that makes the back of my neck tingle with warmth.

I don't want to be *just friends* with Jamie Forta.

What would happen if I leaned over and kissed him? Do I have it in me to do that? Would he stop me?

I suddenly hear myself breathing too hard and too loud. I start to feel stupid, dumb, needy. Fifteen minutes ago, Jamie Forta said we were just friends, and so what do I do? Fantasize about kissing him. It's crazy. This whole thing is crazy.

**Books by Louise Rozett
from Harlequin TEEN**

CONFESSIONS OF AN ANGRY GIRL
and coming in 2013
CONFESSIONS OF AN ALMOST-GIRLFRIEND

LOUISE ROZETT

confessions of an

ANGRY
GIRL

HARLEQUIN®
entertain, enrich, inspire™

Recycling programs for this product may not exist in your area.

ISBN-13: 978-0-373-21048-0

CONFESSIONS OF AN ANGRY GIRL

Copyright © 2012 by Louise Rozett

This edition published by arrangement with Harlequin Books S.A.

For questions and comments about the quality of this book, please contact us at CustomerService@Harlequin.com.

® and TM are trademarks of Harlequin Enterprises Limited or its corporate affiliates. Trademarks indicated with ® are registered in the United States Patent and Trademark Office, the Canadian Trade Marks Office and in other countries.

www.HarlequinTEEN.com

Printed in U.S.A.

For Alex Bhattacharji,
who helps me—in so many ways—to do the work I love

PROLOGUE

THIS, DEAR READER, IS A TALE OF THE HELL OF HIGH
school. Of being dropped into a world where it seems like
everyone is speaking a foreign language. Where friends become enemies and enemies become nightmares. Where life
suddenly seems like a string of worst-case scenarios from
health-class movies.

This is a story about a girl with a stellar vocabulary who is
four years away from college and a year and a half away from
a driver's license. About a girl trapped in a hostile universe
where the virginity clock is ticking down—relentlessly—
with zero consideration for her extenuating, traumatic, life-
altering circumstances.

This is a story about death. About the occasional panic attack, the inability to shut up and high school in the suburbs
without a cell phone.

Read it and weep.

FALL

plummet (*verb*): to fall suddenly, sharply, steeply
(*see also:* to start high school)

———

1

"JAMIE. YOU GONNA EAT THAT? JAME. THAT BAGEL. YOU gonna eat it? 'Cause I'm really hungry, man. My mom threw me out before I could eat my cereal. And she didn't give me a dime."

Jamie slides the half bagel dripping with butter over to Angelo without looking up from drawing on the back of his notebook. Angelo is silent for thirty seconds, and then he's on the make again, looking for someone else's leftovers. The PA system screeches with feedback, and the din gets louder as everyone tries to talk over it.

"Good morning, Union High. Please rise for the Pledge of Allegiance." The brightly colored riot-proof seats welded to the cafeteria tables left over from the 1970s creak as period-one study hall drags itself to its feet to say words that we haven't thought about and don't understand—or can't make ourselves say. Jamie stays seated, his pencil slowly tracing the lines of his drawing.

"Forta, is that your assigned seat?" Jamie nods at Mr. Cella, the gym teacher who would probably rather be anywhere other than chaperoning first-period study hall. "Then get out of it and join the rest of us in pledging allegiance to this fine country of ours," Mr. Cella says kind of sarcastically as he moves on to the next table.

Jamie looks around and sees that people are in the middle of the pledge. By the time he stands up, everyone is sitting down already.

"Jame, you got any money? I'm still starvin', man. I just need another bagel or a piece of toast or something. I'll pay you back tomorrow. I just need, like, a dollar. You got that? Could I have it?"

Jamie reaches into his pockets for change, coming up with a quarter. He hands it to Angelo, who looks majorly disappointed.

"This all you got, Jame?"

"Here. Here's seventy-five cents." The slightly sweaty freshman girl in the blue cotton sweater at the end of the table, also known as me, reaches out three quarters, glad to have made it through another pledge to the flag without throwing up. I don't exactly feel like swearing my allegiance to America these days, and I probably won't for a long time, if ever.

Angelo looks at the quarters suspiciously. Maybe he's unsure why I'm suddenly talking to him after not speaking for the first three days of school. He probably thinks I'm a snob, but I'm really just afraid to look up from my books. I just survived the worst summer of my life, and I don't remember how to talk to people. Plus, I just started high school—this guy has probably been here for more than his share of four years.

The PA system squawks, "Have a good day," before shutting off. Angelo takes the quarters from me slowly.

"Thanks. Do I gotta pay you back?"

"Um, not if you…can't."

Angelo stares hard, keeping his eyes on me as he swaggers backward over to the pile of bagels on the counter. He picks one and then smiles at me. I quickly look back down at my books, thinking I might have made a mistake, being nice to one of the vocational-technical guys. Especially one of the older "vo-tech" guys. He pays and makes his way back to the half-empty table for six, sitting across from Jamie. His jacket is too small for him, and he wears a ratty Nirvana T-shirt that looks like it belonged to an older brother when Kurt Cobain was actually still alive.

"Good bagel," Angelo says to me, while I pretend to be lost in my biology textbook. "What are you reading?"

"I'm studying for a biology test," I say without looking up.

"You already got a test?" he asks. "We only been back a few days. You in those smart classes?"

I decide not to answer this time, but it doesn't do any good.

"Didn't you study at home? You look like a girl who woulda studied at home."

"I did. But I don't think it was enough."

"Want me to quiz you? I could quiz you."

"No, thanks."

Angelo slides over so he's sitting right next to me. He leans in. "I bet it would help," he says. I shift back slightly. He's got a ton of sharp black stubble, and he smells like cigarettes and Axe. He looks like he's at least twenty.

"That's okay."

"You sure?" He reaches for my textbook. "I know a few things about biology."

"Leave her alone," says Jamie without looking up from

his notebook. Angelo turns, raising his eyebrows. "She don't wanna talk to you. She's studying."

"Fine, man. I'll leave her alone." Angelo gets up and moves toward another table. "See ya later," he says to me. "What's your name, anyway?"

I start to answer, but Jamie lifts his head from his drawing to stare at Angelo.

"What, man?" says Angelo. "What's the deal? She your girlfriend or something?"

I can feel the blush start at my collarbones and work its hot way up to my cheeks. Jamie looks directly at me for the first time ever, as far as I know, and I have to look back down at my book. The words blur before my eyes as I try to focus on something, anything but what's going on right next to me.

"I'm just tryin' to be nice. She gave me some money." Nobody says anything. Jamie studies the tip of his ground-down pencil. "All right. See ya in shop, Jame. Bye, Sweater," Angelo says.

Jamie goes back to his work. I can barely breathe. Tracy, my best friend since the beginning of time, is suddenly in the seat across from me. I kind of can't believe she's here— upperclassmen get to go where they want in study hall, but the freshmen are supposed to stay glued to their seats.

"Did you study last night? It's going to be so hard. Are you okay? You're all red." She brings a spoonful of yogurt to her mouth, studying my face in that weird, concerned way that I've seen a lot these past few months. Then she looks sideways at Jamie, at his construction boots and the ragged, dirty cuffs of his too-long jeans. "It's too bad you got stuck at this table. We're all studying together over there." She points to a big twelve-seater full of freshmen who are probably talking about the keg party that they won't get into at the nearby private school's polo fields tonight. Why they even want to go is beyond me. But I've been trained by Tracy not to say that stuff out loud. It doesn't do anything to increase my popularity, according to Miss Teen Vogue.

"I study better by myself."

"Yeah, I know, you *always* say that. Maybe that's why you *always* get A's."

"I don't always get A's."

"Oh shut *up*. Have you thought about what we talked about?"

Tracy is referring to whether or not she should have sex with her boyfriend, Matt Hallis. We've been talking about this nonstop for the last few weeks, and it's become my least favorite topic ever—for a lot of reasons. At first I thought she was bringing it up all the time to distract me and give me something to think about. But now I realize that she's totally obsessed. It's like she decided that the second she started high school, she had to lose her virginity or she'd never fit in. Or be cool. Or be…whatever.

Mr. Cella materializes out of thin air behind Tracy, who notices me looking past her and freezes.

He consults his seating chart. "Ms. Gerren, would you care to go back to your assigned seat?"

"We're just talking about our biology test, Mr. Cella."

"You had ample time to do that last night via text, or cell, or IM, I'm sure. Back to your seat."

Tracy gets up. "You're okay, right?" she asks. I nod. "Sorry you're stuck over here," she says again, before Mr. Cella escorts her back across the cafeteria without so much as a glance at me.

It took only two days for the teachers to stop looking at me like some sort of pathetic freak. Which is exactly what Peter said would happen, when I was complaining to him about starting high school barely three months after burying our dad.

What was left of him, anyway.

I try to concentrate on biology and ignore the flush in my cheeks that is taking its time receding.

I sneak a glance at Jamie.

Jamie Forta.

I know who Jamie is. I know because of Peter. Jamie and Peter were on the hockey team together when I was in seventh grade and Peter was a junior. Jamie was a freshman then. Dad and I used to come to the games to watch Peter, but after getting a good look at Jamie in the parking lot after a game once, I mostly watched Jamie. The next year, Jamie got thrown off the team during the first game of the season for high-sticking a West Union player named Anthony Parrina in the neck.

Although I hadn't seen Jamie in a year, I recognized him the second I was assigned my seat at this table. Even without the hockey gear.

I can hear the scratch of Jamie's pencil as he draws, grinding graphite down to wood. My gaze finds its way across the pages of my book, over the table and onto his notebook. It takes me a second to recognize the upside-down image as a house, a strange-looking house in the woods with a porch and a massive front door at the top of a wide staircase. I lean over the table to get a better view. And I realize he's no longer drawing.

I'm afraid to lift my eyes from the page. When I do, Jamie is looking at me, his pencil in midair. Again, the flush rises from my chest, up over my neck and into my cheeks. Before I look away, I think I catch the slightest, tiniest, most minuscule glimpse of a smile in his eyes.

"That's a really nice picture," I whisper, unable to get any volume.

He looks at the pencil and shakes his head at its wrecked point, dropping it next to his notebook. He reaches into his pocket and draws out a dollar as he gets up from the table and starts toward the food. Apparently he's learned to keep some of his money for himself, rather than give it all to Angelo.

"You should be studying," he says with that hint of a smile in his eyes, and walks away. I feel the heat intensify at the sound of his voice, making the skin on my face tight with imaginary sunburn. He disappears in the rush of upperclassmen who have just come in from the cafeteria courtyard to get food before the bell rings.

I close my book and put it in my backpack, hoping to spy a piece of gum at the bottom somewhere to erase the dryness that goes along with humiliation. I rifle through my new makeup bag, which Tracy put together for me ("You *can't* go to high school without a makeup bag") and find an old piece of partly wrapped gum stuck to a busted eyeliner (apparently I got her hand-me-downs). I take the eyeliner out with the gum and separate the two, deciding the gum looks clean enough to chew. Weirdly, it tastes like lipstick. I rifle a little more, searching for something to help me find solid ground again. My fingers brush the eyeliner sharpener.

I take the sharpener out and look quickly over my shoulder for Jamie, who's in line waiting to pay for a coffee. I grab his pencil and jam it into the sharpener, twisting and twisting and twisting, watching the yellow wood shreds peel off and fall to the table. I take his pencil out and look at its now-sharp point. The bits of eyeliner stuck in the sharpener have left a few electric-blue stains, but the point is truly perfect.

I quickly put it back where I found it, looking again just in time to see Jamie turning away from the cashier to start back to the table. The bell rings. I grab my bag and run.

blunderbuss (*noun*): clumsy person who makes mistakes
(*see also:* me)

———

2

"MY GRANDMA SAYS IT'S BETTER NOT TO BE BEAUTIFUL, because then you have nothing to lose. And you know that the guy who married you married you for the right reasons," Stephanie says.

"Or you just know that he's ugly, too," Tracy responds.

"I assume the level of conversation in the room means that everyone has finished his or her exam?" Mr. Roma says from his position by the blackboard. "Ah, Robert still has his paper, girls, so no more talking until he's done. You have ten minutes, Robert. Is Robert the only one?"

No one else says anything. Robert looks up, catches my eye and winks. I look away. Tracy and Stephanie laugh.

"Enough, girls. Let the man finish."

"Genius takes time, Mr. Roma," he says.

"You have nine minutes, Robert."

I suddenly remember the answer that I needed for the fifth question, and I become convinced that I failed. But I'm always convinced I failed, and it has yet to happen. The class has been sitting in silence for two minutes when a note lands on my desk. I can tell by the way it's folded that it's from Tracy.

Students are not allowed to bring cell phones or smart phones or anything like that into classrooms. This drives a lot of people crazy, including Tracy, who is addicted to texting and IM-ing. But I couldn't care less about the ban because a) I'd rather get a nicely folded note with words that have all their letters than a stupid text any day of the week; b) I hate people who cheat, and cell phones make it really easy to do that; and c) I don't have a cell phone. Tracy thinks it's really lame that I'm so far behind the curve.

I was going to get one before school started this year, but other things came up. Like death.

I try to open the note without making any noise, but Mr. Roma hears me. He raises his finger to his lips to silently shush me, but he doesn't get up to claim the note and read it out loud, which is what he did yesterday to Stephanie. Instead, he gives me a frowny smile. Apparently, Mr. Roma still thinks I'm a pathetic freak in need of sympathy even if Mr. Cella does not. I look down at the note.

What did you do to that guy at your table in study hall? He asked me where your last class was.

My heart stops. *Where's your last class?* can be code for several things: *Where do you want to meet so we can walk to practice together?* or *Where should I meet you so I can sell you those drugs?* or *Where can I find you so I can beat you up?* Since Jamie and I aren't on a team together—I'm not on one yet and, in fact, I don't think he's allowed on any team anymore—and I have no interest in buying drugs from him—not that I know he actually sells drugs—that leaves one option. But that doesn't make any sense, either. All I did was sharpen his pencil.

I turn to Tracy. *Did you tell him?* I mouth. *What?* she mouths back. I point to the note and mouth my question

again, more slowly this time. She nods seriously and then
shrugs at my panicked expression.

"What was I supposed to do? He creeped me out," she
whispers.

"Was he mad?"

"Kinda—"

"Tracy Gerren! Enough! Go sit by the window."

Tracy rolls her eyes, gathers her things and heads toward
the back of the room. "Thanks a lot," she mutters in my direction. Robert places his paper down on Mr. Roma's desk
with a flourish.

"I am officially finished, ladies and gentlemen. You are
free to talk."

"Sit, Robert. And be quiet. In fact, everyone stay quiet
until the bell rings. I've decided that I like this class best
when it's silent."

Three minutes until the bell. I have no idea what's going
to be waiting for me out there. I feel sick to my stomach,
which gives me a great idea. I slide out of my seat and head
toward—Mr. Roma's desk. Robert tries to grab my hand as
I walk by. He smells like cigarettes. I ignore him. I've been
ignoring him since sixth grade.

"Mr. Roma, I know the bell's about to ring, but I need
a lav pass."

Mr. Roma hands me the pink pass after writing the time
on it without so much as a raised eyebrow.

I guess there are some benefits to freak status after all.

I'm in the bathroom by the gym—the bathroom farthest
from the school's main front doors—when the final bell
rings. Two girls are smoking in a stall at the end. It's hard to
breathe. I wait until they leave, and then I wait a few more
minutes. It's still hard to breathe. I wonder if I'm having one

of those panic attacks my mom is convinced I get now. To distract myself I read the graffiti on the wall, which says *Suck it,* among other things, in hot-pink nail polish.

Such originality here at Union High. Such excellent use of vocabulary.

When I can breathe again, I leave.

The halls are basically empty. I go to my locker. I get my books. I grab my French horn out of the orchestra room so I can practice later, and I leave by the front doors because there's no other way to leave at the end of the day; they funnel us out through the front to keep an eye on us. I'm waiting at the crosswalk when I see him on the other side of the street. He isn't holding any books. The crosswalk light goes from the red hand to the silver guy, and I'm afraid to move, but I do anyway. I get closer and closer and closer, but he doesn't say a word. In fact, I just walk past him as if I don't see him, and a few seconds pass. My legs are still moving when he says, "Rose."

I've never, ever heard anyone say my name like that in my entire life. I didn't even know that was my name until he said it like that.

"Yeah?"

He holds out his pencil. "What did you do?"

"I…just…it was…" I falter.

"What's this stuff on it?"

"Oh, um, sorry—it's eyeliner."

He takes a few steps closer and looks carefully at my eyes. "You don't wear that stuff."

The flush starts. It's slow-moving, but it's going to be a huge burn—it stretches from shoulder to shoulder and it's going to spread above my collar in about three seconds. I notice that his eyes are hazel with gold specks and then I can't look anymore.

"Sometimes I do."

"Like when?"

"If I'm going out with my boyfriend or something."

"Oh, yeah? Who's that?" I have nothing to say. "You're a freshman, right?" he asks.

"I'm fourteen," comes out of my mouth. And then, like we're playing in the sandbox, I ask, "How old are *you?*"

That glint of a smile shows up briefly again but disappears before I'm sure it was real.

"Come on, I'll take you home."

"You don't know where I live."

"Yeah, I do," he says. I stare at him dumbly. "How's your brother?" he asks.

The question surprises me. Even though Peter and Jamie played hockey together, I assumed they never talked off the ice. "Okay, I guess. He's at Tufts. Are you guys friends?"

"I drove him home when Bobby Passeo skated over his fingers," he says, not answering my question.

"I saw you, you know. Play hockey. When you were still on the team." I become very interested in my shoes, realizing that I sound like exactly what I am—a babbling fourteen-year-old. He looks at me, waiting. When I don't say anything else, he says, "So do you want a ride?"

"I can't get in the car with you," is my response. I'm no longer a babbling fourteen-year-old. I'm now ten. Or maybe eight.

He can't help himself this time. He breaks into a huge smile. My heart skitters for a second.

"What do you think is gonna happen?" he asks, taking my French horn from me. I feel like an idiot. "Come on, freshman. I'll drive you home."

His car is old, and rusty and a strange, flat green. But the inside is clean, and black and smells like cold rain. I'm sit-

ting far away from him, embarrassed that I was embarrassed
when he opened my door for me in the school parking lot.
The radio is playing Kanye, but Jamie changes it to a classic
rock station. Pearl Jam. When I was in kindergarten Peter
used to play Pearl Jam for me and make me recite the band
members and the instruments they played. Eddie Vedder,
singer. Mike McCready, guitarist. I can't remember the bass
player's name. Jeff Something. Peter got me addicted to good
music and real musicians at a very young age, which, to be
honest, hasn't done me any favors socially.

I can't believe I'm in a car with Jamie Forta.

"Are you cold?"

"No."

"You look cold."

"Not really." He's right. I am cold. But not because of
the weather—September in Connecticut still feels like summer. I always spend the first three weeks of school sweating through my new fall clothes because I couldn't stand to
wear my summer clothes for another minute. I'm probably
the only person in my entire school of 2,500 who wore a
sweater today, willing the weather to be cooler.

Well, I sort of got my wish. I'm cold now. Fear does that
to me.

I look at him and he's looking at the road. He stops at a
yellow light. I'm surprised. I guess I expected someone like
Jamie Forta to just blow through a yellow light without
even thinking about it. He's still looking at the road. Nobody seems to have anything to say. I'm embarrassed again.
I've been embarrassed a lot today. Mostly because of him.

"Where's your notebook?" I ask.

"Locker."

"Don't you have any homework?"

He looks at me like I've said something funny. The light

turns green, and he turns left. I realize that he actually does know where I live.

Silence. Silence, silence, silence.

"I liked the house you were drawing."

"Yeah?"

"You're a good artist."

He takes another left. We drive by Tracy's brown house with the red trim, where I will spend the first part of tonight lying on her bedroom floor, continuing our endless conversation about sex. After she decides she'll sleep with Matt "soon," since they've been going out since the beginning of eighth grade, she'll move on to whether I should go out with Robert or not. The answer is usually no, but sometimes she says he'd probably treat me really well. Then I remind her that I hate cigarettes. She suggests I convince him to quit. I reply that people only quit if they want to. She says he'd definitely quit for me.

Robert, according to Tracy, has been in love with me since the sixth grade. I tell her that that's impossible, because how did we know what love was in elementary school? She tells me that just because we couldn't identify love when we were eleven, that doesn't mean we weren't capable of feeling it. Maybe she's right. I have no idea. But I do know that I've never been in love with Robert. And I have no intention of going out with him just because he's "in love" with me. Which he's probably not. Because why would he be? I'm not pretty, and I like to use words with a lot of letters in them—two big turn-offs for guys.

My dad always got mad at me when I said things like that in front of him. "First of all, Rose, you *are* pretty," he'd tell me. "And second of all, never look twice at a man who doesn't appreciate a smart woman. Never." He was always full of good advice that was impossible to follow.

For a while after he died, I saw him almost every night. I'd dream that I was in an empty movie theater, sitting by myself in a sea of red seats, watching him on a huge screen like he was a star. He was twenty-feet tall, his brown hair sticking out every which way, his blue eyes burning like neon when he looked at me, pinning me to my seat with his stare like he was waiting for me to do something, to fix the situation, to get him out of the action flick or Western he was stuck in and back into the real world. Sometimes I'd see things that really happened, like when I was ten and he took Tracy and me to a Springsteen concert, and I was embarrassed by his weird dancing but also kind of proud that he was so into the concert. Or I'd see us looking at his twenty-volume Oxford English Dictionary, studying the history and derivation of some crazy word that had come out of his mouth, like *erinaceous*. One night at dinner he'd said, "Pete, you seem to have inherited the erinaceous hair Zarelli men are often cursed with—consider cutting back on the product." Later, when Peter found out that Dad had basically said his hair looked like a hedgehog, he didn't talk to my dad for almost a week.

I bet Peter regrets that now.

Other times when I was having the movie theater dream, I'd see things that I didn't experience. Like when the convoy Dad was riding in blew up, killing everyone within fifty feet.

Dad never should have been in Iraq. He wasn't a soldier. He only went because when the economy tanked, he lost his job as an aircraft engineer, and the military recruited him as a contractor, offering him a big salary for a short tour of duty. Mom was freaking out about money, and they had eight years of college tuition to look forward to, thanks to Peter and me, so he went.

Peter and I never said it to them, but we both thought they

had gone completely insane. And we were right. Dad got to Iraq in February and was dead by June, when the truck he was in hit a homemade roadside bomb. He died instantly they told us, to make us feel better. But it didn't make us feel better—well, not me, anyway. It just got my imagination going, wondering exactly what that meant.

Dreaming about exactly what that meant.

The dreams about the convoy didn't have sound. I never heard the explosion, or the dying, or anything. And there was no blood. I just saw Dad, sailing through the air with his eyes wide open, twisting and turning, and then landing on his back on the ground and cracking into sections like a piece of glass that had been dropped from just a few inches up, shattering but still keeping its shape.

The dreams stopped after a while, and I was relieved— until I started to miss them. Now that I don't see my dad at all anymore, I worry that I'm forgetting everything about him.

Jamie takes a right and then a quick left, and ten seconds later we're at my house.

"This is it, right?"

"Yes." Silence. "So, when did Bobby Passeo skate over Peter's fingers?"

"I don't know. Two years ago, I guess."

I can't believe he still remembers where we live.

"Wait, you had your license two years ago?"

He shakes his head and leans back against his door, looking at me with those perfectly hazel eyes that make me nervous.

"You okay?" he asks, a cloud passing across his face. His question and dark expression catch me off guard, as I'm still thinking about him driving without a license. A thousand people have pissed me off by asking that question in the past few months. But I don't seem to mind it when it comes from Jamie. "I'm sorry. About your dad," he says.

I nod, but that's all I can do. I'm not going to risk crying in front of Jamie. I can't really predict when I'm going to cry, but when I do, it involves a lot of snot. "Well, thanks for the ride," I say, reaching for the door handle.

"Rose," he says. "You know my name, don't you?"

His name? He thinks I don't know his name? The idea that I'm so in my own universe that I haven't heard Angelo call him "Jamie" and "Jame" every two minutes in study hall—that I wouldn't know his name, that I wouldn't know who he was after watching him play hockey all those times—is crazy. But should I admit that I know his name? If I know his name, will he think I...like him?

"Um..." I say.

His expression quickly goes blank. He turns back toward the steering wheel and puts the car from Park into Drive as if he were planning to gun it the second my feet hit the pavement.

"Jamie," he tells me as he stares straight ahead, waiting for me to leave.

I'm an idiot. But if I now say, *Of course I know your name, I've always known your name,* he won't believe me. "Thanks again for the ride," is all I can manage.

I get out as fast as I can, and he takes off, leaving me standing in the street, feeling like a complete loser for pretending not to know the name of someone who just went out of his way to be nice to me, who seemed genuinely sorry about what happened.

Nice going, Rose. Way to make friends. Keep up the good work.

belligerent (*adjective*): inclined to hostility or war
(*once again, see also:* me)

———

3

A FEW HOURS LATER, I'M IN MY USUAL FRIDAY-NIGHT SPOT, sprawled on Tracy's bright orange shag carpet that we got at Target, waiting for Robert and Matt to show up so we can go to Cavallo's for pizza. I am very carefully not talking about Jamie, although I feel like I'm going to explode if I don't. He was being so nice, and I messed everything up. I want to ask Tracy if she thinks he actually likes me or just feels sorry for me, but I can tell she doesn't like him by the way she looked at him in study hall today. It's easier just to say nothing.

Tonight, predictably, Tracy and I are covering three topics during our session in her room: her virginity, Robert and her cheerleading tryout. To be honest, I can't believe Tracy is going out for cheerleading at Union High. First of all, our cheerleading team is not one of those amazing, superathletic competitive teams—there are no backflips off crazy-high human pyramids at halftime. The most acrobatic thing that goes on here is a synchronized hair flip. And being on the cheerleading team at our school isn't like being a cheerleader at the private school in Union— Here, it doesn't mean you're at the top of the food chain. Yes, some of the cheerleaders are beautiful and go out with hot jocks, but some are average-looking girls who just happen to know how to dance. Some are smart, some not. Some have money, some don't. In other words, not all of them are popular. And to top it all off, Union High cheerleaders have kind of a slutty reputation on the whole. At least, that's what I heard Peter say once.

So even if Tracy does make the team—and I kind of don't think she will—she's not automatically granted access to the top tier of Union High popularity. But I'm not about to tell her that. She'll just accuse me of being a snob. And in some ways she's right—after all, I think Union High's brand of cheerleading is a waste of time and teenage girls.

But I'd still rather talk about cheerleading than virginity.

"I don't think fifteen is too young to lose it, do you?"

I hate this part of the conversation. "I don't know," I mumble.

"You always say that."

Well, what do I know? I can't really imagine letting a guy see me naked, never mind letting him do *that* to me while I'm naked. So I don't really know what to think. I don't want to think about it at all, most of the time. Which makes me think that fourteen is probably too young. And is fifteen really that different from fourteen?

"Maybe I should go on the pill," she says.

I nearly fall through the floor. I suddenly feel like she's thirty and I'm still in nursery school.

"Tracy, you can't go on the pill."

"Why not?"

"You know why not. You have to use condoms. It's too dangerous not to," I say.

"You're so paranoid about sex, Rosie. You always have been. You better relax."

She's right about this, too. I am paranoid about sex. Maybe it's because I have an older brother who decided to tell me all about the dangers of sex the night before he left for college. I'm not sure why Peter was so worked up about the whole thing, but if I had to guess, I'd say it was because he felt he had to fill the parental void. Since Dad died, Mom hasn't exactly been "available" or "present" or whatever you say, which is kind of ironic, since she's a shrink. Who specializes in adolescent psychology. When she does talk to me these days, she uses her therapy voice, which makes me go deaf almost instantly.

Thanks to her job, we have enough books on teenagers in the house that I could find the answer to pretty much any question I might have, if I felt like looking. Which I don't. Maybe that's why Peter called me into his room to talk about sex while he was packing.

He was listening to Coldplay and I assumed he just wanted to dissect the album and explain why he thought Chris Martin was such a hack. But, no. "Never, ever let some guy talk you into sex without a condom," Peter had said without any sort of warning. I froze in the middle of his room. "He'll try to tell you that he can't feel anything, and that it will be better for both of you if you don't use one, but he's just being a selfish asshole. You can get all sorts of diseases from sex. Girls can even get cervical cancer from sex. So don't listen to some loser who claims he can't get it up with a condom on. That doesn't happen to guys until they're, like, old. And don't go on the pill for anyone. But you'll learn all about this stuff in Ms. Maso's class—she's the bomb."

Peter scared the crap out of me, even though I didn't understand half of what he said. Or maybe that's *why* he scared me so much. I barely know what a cervix is. For someone with the aforementioned abnormally large vocabulary, I can be intentionally dumb sometimes.

Tracy hops off the bed and goes to her full-length mirror to check out how her butt looks in her new Rock & Republic jeans—again. You'd think we were going to a fashion show, not out for pizza. I suddenly notice that all of her boy-band posters are gone. Her walls are blank. I can't believe it, given the amount of time we spent decorating and redecorating our walls last year. I open my mouth to ask about the posters when she says, "Matt *wants* me to go on the pill."

Peter's words about guys who don't want to use condoms replay in my mind, and I instantly want to punch Matt. "That's insane, Tracy. Why?"

"How about not getting pregnant? The pill protects better than condoms, you know."

"Not against STDs."

"Rosie, Matt and I are both virgins. He's not going to give me anything."

Apparently I'm not the only one who is intentionally dumb sometimes.

The words form in my mind, and I know I shouldn't say them out loud. But I kind of can't help myself these days. If I want to say something, I say it, for better or worse.

"Do you really know he's never done it before, Tracy?"

She turns from the mirror and looks at me suspiciously.

"Do you know something I don't know?"

"No!"

"Because if you do, Rosie, you'd better tell me now—"

"I don't! But I'm just saying, Trace, how do you know Matt is a virgin?"

"Because he told me so. And I trust him," she says slowly, as if speaking to someone who doesn't understand English.

I can already tell it's going to take her days to forgive me for this one. "Okay, okay, sorry."

She stares at me for another second and then turns back to the mirror, brushing her straightened brown hair so hard I'm amazed it stays in her head.

"And he's not going to cheat on me, either."

At least she's thought about that possibility. That's a positive sign, even if she is in denial.

"I'm just saying that things happen. And it's never a bad idea to protect yourself." I impress myself for a minute— I actually sound like I know what I'm talking about, which is ironic because Tracy is way more experienced than me, as she often likes to point out. Even if she did get all her "experience" this summer. Which was basically last month.

The doorbell rings downstairs, and Tracy's mom calls up to let us know that the boys are here. Tracy finishes putting on more eyeliner and leaves the room without another word to me. I grab the bag she lent me when she insisted I'd look like an idiot if I brought my backpack, and I follow her. It's definitely going to be one of those nights.

Cavallo's is packed. Matt stops to talk to some of his friends from the swim team—they're seniors and they're huge. If I didn't know any better, I'd think they were on steroids. But as I've noticed these last four days, there is a pretty big physical difference between a fourteen-year-old and an eighteen-year-old. It almost makes competitive sports in high school seem like a joke. The senior who held the cross-country team's informational meeting the other day had legs that were at least twice the length of mine.

My dad would have told me not to worry. "It's not the length of the leg, it's the length of the stride," he used to say. He was always telling me to take bigger steps when we ran together. Dad made the mistake of taking me to see a half marathon when I was nine, and right then and there I decided that I was going to run the race the next September. He said he'd train me, which basically meant he spent the summer being really late for work and running twice as much as I ever did. We'd go on runs early in the morning, before it got too hot, and of course it took him a while to get me out of bed, so we never started as early as he wanted to. And then, when we were running, I'd get slower and slower as the longer runs went on, and he'd have to double back for me. I don't think it was much fun for him, but he was pretty proud of me when I finally ran the race at the end of all that. It took me forever, but I finished. I was the youngest girl running that year.

I haven't run since he died. Peter pulled me aside this summer after Mom had asked me for the millionth time when I was going to go for a run, and he told me that I never had to run again if I didn't want to. But I do. I will… I think.

Robert and I grab a booth, but Tracy hovers near Matt until she realizes that he's not going to introduce her to the swim thugs. Then she comes over, trying to look fine but mostly looking mad. And sad, too.

"So, Rose," she says. I know I'm in trouble when she calls me Rose and not Rosie. Well, that, and also the fact that until now she hadn't spoken to me since we left her room. "I saw you with that guy today in the parking lot after school."

Robert looks at me. The waitress with the crazy beehive hairdo arrives to take our order. She's famous for demanding that kids pay before she puts their orders in—including tip. We must look trustworthy, because after we order our pizza and sodas, she just leaves.

"What guy?" Robert asks.

I'm staring at Tracy. So this is how she's going to get revenge for me saying that Matt might not be her knight in shining armor. I realize that she has had this information about me since the afternoon and she's been saving it. Clearly Tracy has been studying *Gossip Girl,* absorbing lessons in how to treat your friends like crap.

"Jamie Forta. You got in a car with Jamie Forta," she says. How interesting that, when it's convenient for her, she knows his actual name. Her eyes are glued to Robert's face, searching for a reaction. He must look appropriately shocked or hurt because she appears to be very satisfied. I decide to focus on the blackboard menu above the counter, even though we've already ordered and I know the menu by heart.

"What the hell were you doing with Jamie Forta?" Matt asks as he finally sits down at our booth. "That guy's such a loser. I hear he's been trying to graduate from high school for, like, three years or something."

I used to like Matt, way back in eighth grade. But something changed over the summer when he started preseason training with the swim team. He partied with them and now he thinks he's such a big deal, it's annoying. I started hating him the second I realized he was pressuring Tracy to have sex. But tonight, right now, I hate him for an entirely new reason.

"He's a junior, Matt. And you don't know anything about him."

"There's definitely something wrong with that guy," Matt says. "He's a moron."

"Do you know him, Rose?" Robert asks.

The waitress drops off four sodas. Matt reaches for his wallet, but she still doesn't ask for money. He looks puzzled. I sip my root beer and try to buy myself some time.

"Rosie?" Robert says.

"Yes," I finally say, hiccupping because of the carbonation. "He was on the hockey team with Peter."

"Peter knew him?" Tracy asks, blushing a little bit. Matt gives Tracy a sharp look. She's had a crush on Peter since the day she became my best friend. Coincidence? Doubtful. But maybe that's just my cynical side coming out.

"Jamie drove Peter home once, when Bobby Passeo skated over his hand." I know that no one here could possibly know who Bobby Passeo is, but I figure he could work as a diversion from the current topic.

"Jamie's weird," Tracy says, ignoring Matt. "What did he want with you?"

So much for a diversion. "Nothing. He has a right to talk to me, Trace. He even has a right to offer me a ride home."

"He's a junior," Robert says, sounding alarmed.

"So what? We're not supposed to talk to people who aren't in our class?"

"He must have wanted something from you," Tracy says again.

"Nope." I am determined not to give her anything. Two can play at this game.

"Fine. Don't tell me if you don't want to," she snaps.

"There's nothing to tell," I snap back.

The guys are now watching our conversation like it's a tennis match. Matt looks amused, Robert looks confused. Tracy is staring at me, hard, and then she plays her trump card. I don't actually know if she knows it's a trump card, but it is.

"He goes out with Regina Deladdo, who's friends with Michelle Vicenza. They're both on the squad," Tracy says, using her favorite, extremely annoying nickname for the cheerleading team. "Michelle's the captain. Regina's her lieutenant."

You'd have to live under a rock three towns over to not

know who Michelle Vicenza is. She's Union High's prom and homecoming queen. It's been that way for four years. She might have been born with those titles. Every girl in Union secretly—or not so secretly—wants to be Michelle. She goes out with Frankie Cavallo, who graduated two years ago and now runs Cavallo's, which is his family's place. Peter introduced me to Michelle last year at his graduation party—I thought she was the prettiest girl I'd ever seen.

But I have no idea who Regina Deladdo is.

Or why Tracy suddenly seems to know everything about Jamie Forta when she was calling him "that guy" just two minutes ago.

The waitress brings our pizza over and takes a moment to rearrange everything on the table so it fits. I'm glad, because I need a second to get over the fact that Tracy knows more about Jamie than I do. The way she's doling out information tonight makes me want to kill her. How does Tracy already know that Regina Deladdo is dating Jamie? She must have been studying up from the moment we started school on Tuesday.

Jamie goes out with a cheerleader? My brain hurts.

I try very, very hard not to let anything show on my face.

"Wow," Robert says. "I know who she is. She seems a little…" He takes a sip of his drink as he searches for the right word.

"Insane?" Matt says, shaking his head as he takes a bite of pizza. "Imagine screwing that harpy," he adds. Robert nearly spits out his soda. Tracy stares at the table.

Matt, a virgin? Uh-huh. Sure.

"They're perfect for each other," he continues. "They're both idiots."

For the second time in one night, I know I'm about to

say something I shouldn't, but I can't stop the words from coming out.

"Just because you got drunk with a few seniors over the summer, does that make you better than everyone now?"

Matt slowly puts his pizza down. "What's your problem?"

"My problem, Matt, is that you're being a jerk! And you've been a jerk for, like, two months now."

"Anything else?" he asks.

I'm on a roll, and when this new me is on a roll, nothing can stop me. It feels so good to say exactly what I'm thinking.

"Yeah, actually, there is something else. Stop treating my best friend like dirt. Introduce her to your friends when you're talking to them and she's standing right next to you. And you might want to—"

"Stop!" yells Tracy, kicking me hard under the table. Matt looks from me to Tracy and back, and then gets up and goes to sit with his swim thugs. Tears pool in Tracy's eyes.

"You don't get to just say whatever you want, no matter what happened to you this summer," she hisses as she grabs her bag and marches out the door. Matt watches her leave but doesn't go after her. I'm suddenly really, really embarrassed.

"Nice work," Robert says.

I'm trying to backtrack in my head and figure out what set me off and made me act like a lunatic. The waitress comes over.

"You're Peter's little sister, right?" she asks. I nod. "Sorry about your dad, hon. Soda's on the house." She slaps the bill down on the table and walks away. If I were in a better mood, I might laugh at how one dead dad equals four free sodas here at Cavallo's.

"Rosie, I think you should go after her," Robert suggests, reaching for the bill, an unlit cigarette already in his mouth. "And you should probably say you're sorry."

He's right. I should. And I do.

lachrymose (*adjective*): sad; tearful
(*see also:* being a crybaby)

———

4

JAMIE HASN'T BEEN IN STUDY HALL SINCE FRIDAY. IT'S NOW Wednesday. Since Monday, I've spent the period pretending to read *A Separate Peace* while trying to come up with something to say to him, something that will right the wrong I committed on Friday by stupidly pretending I didn't know his name. As lame as it sounds, I'm not used to having to come up with answers to these kinds of dilemmas by myself. I usually talk to Tracy, but I can't do that this time.

I ran after her on Friday night, catching her just a few blocks from her house. I told her I was sorry for what I did but that I meant what I said—Matt was acting like a jerk. She didn't agree, but she didn't disagree, either, and we've had a truce since then. She hasn't asked me any more questions about Jamie, and I'm not about to bring him up. She'll want answers, and I don't have any.

I look across the cafeteria and see her sitting next to Matt, looking up at him adoringly while he barely acknowledges her existence, as usual. She waves at me, and if I had to guess,

I'd say that she kind of likes the sight of me sitting by my-self. Freshmen at the end of the alphabet always get screwed when it comes to assigned seats in study hall. You get stuck anywhere there are leftover seats, which is at the juniors' and seniors' tables. They get to pick their tables first, which is considered a privilege, and then tables are assigned to the sophomores and then the freshmen. The freshmen at the top of the alphabet end up at the few remaining empty tables together, but the freshmen at the end of the alphabet—like someone named, say, Rose Zarelli—get assigned wherever there are leftover seats. Jamie and Angelo and I have a whole table for six to ourselves.

I wave back at Tracy, and she frowns, pointing behind me. I turn.

"Hey, Sweater. I got those quarters for ya."

Angelo shaved this morning, and it didn't work out so well. He has little dots of dried blood all over his face, and his stubble is already growing back.

"Oh. Um, that's okay. You don't have to pay me back."

"Really?"

"Keep them. I don't need them."

"I don't need them, either, Sweater."

"No, I mean, I have money today."

"So do I. Whaddya think, I'm poor or something? I got paid yesterday."

"I mean, my mom never kicks me out of the house with-out letting me finish breakfast, and she always gives me lunch money," I say, instantly cringing at the fact that I just said *lunch money*—couldn't I have just said *money,* without the *lunch* qualifier? No, of course not. "Um, so you should keep it in case your mom does that again."

He says nothing.

"I'm…I didn't mean… Sorry."

"How'd you know that?"

"Well, um, I mean, that was Friday."

"I told you about that?"

"Not exactly."

"I was talkin' to Jamie," he says suspiciously.

"Yeah, but I sit here, too."

"I guess you do, dontcha." He leans over me, and I notice that he opted not to wear Axe today. "You're listenin' even when you pretend you're not, ain't ya?" He takes his jacket off and hurls it on the table, revealing a Metallica T-shirt as ratty as his Nirvana shirt, and a lighter falls out of the pocket. He grins at me. "Want anything? I'm buying today."

"No, thanks."

"You sure? I'm gettin' a coffee for Jame."

My stomach drops like I'm on the first plunge of a rollercoaster ride. "He's here today?"

"Yeah. Even vo-tech guys can only cut so many times before someone catches on."

"Where is he?" I say too quickly. Angelo, who was walking backward toward the food line, now stops.

"Outside," he says, looking at me very carefully. "Why? You miss him?"

I'm blushing, but I'm too busy backtracking to pay much attention.

"I just didn't think he was here, that's all."

"You been looking for him."

"No, I haven't—"

"What's the deal with you two? You doin' it?" He sits down and whacks me too hard on the shoulder. "Come on, you can tell me. I know everything about him. He won't care."

"Why are you asking me if you know everything about him?" I say, sort of proud of myself for a second.

He's a little puzzled until his brain catches up with his ears. "All right, I don't know everything about him. But he tells me about all the girls he bangs, so you can tell me if you're doin' it."

I'm unprepared for the jealousy. It dries out my mouth. A slow smile crosses his face.

"Look at you. You're all pissed off that he's with other girls."

"I'm not pissed off. I don't care. He can do whatever the fuck he wants." I figure if I throw in the F-word, it'll sound better, but of course, since I'm not really practiced at throwing in the F-word, it just sounds stupid.

"You two *are* doin' it! Did he 'pop your cherry'?" he asks with air quotes. "How old are you, anyway?"

I amaze myself by starting to cry. It comes out of nowhere. Tears pool in my eyes, and I know that if I move my eyeballs at all, or if I blink, those tears will spill on the table. So I look down, trying to be still, concentrating on keeping my last little shred of pride intact.

He whacks me again, a little more gently this time. "Sweater, gimme the details," he says, conspiratorially. "Jamie's gonna tell me anyway."

"Tell you what?"

I've wanted to see Jamie for five long days now so that I could apologize and set the record straight about the name thing. And any other time, I'd be thanking god that he showed up to get Angelo away from me and off the topic of my "cherry." But right now, I'd rather be taking a test I didn't study for than have to see his face. I make the fatal mistake of turning my head slightly, and a fat tear splats on the table. I glance up. Then two more fall. Angelo, to his credit, looks a little mortified by the waterworks.

"I'm just trying to get Sweater here to tell me what's goin' on, that's all. I didn't do anything. I swear, Jame. I didn't touch her or nothin'. Well, I hit her on the shoulder but not hard. I didn't hit you hard, did I?"

I can't answer, even though I feel bad that he feels bad. We all just sit there. Teenage boys don't know what to do with a crying girl. Even the crying girl doesn't know what to do with the crying girl.

"I'm gonna go get that coffee now, Jame."

"Yeah, you do that."

"I hate when I make girls cry. Fuck," he says. He wanders off, looking over his shoulder, completely bewildered.

The cafeteria seems to go silent as Jamie sits down across from me. "What did he say?"

I'm memorizing the initials scratched into the top of the table. JH, JG, SW, SR, TR. My throat is so constricted from trying not to cry that it aches like the worst strep ever, and I'm afraid of what my voice will sound like if I talk. Mostly, I just want to keep my nose from running in front of him.

"Rose." I love the way he says my name. It starts somewhere in his chest and it has a Z instead of an S. My eyes rise to meet his, and he looks so concerned that I almost start to cry again. "What did he say to you? Was it about your dad?"

It would be a lot easier to explain my reaction if I were crying about my dad. And maybe I am for all I know. My mom warned me in her annoying therapy voice that I might cry about him without even realizing that that's why I was crying. Maybe that's what's happening now.

Jamie reaches out his hand, but it stops just short of mine on the table and rests there. He's got ink on his thumb, but other than that, his hands are immaculate. Beautiful. Strong. I can see the blood in his thick veins. I want to run my finger along them. I bet the insides of his forearms look the same way. I imagine pushing up his sleeve to look.

I shake my head and wipe my face. "Angelo was just teasing me," I say.

"About what?"

I take a deep breath. "You."

"Me?"

"He wanted to know if you and I were having sex. And whether I was a virgin." The word sets my blushing mechanism off at full force. I can't believe I put the issue of my virginity on the table, but I want him to hear my version of the story— Who knows what the heck Angelo will tell him.

Jamie smiles a little. "He just can't get any, so he always wants to hear what everybody else is doing." He pulls his hand back. "Not that we're doing anything."

Another tear, hopefully the last one, begins its descent, and I wipe it away before it hits my cheekbone.

"That's why you're upset?" he asks.

I nod my head. And it could end right there. I could just call it a day. But my mouth won't stop running. "He said you tell him everything, about all the girls you…" My throat closes up again, and I can't finish the sentence, never mind ask him about Regina.

"'All the girls'? What girls? Do you see any girls around here?"

"He said that you…that you're with a lot of girls."

"Forget him."

"You're not with a lot of girls?"

He looks at me with mild curiosity and he's about to say something when it occurs to me that I've been waiting for five days for the opportunity to apologize to him. "I'm sorry, Jamie," I blurt out.

"For what?"

"For the other day. In your car. I knew your name. I've

known your name since I was in seventh grade. But I was too—"

Angelo puts Jamie's coffee and a doughnut between us.

"The doughnut's for you, Sweater," he says, and he sits at the end of the table, purposely looking the other way. Jamie takes his coffee and stands.

"I'm goin' outside." I'm not sure who he's talking to. "Angelo," he says sharply. Angelo gets up fast, without saying a word or looking at either of us.

I watch them walk toward the courtyard door. Angelo pushes the door hard, a cigarette already in his mouth, and disappears. Jamie turns, and I think, but I'm not sure, that he winks at me. He's gone before I can manage a smile. I'm so exhausted and confused that I can't even eat my doughnut.

prevaricate (*verb*): to stray from the truth
(*see also:* to lie like a jerk)

———

5

"HEY, WAIT UP!" ROBERT YELLS AS I'M WALKING TO SCHOOL.
It's the middle of October. It's cold, I'm miserable and Robert is the last person I want to talk to. I crank up the volume on my iPod and pick up my pace as some old-school Public Enemy blares in my ears—Peter would be proud.

If anyone ever tried to figure out who I am based purely on my iPod, they'd never be able to do it. Public Enemy is followed by the Pussycat Dolls and preceded by Patty Griffin. I love my Florence + The Machine as much as my Rihanna, my White Stripes as much as my Black Keys. I pride myself on my eclectic musical taste, which has everything to do with Peter and probably not that much to do with me.

"Hey!" Robert yells again. I look over my shoulder. He's trying to catch up with me. I start running, my backpack smashing against my shoulder blades.

"Rosie! Come on!"

Nothing is the way it was supposed to be this year, and it's really pissing me off. Tracy was one of two freshmen who made the cheerleading team, and she has totally abandoned our Friday nights at Cavallo's to hang out with her "squad" friends. Jamie was pulled out of study hall and put in remedial English, and now I only see him in the halls between classes, if at all. Angelo drives me crazy in the mornings, talking my ear off. And yesterday, I went out for the cross-country team.

The tryout was a disaster, a runner's nightmare come to life. My legs wouldn't work. My timing was off—I had to tell my brain to tell my legs to move. And when they did move, I couldn't lift them high enough to take a real step, like I was wearing metal running shoes and there was a giant magnet underneath the ground. It wasn't even that I ran badly—it was like I didn't know how to run at all. Before I tried out, I was pretty sure I wouldn't make the official team, but I was confident I'd make alternate. I mean, I've been running long distance since I was nine—how could I *not* make alternate? But I'm guessing the coach prefers that his alternates actually know how to put one foot in front of the other, which I clearly do not.

On top of all that, I now know exactly who Regina Deladdo is because I've had to sit through a million football games to watch Tracy cheer—or try to watch Tracy cheer. Since she's new on the team, she's always in the back row. Not that I care. Tracy introduced me to Regina after one of the games, probably to make a point. I could practically see the thought bubble above Regina's head that said, *Tracy, why the hell are you wasting my time introducing me to a nobody freshman?*

And last but not least on my Things That Suck This Year list: yesterday my mother told me she wants me to see a shrink to talk about the panic attack I had over the summer. But I'm not even sure that what happened to me at the movie theater *was* a panic attack. Maybe I just couldn't breathe because the theater was crawling with mold or mildew or something. Anyway, I've been fine ever since. Except for that day in the bathroom when I was hiding from Jamie after school. But that was probably just from the smoke.

Whatever.

I hate my life. And this morning, I feel like taking it out on Robert.

"If you didn't smoke cigarettes," I yell back at him as I run faster, "you could probably catch up with me!"

"Come on, Rosie! Rosie the Rose! Just wait up for a second!"

I stop running. He drops his cigarette and keeps walking toward me. I point at it. He stops, turns, steps on it and starts toward me again.

"You're such a Goody Two-shoe."

"Two-*shoes*. Two. Shoes. Plural."

"Want me to carry your books for you?"

"What is this, the 1950s?" I ask.

"Going to homecoming?"

I bust out laughing. "You're chasing me down the street at 7:00 a.m. to find out if I'm going to a dumb dance that's, like, two months away?" I say, walking faster toward school. I'm well aware that I am being unnecessarily mean, but I can't help it. "It's only October, Robert. Homecoming is before Christmas."

"Yeah? So?"

I sigh. "Just ask me if you want to ask me," I say bitchily. Robert has the ability to bring out the absolute worst in me. Lucky him.

The fact of the matter is, all the freshmen are talking about homecoming already. We started talking about it in elementary school because of the big fight that happened during

Peter's freshman year. Well, not just because of that—also because it's the first big dance in high school, and it's cooler than prom because all the alums come back. But the fight was a big deal.

Most normal schools have homecoming at Thanksgiving, but Union High had to change its homecoming after a bunch of alums from rival high schools practically started a riot. Now all the neighboring towns stagger their dances so that no two homecomings are on the same night. This year, ours is right before Christmas break. There are still fights, but at least the fights don't involve morons from multiple schools. Only morons from one school.

"I don't want to ask you," Robert says. "Jamie Forta asked me to find out." My teeth suddenly hurt from the cold air, and I realize my mouth must be hanging open. "Huh. So it's true."

If I'd thought about it, I would have guessed that a) Jamie would rather die than go to homecoming, and b) he would never ask Robert to do anything for him. He probably has no idea who Robert even is. If I'd thought about those things, my mouth would have stayed closed. "You're a jerk, Robert."

"But it's true, isn't it?"

"No, it's not."

"You don't even know what I'm talking about."

"All right, what, then?" I say, so annoyed with him that I want to shove him like I did in sixth grade when we had a fight over a game of four-square on the playground. He wanted to shove me right back—I could tell—but instead he lectured me about how a gentleman does not shove a lady. And he did it in the bad British accent that he used for the school's abridged production of *My Fair Lady* that year. Girls from that year still call him Henry occasionally, and he loves it—"Good day, Ladies," he replies, sounding like

Prince Charles. In junior high, girls giggled when he did that—now they roll their eyes and make fun of him. But he keeps doing it.

"I'm talking about you and Forta," Robert answers, reaching into his pocket for another cigarette.

"Don't smoke those things around me. It's too early in the morning."

"I can do whatever I want."

"Fine. Start killing yourself at fourteen—"

"Fifteen. Soon to be sixteen."

"Whatever. See if I care."

"Are you going to homecoming with him?" Robert asks.

"Why would you think that?"

"I don't know. I just get the feeling that he likes you."

"He doesn't like me, Robert. He doesn't even know me." My face is getting hot.

"I saw him watching you at track tryouts yesterday."

I'm kind of astounded, but not so astounded that I can't correct Robert. "Cross-country. Track is in the spring."

"Well, yeah, but you were running around the track."

"Where did you see him? And what were you doing there?"

"I was just hanging around," he says a little sheepishly. "I saw him going to his car in the parking lot, and he just stood there for a minute, watching you run."

My brain is so scrambled that I don't know what to say. The thought of Jamie watching me run is too much to process. I try to remember what I was wearing yesterday. My favorite gross sweatpants; a Devendra Banhart T-shirt; my old Union Middle School sweatshirt. Hopefully, by the time he was watching, I'd taken off the middle school sweatshirt. Although that would mean that I'd been feeling pretty hot and sweaty at that point, which is not when I'm at my most attractive. Not that I have any idea when I'm at my most attractive. Or if I even have a most attractive.

"Do you know how old that guy really is, Rosie?"

Not this again. "Why are people obsessed with how old Jamie is? He's a junior."

"He's an old junior."

"Aren't you the oldest person in the freshman class, and about to become the first person in our class who can drive? Isn't that a little unusual?"

He looks at the sky, squinting into the morning sun. "My credits didn't transfer," he mumbles.

"That's why you had to do sixth grade again when you moved here? It wasn't because you were held back?" I ask. He doesn't respond. "Stop talking about Jamie like you're automatically better than him, okay?"

He lights his cigarette and turns his head to the side to exhale while keeping his eyes on me. I am sure he saw Chuck do this on *Gossip Girl,* and I bet he's been practicing in the mirror ever since. I suddenly hate that stupid show.

Apparently I hate everything these days.

"I don't know what you see in that guy. Especially since you could have me."

Robert has crystal-blue eyes and jet-black hair. There's no doubt that he's cute. Last year, he had gaggles of little drama-department geeks trailing him like a Greek chorus. Actually, after he played Jason in *Medea,* he literally did have the Greek chorus following him around, giggling over everything he said or did. Of course, the irony is that Jason is not exactly the most honorable character in Greek tragedy. He left his wife Medea for another woman, and she went mad and killed their children to piss him off—or, more accurately, to destroy him.

You would think that the actor playing Jason would become less attractive due to his character's misdeeds rather than more attractive, but the Greek chorus could not get enough of Robert. Maybe the anachronistic biker jacket and leather boots he wore on stage canceled out the fact that he played a two-timing jerk.

Sometimes Robert used the Greek-ettes to try to make me jealous. It never worked.

In June, Robert came to my father's memorial service. He sat right behind me and handed me a clean tissue every few minutes. My mother will always love him for that. I try to remind myself of that kindness every time I want to tell him to get lost. I usually end up telling him to get lost anyway.

"You *could* have me, you know," Robert repeats.

"You're just what I need, Robert. A convicted felon."

"Stealing from H&M is not a felony."

"You mean stealing from H&M twice is not a felony."

"Sure, that, too."

Robert has a crappy life, and sometimes he does bad things, like steal and lie. He lives with not one but two stepparents. His mother bailed and his father got remarried. Then his father bailed, and his stepmother remarried, and Robert ended up with her and her new husband. Is that even legal? I have no idea. But it definitely seems crappy to me. As annoying as Robert can be, even he doesn't deserve that.

He makes another big show of inhaling and exhaling, blowing the smoke through his nose. "Forta likes you."

"I am not the kind of girl he likes. He likes the Regina Deladdos of the world."

"Tracy said he carried your horn and opened the car door for you that time."

"Maybe he was raised well."

"He doesn't look like it. He wears the same clothes to school every day."

"That's the kind of thing a girl would say."

"Tracy said it," he admitted.

"She would notice."

"Robert and Rosie sounds better than Jamie and Rosie."

I look at him for a second, this guy I've known since I was eleven, and he looks hurt. To be honest, I like the sound of Jamie and Rosie. Robert and Rosie is too much alliteration for me. But I'm not going to say that. I've already been mean enough for one day, and it's only seven-fifteen. Besides, I don't feel like reminding him what alliteration is.

"I've always aspired to select my relationships based on how they'll sound inscribed on the wall in the lavatory," I say.

"Stop talking like that, AP English." He grabs my coat to make me stop walking. "Will you go to homecoming with me?"

I knew this was coming. And even though homecoming is two months away, I'm kind of surprised it took him this long, considering he's been suspicious of Jamie since the first week of school, and also considering that everyone we know has already decided who they're going with. Tracy's going with Matt, who still isn't speaking to me, which is fine, because I'm not speaking to him, either. Stephanie is going with the swim-team thug that Tracy and Matt set her up with this summer, Mike Darren. Everyone knows who they're going with except me. And Robert.

To be honest, I don't want to go. I'm not in the mood for dancing these days—go figure. But I have to, or I'll never hear the end of it from Tracy. Or my mother, for that matter. My mother expects me to go on living as if everything were still completely normal. She seems incapable of understanding why I might not feel like going to a dance right now. She seems incapable of understanding me in general.

I look at Robert. "Do you promise not to lie to me ever

again?" I ask, knowing full well that this is not a promise he'll be able to keep.

"I didn't lie about anything!"

"You told me Jamie Forta asked you to find out if I was going."

"That wasn't a lie, that was a tactic."

"It was a lie."

He drops his cigarette and concentrates hard on putting it out with his thrift-store Doc Martens. I wonder if he paid for those boots or if he acquired them on one of his "excursions."

"Sorry," he mumbles. "But I was only using it as a tactic. It wasn't going to stay a lie."

I'm not entirely sure what that means, but I get the gist. I start walking again. He follows me.

"Do I have to wear a dress?" I say.

"It would be nice."

"Do I have to wear makeup?"

"I don't care."

"High heels?"

"Rosie!"

"Okay, I'll go."

"Don't sound so excited," he says.

"I don't like dances."

"What are you talking about? You love dancing!"

"Dances and dancing are two separate things."

He rolls his eyes. "But you'll go?"

"Yes, Robert. I'll go."

"Okay," he says, looking so happy it makes me regret saying yes.

envenom (*verb*): to make bitter, to fill with bad feeling
(*see also:* Regina's specialty)

6

TRACY'S HALLOWEEN PARTY ALREADY SUCKS AND IT HASN'T even started. She decided to throw the thing as soon as she made cheerleading last month because apparently it's important for the new girls to kiss up to the older girls. She doesn't put it that way, though—she says the younger girls have to pay their dues by hosting parties and things like that.

She keeps talking about how pretty the cheerleaders on "the squad" are, like being pretty is the most important thing in the world. When I roll my eyes, she just shakes her head like I couldn't possibly understand how important all this stuff is. And she's right—I don't. I don't think we should still have cheerleaders that prance around in short skirts repeating stupid rhymes, flashing their underwear to cheer on boys without doing so much as a cartwheel. It's the twenty-first century—shouldn't we be more evolved than this?

If Tracy weren't my best friend, I wouldn't be here hanging decorations for a "cheer party" while she and Stephanie finish putting on their costumes and looking for the key to

Tracy's parents' liquor cabinet. I'd be home, probably, secretly wishing I were still allowed to go trick-or-treating and watching something on HBO without permission while my mom was locked away in her office writing up her notes on all the crazy kids she listened to that week. Or I'd be... I don't know where else I'd be. I spend all my time with Tracy, so it's kind of hard to know what I'd be doing if she weren't my best friend.

This is the first time Tracy's parents have ever left her home alone, and I know it will be the last. I tried to tell her that this party is a bad idea and could get her into serious trouble, but I don't think she actually hears me when words come out of my mouth anymore. Her house is beautiful and her parents collect antiques. Like, real antiques, shipped over from England and Portugal. When I mention this to Trace, she just says, "That's why we're having the party in the basement! There's nothing valuable down there."

I refrain from asking her if she's going to lock everyone in, making them come and go through the little windows that are high up near the ceiling.

Something tells me that the two of us are not going to have an easy year.

We had a big fight earlier, when we were making chocolate-chip freezer cookies for the party. She told me that she and Matt were going to do it tonight. I told her that I had finally decided that fifteen *is* too young. She didn't like that at all. She changed the subject, saying that I need to find an activity, or a group, or something so that people will know who I am. "Like, you know, I'm known as a cheerleader now," she said. "What are they going to say about you? And don't say, 'She plays French horn in the orchestra' because, I'm sorry, but that's just lame." I shoved some candy in my mouth to stop myself from saying, *At least playing French horn takes some talent.*

Instead I said, "I'm a runner" to which she replied, "Not on a team, you're not," to which I replied, "Well at least running is a real sport, not like cheerleading," to which she replied, "It's good enough for Regina and she's Jamie's girlfriend."

I almost punched her.

She hasn't mentioned Jamie in a long time, probably because the last time she brought him up, I still wouldn't tell her anything. That made her so mad that she started texting someone on her stupid phone right in the middle of our conversation, which she totally knows makes me crazy.

Of course, what she doesn't know is that there's nothing to tell about Jamie. Except maybe that a few weeks ago he watched me run laps around the track during tryouts, according to Robert. But now that Jamie and I don't have study hall together anymore, we never talk. If he makes eye contact with me in the hall, maybe he'll give me a little nod, but that's it. I wonder if he's freaked out by our last conversation. I guess I can understand that—I mean, we don't even know each other, and I basically asked him how many people he's had sex with. Dumb.

"Rosie, where's your costume? It's almost time," Stephanie says, coming downstairs to the basement where I'm about to fall off a ladder, hanging fake spiders from the ceiling. She's dressed as Lady Gaga. Or maybe Katy Perry. I'm not really sure which, since they both like crazy wigs, corsets and stupidly high heels.

"Um, I don't... I'm not dressing up this year." As I hang the last spider, I notice the blue nail polish I put on in honor of Halloween is already chipped.

"You have to! Oh, my god! Tracy will kill you if you don't!"

"I'm not staying, Steph. I'm not in the mood for a party."

Stephanie sort of shuffles her patent leather platforms

around on the floor and then squints up at the orange-and-black streamers that run the length of the ceiling, twisting around each other with the spiders poking through. She takes a single blue M&M out of a bowl on the food table and pops it in her mouth.

Stephanie is truly one of the nicest people I know, which means that she gets caught in the middle a lot. Tracy and I met her in middle school last year, when she moved from southern Illinois with her mom after her parents got divorced. She's more Tracy's friend than mine, especially since she started dating Mike over the summer. I've wanted to ask Tracy for a while now why she and Matt didn't set me up with anyone this summer, but I'm not sure I want to hear the answer.

"Are you leaving because Tracy's mad at you?" she asks.

I have to think about that. Is that why I'm leaving? I think I'm leaving because I don't feel like having Tracy flaunt her new friends in my face as if I'm not worth anything anymore. And because she's making a big mistake by having sex with her stupid boyfriend when she barely even knows what sex is. And because he's a jerk who is probably already doing it with half the girls' swim team when she's not looking.

Matt morphed into something gross this past summer. Tracy didn't notice. But I did.

"Tracy's mad because I told her I don't think she should do it with Matt tonight."

Stephanie shuffles some more and yanks down her purple-and-black striped skirt, which rides up every time she inhales. Or exhales. Or moves. Or thinks about moving.

Am I a prude? I wonder.

"You told her that?"

"I mean, Steph, isn't fifteen, like, *young* to be worrying about this stuff?"

"Not really. It seems like everyone has had sex already, except us."

"Everyone who? Who's everyone?" I ask, a sick feeling flooding the pit of my stomach. Am I completely behind, and I don't even know it? Am I totally out of the loop with no idea who's doing it and who's not? Part of me shrieks, *Who cares?* and the other part of me whispers, *Chicken....*

"Well, like, Tracy says all of Matt's friends, and, like, most of the cheerleaders—"

"But they're all—" I stop myself from saying, *They're all older, we're just freshmen,* because that argument has gotten me nowhere, especially in my conversations with Tracy. I guess I'm not supposed to *be* a freshman. I'm supposed to pretend to be older than I am at all times, I'm supposed to want to do things that don't even make sense to me yet.

"You know what?" I finally say. "I don't care what Tracy or her new friends do."

"Come on, Rosie, Tracy's your best friend. You don't mean that."

"She should do it or not do it, but either way, it'd be great if she'd stop making such a huge thing out of it. Why is it such a big deal?" I listen to my voice falling flat in the unfinished cement basement and realize I sound like a whiny, jealous brat. What is wrong with me?

When I hear Tracy trying to navigate the basement steps in her ridiculous spiked heels, I just know she's been standing at the top of the stairs for the previous thirty seconds, listening. I'm suddenly very tired of myself. I need a lot more candy if I'm going to make it through this night.

She appears, looking an awful lot like Stephanie. Maybe they're both supposed to be Lady Gaga or Katy Perry—again, I can't tell. She takes one look at the table covered with the "spooky" Halloween tablecloth I brought that suddenly looks like it's for two-year-olds and starts rearranging everything to cover it. She turns, looks right through me and asks, "Steph, did you get the vodka?"

"I almost forgot," Stephanie says, practically running toward the stairs. Then the doorbell rings, and Stephanie stops in her tracks, screaming in unison with Tracy, "They're here!" Tracy flies up the stairs behind Stephanie, yelling over her shoulder, "Get dressed, Rose! *Now!*"

"I *am* dressed," I shoot back, but she's not listening to me. She never is.

I hear the front door open. There's a lot of high-pitched squealing that makes my ears hurt even though I'm still in the basement. The cheerleaders have arrived.

I need to get out of here.

I can practically hear Tracy's voice in my head, calling me a snob. She's always called me a snob, ever since we were five and I told her the Wiggles were dumb. I'm not a snob, I just don't feel like spending the evening with Tracy's new best friends.

The entire squad starts making its way down to the basement, and my first instinct is to find a place to hide. But I freeze when I hear Regina's nails-on-a-blackboard voice say, "Put the keg over there."

A familiar pair of construction boots descends the stairs behind the gaggle of pop-star wannabes in wigs and heels. Jamie appears, carrying a keg. It didn't even occur to me that he would be here. I'm so happy to see him that I smile and wave before I actually think it through. Regina is standing two steps away, and I don't want to give her any reason to ask why I'm waving at her boyfriend. My hand freezes in midwave, and he looks at me, slightly puzzled. I stop smiling and turn away as the girls coo over how great Jamie is for getting the keg with his fake ID.

Matt comes down wearing a baseball hat with horns on it, carrying a tub of ice. He looks me up and down and says, "Scary costume. What are you supposed to be?"

I'm about to tell him to shove it when Stephanie runs in with a huge bottle of vodka and goes straight to Tracy, carrying it like it's a beating heart needed for a transplant operation.

"Here it is!" she squeals, jumping from one foot to the other, nearly falling over with excitement and balance problems, thanks to her shoes. Stephanie is an extremely enthusiastic person.

Tracy takes the bottle and holds it up like a trophy while everyone in the basement—except Jamie and me—cheers like morons. I'm not sure why a bottle of vodka is so much more exciting than a keg, but then again, I'm not much of a drinker.

Tracy unscrews the cap and starts pouring the vodka into a bowl of punch.

"Don't pour the whole thing in there, Trace—save some for later!" screeches Regina, slapping her hard on the arm. Tracy laughs her embarrassed laugh while rubbing her arm. Someone jams an iPod in a dock and the Crash Kings starts playing so loud that I can feel my skull vibrating. I stick my fingers in my ears and realize that I'm acting like an old lady.

Regina screeches again, making some sort of weird, unearthly cheer call that reverberates off the concrete walls, and suddenly the cheerleaders turn on Tracy like a coven of witches who just happen to wear tight spandex skirts and push-up bras. They grab her, cackling as they pin her down on the table. Regina takes a plastic funnel from her bottomless bag. For a second, I can't figure out what she's going to do with it—at my house, we use funnels to transfer maple syrup from a huge tin canister into a carafe that looks a lot nicer on the breakfast table than the canister does. But there's no maple syrup transfer going on here.

Regina jams the funnel in Tracy's mouth while Kristin, her evil little freshman protégé and kindred spirit, lifts up the punch bowl and starts pouring it into the funnel. It takes about two seconds before Tracy can't swallow it fast enough, and it spills all over her face and costume. She starts choking, which makes the witches laugh even harder.

I look at Stephanie, who is tugging on her skirt and twirling a lock of her red hair—peeking out from under her purple wig—which is what she always does when she doesn't know what to do. I look around for Matt to see if he has any plans to help out his girlfriend, but he's in the corner flirting with Lena, a junior, and has no clue that Tracy is being force-fed vodka. Or maybe he just couldn't care less. I stomp over to the punch bowl table and yank the funnel out of Tracy's mouth, knocking over our platter of cookies and sending punch flying. It splatters across everyone holding Tracy down.

"What the fuck?" says Regina, staring at me as if no one has ever taken anything away from her before.

"You're choking her!" I yell.

"This is her initiation, bitch, so back off," she says in a quiet, scary voice.

Even though I can tell Regina is about half a second away from ripping my eyes out, I stand my ground. Tracy turns over, still coughing and spitting out punch, her eyes watering, her triple-action mascara running down her face. The other cheerleaders are frozen, looking at Regina—who is staring at me—waiting for their cue to do something. Kristin is watching me like she's never seen me before, even though we've been in all the same classes for almost two months now. For some reason, she's not dressed as a pop star. She looks more like a demonic fairy princess, with iridescent wings sprouting from her shoulders and a nasty scowl on her face.

I reach over and whack Tracy on the back a few times, trying to help her get the vodka out of her lungs. But her choking turns into giggling, and she whirls back around, yelling, "Hit me again!" The banshees scream and throw her back down on the table.

And suddenly I can see the future so clearly I can't believe I couldn't see it before. There is no room for me in this world of vodka and cheer-witches, which is fine, because I don't want to be in it anyway. At least, I don't think I do. But is it possible that, even though we've been friends since before we could read, Tracy and I might not make it through this year?

As they jam the funnel down Tracy's throat again, Matt and Lena sneak up the stairs, not even bothering to go separately so no one gets suspicious. Regina leaves the funnel ritual to her minions and plops herself down on Jamie's lap on the couch, shouting instructions to the girls. My heart sinks. I didn't want to believe that he was with her, but if he wasn't, he probably wouldn't let her do that to him. Not to mention that he wouldn't be in Tracy's basement in the first place.

Jamie is watching Tracy's initiation, looking like he's confused about what he's doing here and wondering if he should attempt to stop the madness. I understand the feeling. And then, without any warning, he looks up at me.

I can't look away. And of course that is the very moment Regina stops squawking for a second, turns on Jamie's lap to say something to him and then follows his gaze to me. She looks at me for a good long time, as if everything is clicking into place in her brain, and then she turns back to him and forces him to kiss her. Literally. She grabs his head and pastes her mouth on his, wrapping her arms around his neck as if she wants to suffocate him. I keep looking. He doesn't really kiss her back, but he doesn't not kiss her, either.

I want to rip her stupid bustier right off in front of everyone. Instead, I grab my stuff and head up the stairs, waiting for Tracy or Stephanie or someone to call after me and tell me to come back. For a second, I even imagine Jamie calling my name, but when I think about the fact that he's got a girl on his lap making out with him, I'm pretty sure he's forgotten all about me. And suddenly, the reason I've been so mad at everyone and everything for the past few weeks is very clear to me: I don't understand any of this. The rules of high school are completely, entirely, disturbingly mysterious to me.

But everyone else seems to get them.

I let the door slam shut behind me.

execrable (*adjective*): very bad; deplorable; appalling
(*see also:* Peter)

———

7

AT FIRST, IT'S JUST A NORMAL SATURDAY MORNING AFTER a bad Friday night. I'm sitting on my bed with my laptop, watching an animated short about photosynthesis for a biology project. Then suddenly, out of nowhere, I'm doing a search for my dad.

I've typed his name into the blank box a few times before, but I've never had the courage to hit the search button. I was afraid of what I'd find. Would a picture of him I'd never seen before pop up? What if someone posted footage of the explosion that they'd taken with their phone? What if I saw a photograph of him dead? I already had plenty of images in my head—did I really need more?

Today, however, before I take any time to think about it, I type in "Alfonso Zarelli" and hit Search.

Too quickly, the photosynthesis cartoon vanishes, replaced by a results page. Google claims that there are about eight thousand "Alfonso Zarelli" results, but most of those results beyond the first few pages won't have anything to do with my dad. As I scroll down, I see links to articles on news sites about the explosion and pages from his old company's website where his name is still listed. Nothing weird or unexpected—until I see the memorial sites.

At first, I'm confused about why his name is listed on pages for other people who died—I don't want to take in what's right in front of me. But I can't stop looking and reading, and as I do, I realize that these are the soldiers and contractors who died with my dad. Their friends and families built websites for them and took the time to list the names of everyone who died in the explosion.

How have I gone this long without even thinking about these people? I didn't know any of them. I don't even know if Dad knew them—he could have just been riding with them, like people on a train or a bus who, if they met tomorrow, would have no idea that they'd actually seen each other for the first time the day before. So should I feel bad that I never thought of them until just now?

Yes, I decide. I should.

I click on a site dedicated to a twenty-one-year-old sergeant. There are three photos of him on the home page—his graduation photo from a military academy in California, a picture of him in uniform sitting next to a girl who seems to be laughing at something he said, a photo of a memorial service that his unit had for him, a rifle jammed into the sand, a helmet resting on the butt of the gun. There's a link to letters from his father, his sister, his best friend—some were written while he was still alive, some after he died—and an email he sent to his sister the night before the explosion. And then there's a page with a description of what happened to his unit the day he died, and a list of the people who were killed alongside him.

My dad was one of those people.

I close my laptop and push it away from me on the bed. I look at the clock. It's time to call Peter. We always talk on Saturdays around eleven.

Usually when we're on the phone, I can tell he's fishing for information about how I'm doing. He never seems to believe it when I tell him I'm fine. But I get it—I don't believe him when he says it, either.

Sometimes he's not awake when I call, so I leave him a totally random, incomprehensible message in the weirdest voice I can come up with, and he calls me back later. But today he answers right away, on the first ring, which is good because I don't have it in me to come up with a weird voice right now.

"Rosie?"

"Hey."

"You don't sound so good," he says, coughing a little, his voice rough.

"You sound like you just woke up two seconds ago when your phone rang. Did you go out last night?"

"Friday nights in college rock, Rosie. So do Thursday nights. And Saturdays. And the rest of them. It's awesome," he says. I can tell he wants me to believe what he's saying, but the way he sounds, he might as well be talking about doing his laundry.

"It sounds awesome," I say, playing along anyway. I realize that even though I'm fourteen, and I'm supposed to be into the idea of going out every night of the week, I have no desire to do so. Zero. Zip. None. I guess that means I'll be a social loser in college, too. Something to look forward to.

As Peter tells me about the party he went to last night, I lie back on my bed. The corner of Peter's old PSAT book digs into the back of my head, and I yank it out from underneath me and start doodling on it with a blue marker I find under a pile of crap on my nightstand. My room is a mess, but my mom doesn't say anything about it anymore. She used to tell me all the time that a messy room shows a lack of self-respect. But I don't think she's even set foot in here since the beginning of summer. My walls are neat, but that's just because there's nothing on them. After Tracy made the squad, I ripped down all the posters she'd made me buy of bands and boys I would never like in a million years, and I tore them into shreds. The shreds are still lying on the floor. I like the way they crunch under my feet when I get up in the morning.

I look at my bare walls and have the sudden urge to draw on them. I wonder if my mother would notice that. Without thinking further, I take the blue marker and draw one petal of a tiny daisy—because it's the only thing I know how to draw—on the wall next to my bed. I wait. Nothing happens—the wall doesn't collapse, no alarm bells go off— so I draw the rest of the flower and start to color it in while Peter continues to talk. Drawing on the wall is oddly exciting. Which means my life is pretty sad and pathetic. But I knew that already.

I look at the green light blinking slowly on and off on my closed laptop, and I think about the sergeant still on the screen. Has Peter ever done a search for Dad? I'm just about to ask him when he says, "What did you do last night?"

"Nothing."

"You stayed home?"

"No," I say, pausing. I know he's not going to like it when I tell him about leaving Tracy's party. He thinks I need to be more social; I think that's the last thing I need. "I went to Tracy's Halloween party."

It's quiet on the other end, and then I hear what sounds like a long exhale. My blue marker freezes in the middle of filling in a petal as I place the sound.

"Are you…smoking?" I ask.

"You didn't stay, did you," he counters.

"Are you smoking?" I ask again.

"Yeah. It helps me wake up."

"Gross," I say, completely thrown off by the image of Peter with a cigarette in his mouth. "Dad would kill you for that, you know."

"Yeah, well, he's never going to find out, is he?"

My marker falls out of my hand and down into the space between my bed and the wall. I expect him to say he's sorry, but he doesn't say anything at all, and the silence is weird, like he's waiting for me to call him out for talking like that. But I can't. I can't even believe he said it in the first place.

"So why'd you leave Tracy's?" he finally says.

"Because I hate her," I say, not meaning it.

"What happened this time?"

I was expecting Peter to say, *What did she do now?* His neutral response pisses me off, and I immediately want to make things sound worse than they are.

"She's become one of those idiot girls who turns her back on her real friends, and who's obsessed with all the wrong things."

"Like what?" he says. I can practically hear him rolling his eyes. This conversation isn't going how I pictured it at all. Peter is always on my side, no questions asked. But now he just sounds annoyed.

"Like sex, and vodka funnels, and being a cheerleader."

"That's called fun, Rose. Look into it. High school is short. So is fucking life, I guess."

I can hardly believe my ears. My brother—the guy who was so worked up about me being safe and taking care of myself and not doing anything stupid—is acting like I'm a dud for not partying like Tracy, who's probably going to end up pregnant or diseased or both by the end of the year.

"I thought...you..." I trail off, confused about how to explain why he suddenly seems like an alien to me. He exhales loudly again. "I can't believe you're fucking smoking." It feels so good to swear, even if I'm not really swearing *at* him.

"So why'd you leave? Did something happen?"

"The cheerleaders were forcing Tracy to drink by pouring vodka into her mouth—some stupid initiation thing. And when I tried to help her, everyone got mad at me, especially Regina Deladdo."

"Oh, man. I forgot about her. She's scary."

"Yeah. You could say that."

"Does she still have her claws in Jamie Forta?"

"She did last night," I say, trying to keep any hint of anything out of my voice. It's strange to hear my brother mention Jamie. But not as strange as what he says next.

"Have you seen Jamie a lot this year?"

"Um, I have study hall with him. Well, I did until he got pulled out for remedial English."

"You guys friends?"

"Not...no, not really. I mean, he gave me a ride home once, but I wouldn't say we're friends." My heart is pounding so loud I can barely hear myself talk. "Why?"

"No reason. I just...I know you had a crush on him back when he and I played hockey together."

I'm blushing instantly. "I never had a crush on Jamie."

"Oh, Rosie, come on. When you came to my games, Dad always teased you about watching Jamie instead of me. Remember?"

I don't remember that. What does that mean?

Did I block it out because I was embarrassed, or is everything I ever did with Dad starting to disappear from my mind? I try to run through my mental catalog of Dad memories but my brain seizes up, and I can only see him lying on the ground, fractured into bloodless sections.

I start to panic. *Think,* I command myself, *remember....*

I can't afford to lose a single memory of my dad—even if it's just of him taking out the garbage—because there aren't going to be any new ones.

"He teased me about Jamie?" My throat feels like it's closing off, and my voice sounds strangled.

"Hey, Rosie, it's not a big deal. Look, Forta's actually a good guy. *And* he's a badass. That's one of the reasons I asked him to keep an eye on you this year."

I'm so shocked by what Peter said that I gasp, which works in my favor, in terms of getting air into my lungs.

"You *what?*" I ask, hoping against hope that I just heard him incorrectly.

"I saw Jamie at a party this summer. He came up and said he was sorry about Dad, which is more than I can say for any of the other Union High assholes. He asked how the family was doing. I told him you were starting at Union and that I felt bad that I couldn't be there. He said he'd keep an eye on you, if I wanted him to."

I'm an idiot. A huge, idiotic idiot. So that's why Jamie has been paying attention to me. Not because he likes me, but because Peter asked him to. How could I have ever thought that Jamie liked me? I'm a freshman. He's a junior. He has a girlfriend.

"Why—why didn't you—ask Tracy or Robert?" I stutter.

"Jamie's older, he knows the school, people are kind of afraid of him...." He trails off, his words lingering in the air.

There's something else, but he's not saying it. I am able to take a few deep breaths, and just as I'm about to give him total hell, he changes the subject.

"Rosie, I have something to tell you."

I can tell by the tone of his voice that whatever he's about to say is not good, and I'm not sure how much more I can take in one conversation. My panic is now complemented by dread, and my head is spinning from overload. I suddenly realize that whatever he's about to say is the reason he answered my call on the first ring, and he's probably spent our entire conversation trying to figure out a way to say it.

Maybe if I don't answer him, he won't say it at all.

"Are you there?"

"Yeah…"

"I'm not coming home for Thanksgiving."

What?

How can he leave my mom and me alone on Thanksgiving? What are we going to do—stare at each other across the turkey while we don't talk about Dad?

"Rosie, did you hear me?"

"I'm not sure. I could have sworn you said you weren't coming home for Thanksgiving."

Silence.

"So where are you going instead, Peter?"

"To my girlfriend's. She invited me to her house."

Going to his girlfriend's house for our first Thanksgiving without Dad. Nice. Real nice. Who is this "girlfriend" he's never mentioned before? And what is *wrong* with him?

It takes everything I have not to hang up. I don't really believe in heaven and all that, but I do believe in some kind of afterlife, and I hope Dad can see this from wherever he is. I hope he can find a way to kick Peter's ass from the great beyond, because Peter deserves it, that's for sure.

"You're mad."

"Bring her here."

"I can't. She always spends the holidays with her family. They're really close and it's important to them. Her name is—"

I stop trying not to hang up on Peter. I pull the phone away from my ear so I don't have to hear the end of that sentence and watch as my finger presses the end button. I slide the phone back into the base and stare at it, half expecting it to ring again. It doesn't.

I'm still watching it when there's a knock at my door.

"Rose?" my mom says.

I get off my bed and open the door. My mother is standing there with her glasses on, which signals that she's about to see a "client," as she calls the incredibly messed-up teenagers she helps in her home office downstairs.

Her gaze flickers past me, but the mess of my room doesn't seem to register. She looks back at me. Her brown hair is pulled up in a clip, and everything about her seems gray—her eyes, her skin, her attitude. Somewhere in the back of my mind, I realize that she's exhausted. If I were a better daughter, I'd ask her if she's okay.

"Did you just get off the phone with Peter?" she says, a sympathetic look on her face.

She already knows. He told her first.

Tears fill my eyes before I can bite the inside of my cheek or pinch myself to make them stop. I look at the floor. I hate this new crying crap—I've never been such a crier in my entire life. She puts a hand on my shoulder and looks carefully at my face. I want to pull away from her so badly it hurts.

"Honey, are you having one of your attacks?"

As soon as she asks me that, I realize that I'm breathing in tiny, sharp breaths. I shake my head and make a conscious effort to slow down my breathing. I don't need to give my mother any more ammunition in her quest to shrinkify me.

"I don't have attacks, Mom," I say, trying not to wheeze

out the words as I slap away the stupid tears on my face. Crying is so unbelievably lame.

"You and I are going to do something fun for Thanksgiving, okay?" she says, still looking at me skeptically. "Start thinking about what you want it to be. Maybe we can go to the city to see *The Lion King*—you want to see that, right?"

I don't have it in me to remind her that we all saw *The Lion King* together for my birthday in April. I just shrug instead.

"I know it's hard, Rose, but Peter's in college now and things are different—he's different. It's just part of leaving home. It's natural."

There is nothing natural about this—not his forgetting to tell me about his "girlfriend," not his choosing her over us and not his telling Mom about Thanksgiving before me. I hate that Mom knew first. It makes me want to never trust Peter with anything ever again.

"So why doesn't he want to see us?" I demand, wiping the snot off my upper lip with the back of my hand, practically daring her to tell me to use a tissue. She doesn't. Instead, she looks at her watch.

"It's not that he doesn't want to see us. It's more complicated than that. Look, we'll talk about it later, okay, honey?" she says.

She waits for an answer, but when it becomes painfully clear to her that I don't intend to speak, she turns and heads down the stairs. I listen as her client knocks on the side door of the house, and my mother greets the person in her therapy voice.

It's just as well. I don't want to talk about Peter now. I won't want to talk about him later, either.

I crawl onto my bed, look at my laptop for a second before deciding that I don't want to face the sergeant right now, and then jam my hand down between the bed and the wall to find that marker. It didn't go very far—it landed in a fold of my beige comforter, which was all too happy to soak up every bit of ink that the marker wanted to give it. I grab the thing and sit up.

I'm no Jamie Forta—I have no artistic talent. I usually draw the daisy over and over again when I'm doodling. I suppose I could do that to my wall, making wallflower wallpaper, so to speak, but I don't like the symbolism, and I'm not exactly feeling flowery at the moment. Instead, I just sit there, marker in hand, staring at the blank wall so I don't have to look at my laptop, waiting for inspiration to strike and tell me what I'm supposed to do now.

consummate (*verb*): to finish, to complete, to make perfect
(*see also:* no comment)

———

8

"SOME OF YOU WILL HAVE SEX THIS YEAR, WHETHER YOU are ready or not."

Ms. Maso is standing in front of the blackboard. *Virginity* is written in her neat handwriting. Well, actually, it says, *Virginity?* Everyone is still.

"If I'd known that statement was going to engender such profound silence, I would have made it a long time ago," she says. A few girls giggle. The guys just continue to stare at her, unable to believe that their fantasies have finally come true: the beautiful, mocha-skinned, brown-eyed, petite but fierce Ms. Maso is going to tell them all about sex.

What they don't know is that she will not be telling them about what they would call the "good" parts. She will be telling them about all the awful things that can happen as a result of having sex. They have short memories, these boys; we already got the Birds and the Bees lecture in middle school, with just a slight mention of death, disease, unwanted pregnancies and babies that ruin teenage lives. Those of us who didn't go to the local Catholic school got a pared-down version of the lecture way back in late elementary school.

But I know what's coming today because of Peter, of course. Peter, like all of these boys, was crazy about Ms. Maso and took her word as gospel. Whoever asked Ms. Maso to teach health class was a genius—boys will listen to her say anything. And they'll retain most of it, too. Probably because they've never had a beautiful woman be so straight with them before about sex. Or anything else, for that matter.

Sex Ed. It's a lot for a Monday morning. Especially a Monday morning when you haven't spoken to your best friend in days and your brother dropped a bomb over the weekend.

Bad choice of words.

Tracy didn't call me all weekend, and she didn't sneak past Mr. Cella to visit me in study hall. And now here we are, sitting next to each other in health class. And wouldn't you know it? Today's topic is sex. I have no idea if Tracy is still a virgin or not. She looks like she is—she doesn't look overjoyed or freaked or depressed or anything. She mostly looks hungover. She's probably lucky to be alive after what those stupid girls did to her.

"This is our sex education week. I'm guessing that you all know the mechanics of reproduction, since you're high school freshmen. Just in case you don't, I'm going to pass out this pamphlet. Any of you who want to stop by my office after school with questions or email me to request an appointment should do that. I mean it. If there's something here that you don't know or don't understand, you come see me. Immediately. Are you listening?"

"Yes, Ms. Maso," we say in unison. She is the only teacher who can get us to do this. We just ignore the other teachers when they ask us if we can actually hear them talking. She walks up and down the aisles between our desks, putting the pamphlets directly in our hands. Ms. Maso wears awesome clothes, and she looks like she's about eighteen, even though she's probably, like, thirty. Today she's wearing her J Brand jeans with brown high-heeled boots, and a gold-and-brown sweater set that sparkles. She's cool.

"But what some of you may not know already, and what I'm going to be talking about in gory detail this week, are the repercussions of having sex before you're mature enough to handle it. Anyone know what I mean?"

Nobody says anything. We all study our surroundings very carefully. Stephanie appears to be memorizing the graffiti on her desk. Mike is reading the posters above Ms. Maso's head, which provide all sorts of useful information about the food pyramid and how to identify people with eating disorders. Robert is staring at me, which is a dumb move. It's too conspicuous.

"How about you, Robert?"

He snaps to attention and turns bright red, sneaking a glance back at me before he manages to say, "Pregnancy?"

Ms. Maso nods and slowly looks my way as she says, "Yup, that's one." Some days I really wish Robert would transfer. Or steal something again and go to juvie till he's eighteen. I can't believe I agreed to go to homecoming with him.

"What else?" she asks. "Matt?"

It is all I can do not to look at Tracy.

"STDs," he says, sounding extremely bored, as if STDs were not anything he needed to concern himself with. I want to punch him. I always want to punch him.

"Exactly. Can anyone tell me what an STD is?" I know what's coming next. "Rose?"

I always know when a teacher is going to call on me. And I have to admit that usually I'm pretty thrilled when it happens. Despite the fact that kids who know the answers get made fun of for, well, knowing the answers, we still like to show off.

But I really don't feel like answering this question.

I take a deep breath. "An STD is a sexually transmitted disease."

"Like?" she asks.

After a long silence, Doug, one of Matt's swim team co-jerks, calls out "Chlamydia" from the back of the room. I probably shouldn't be thinking of him as a jerk since he just got me out of having to say *chlamydia* in front of everyone.

"You would know," says Matt. The boys erupt in laughter.

Ms. Maso stares at Matt until everyone settles down, which happens pretty quickly. Nobody messes with Ms. Maso.

She walks toward Matt, her boot heels clacking on the floor in the silence. When she arrives at his desk, she leans down and gets in his face. If I were a cheerleader, I'd jump on my desk right now and wave my stupid pom-poms for her.

"Here's what I think you don't realize about chlamydia, or gonorrhea, or HPV—they are all really easy to get, and to give." She looks hard at Matt for another second till he looks away and then continues down the aisle. "HIV is harder to get, but not that much harder, and it can kill you. Syphilis is on the rise in this country again, and if it's not treated properly, it can destroy your internal organs and ruin your mind."

She pauses to let this sink in. Pausing at the perfect moment is one of Ms. Maso's specialties. We are all now imagining what it would be like to have an STD. And that's exactly what she wants us to imagine.

"So unless you're interested in getting these diseases—and mark my words, statistics say that some of you will get them, either because you're irresponsible or uninformed, having not paid attention in my class—I suggest you listen up and listen good. If anybody makes another crack like the one Matt just made, I'll throw you out of this class, and you'll have to take it again next semester when everyone else is taking art, or acting, or whatever elective they please." She arrives back at the front of the class, and folds her arms. "Understood? Matt?"

"Yes, Ms. Maso. Sorry."

She pauses again, to excellent effect. Matt starts to squirm a little, which makes me happier than I've been in a long, long time.

"Okay. Rule number one for sexually active people. Can anyone take a guess?"

There's a pause, and then Tracy slowly raises her hand.

"Tracy?"

"Use a condom?"

I can't believe my ears. I'm torn between wanting to kiss her and wanting to cry.

"Excellent. Thank you, Tracy. I'm going to put that up on the blackboard, but I'm going to call that rule number two. Anyone know why?"

I have no idea what she's talking about, but I think I'm still in shock from hearing my best friend, who was so desperate to go on the pill last month, talking about condoms in health class in front of her incredibly irresponsible boyfriend. I want to hug her. But I know that would look a little weird, especially given the context of the conversation.

"Um…is there another rule that's more important?" asks Mike.

Ms. Maso nods, waiting for him to continue. He doesn't. Mike is a sophomore—he must have failed health class last year. I'm really confused about how anyone could fail the easiest class in their high school career, but as Tracy always tells me, things that are easy for me are not always easy for everyone else. Or something like that. I used to hear that as a compliment, but today it just seems like another version of her telling me that I'm a snob.

"What's more important than using a condom, Mike?"

He thinks for a few seconds and comes up with nothing.

"I didn't think anything was more important than that, Ms. Maso," he says earnestly. Some girls giggle, and I look back at Stephanie, whose face is now as red as her hair. At least I'm not the only one with an overdeveloped blushing mechanism.

Ms. Maso studies each and every student as if she is very disappointed in us. "Every year I hope someone is going to get this, but no one ever does. It says a lot about teenagers' sexual priorities, unfortunately."

She turns her back to us and writes, in the number one slot on the board, *Respect yourself and respect your partner.*

"What does this have to do with sex?" she asks.

"Everything," I mutter.

"What, Rose?"

"Nothing. I didn't say anything," I answer, not entirely sure how Ms. Maso heard something that I thought was inside my head, and not exactly knowing what I meant in the first place.

"You did. I heard you. You answered correctly. Tell everyone what you said."

I love Ms. Maso—I really do. I sort of want to be her when I grow up. But I hate it when she does this. I know she's just doing it because she thinks it's good for my self-esteem or my confidence or my something or other, and yes, that's part of her job, but really, I'd rather just sink into a hole in the floor and be done with it. And what do I know, anyway? I've never had sex before. I don't even know if I'll ever want to. So where do I get off answering these questions or having opinions about what rules people are supposed to follow?

"I said, 'everything.'"

"What did you mean?"

Crap. Why am I always getting myself into these situations? What *did* I mean?

"Um, well, I think I meant that, uh, in order to have sex responsibly, and in a way that's meaningful, you have to have respect for yourself and respect for, um, the other person."

"Kiss ass," Matt whispers from a few rows behind me. Of course, this time, Ms. Maso doesn't hear him. That's not the way my life works. But Tracy does, and she turns and glares at him. Then she looks back at me. She smiles, but it's one of those smiles that doesn't take up her whole face, and I can see that something bad happened between Friday night and now. I can also see that she forgives me for all the things I said. I can't tell if she agrees with them, but I'll just take forgiveness for now.

"Exactly, Rose, that's exactly right. One more question. What does it mean to respect someone in the context that we're talking about?"

She's looking at me, but before I can formulate a reply, Tracy's hand goes up.

"Tracy?"

"It means listening to what that person wants and doesn't want, and taking it seriously. And not pressuring them."

Ms. Maso graces Tracy with one of her flawless smiles. "Right. Very nice explanation. Thank you. Now, I know there's a lot of pressure out there to have sex, and a lot of you will do it way before you're ready because of that. And I'm not going to stand up here and tell you that you should wait until you meet the person you want to spend the rest of your life with because I personally feel that that is just unrealistic advice for people your age in this world that we live in today. But the next best thing, if you *are* going to have sex, is to make sure that there is mutual respect. Because if there isn't, I can promise you this—one or both of you will deeply regret it."

The class is silent as Ms. Maso turns back to the board. I don't think anyone was expecting her to say what she said. I'm sure no one was surprised to hear her mention chlamydia, but no one expected her to play the respect card in health class.

"I want you all to take a moment right now, and think about the person you want to have sex with."

"*The* person? As in, only one?" Doug says. The guys snicker. Most of the girls look panic-stricken.

"Yes, Doug, try to limit your reverie to one person," she says, barely managing to avoid rolling her eyes. "Choose someone you like, not just for his or her physical appearance, but for who they are, how they think, what they do. Don't worry, I'm not going to ask you to name names. Just think about the person. And, of course, if you don't want to have sex with anyone, that's just fine. Think about someone you have romantic feelings for."

Jamie is the first—and only—person who comes into my head.

At first I'm embarrassed, thinking about how Peter basically asked him to be my friend this year. But then the embarrassment disappears, and I'm thinking about how good he looked on Friday night, even with Regina plastered to his lap. I remember the conversation we had about sex during study hall, when Angelo accidentally made me cry. I remember how he almost touched me, and how that was the first time I noticed his hands and arms, how beautiful they are. I imagine those hands touching my face, and I blush, hot and fierce. I look up at Ms. Maso standing at the front of the room, watching us. She's smiling, but not in a way that makes me feel foolish. It's like she understands exactly what we're feeling.

"Now, what if you made that person feel ashamed, or scared, or if you hurt that person deeply? How would you feel?"

No one answers.

"I'll tell you how you'd feel. Terrible. Miserable. Like a bad human being. Like you couldn't ever face that person again. And that, people, is why it is so important to take the decision to have sex very, very seriously. It is not just about you, and there is a lot at stake. If you're not careful, not only can there be pregnancy and disease, but there can be shame and embarrassment and a whole lot of pain."

The bell rings, and Ms. Maso shouts over the sound of chairs scraping backward on the floor and nervous laughter, "I want a three hundred and fifty-word essay on Wednesday about what it means to respect yourself in the context of sexuality." The class groans, and she says, "Want me to make it five hundred?" We collectively tell her that no, three-fifty will be sufficient, thank you.

Robert appears at my desk while I'm still getting my things together. He leans over and winks at me. I roll my eyes.

"You know who I was thinking of?" he asks.

"Megan Fox."

"Too bimbo-y."

"Angelina Jolie."

"Too old—"

Tracy steps between Robert and me, grabbing my arm. "I need to talk to you. Will you walk with me to French?"

I look at her eyes and realize that she cried at some point today. I can always tell—her eyes stay red for a while after she cries. I'm so happy that she wants to talk that I don't even bother to act annoyed with her. I give Robert a *sorry* smile over my shoulder, and she pulls me out of the room, saving me from having to answer his next question, which definitely would have been, "Who were *you* thinking of?" He's predictable when he's trying to be sexy, or suave, or seductive, or whatever it is he was trying to be.

Until Tracy made the squad, she and I walked to all our classes together. Since then, she sometimes walks with scary demon-fairy Kristin, or she gets stopped in the hall by Lena or Regina, who ask her to do something stupid for them, like risk getting suspended by cutting class to get them slices at Cavallo's, which is in the mall next to the school.

Today, she wants to walk with me.

"Why did you leave on Friday night?" she asks.

I don't know if I can be honest with her right now. She seems a little fragile, and a tirade on the idiotic behavior of her teammates might not help things.

"I don't know, I just didn't fit in," I say as we arrive at our lockers. She pops hers open and gets her French book off the shelf. "You were doing all that crazy stuff with the vodka funnel. And you were mad at me."

Tracy turns to me, and she looks like she's about to cry some more. "I wasn't mad at you. I mean, I was, but it was stupid. I know you're just worried about me and you want me to be safe." She looks at her shoes. "Matt and I had a huge fight after you left."

"You did?" I say, hoping against hope that we're finally done with Stupid Boy for good. That's what I've taken to calling Matt in my head. Hopefully I will never say it out loud.

"Yeah. I was really drunk and I felt sick, so I went upstairs to lie down for a minute, and I found him in my parents' room with Lena. They weren't doing anything—they were just sitting there talking, and the door was open...." She stops, not wanting to say anything else. I opt not to mention that I saw them sneaking up the stairs together and that I would put money on that door having been opened only when they heard someone coming.

"What did you say to him?"

"I don't really remember. I think I just stood there. And then Lena got up and went downstairs. And Matt asked me what my problem was."

"Trace—"

"I told him he was being a jerk and that there was no way I was going to sleep with him if he was flirting with other girls. You know what he said to me?"

I brace myself.

"He told me there was no way I was going to sleep with him anyway, which was just fine with him because he didn't want to have to use condoms, and…and I think we broke up." She turns to put her face in her locker so that no one will see her crying. I notice for the first time that she has a note from Matt taped on the inside of her locker door, right under her mirror, next to a picture of us. It's a note that Matt wrote her last year on the back of a lav pass. It says, "TRC iz GR8!" The days of Matt writing notes like that are long gone.

"Tracy, he doesn't deserve you. I mean, for him to take Lena to your parents' bedroom at *your* party, even if they were 'just talking,' that's really…bad."

She doesn't turn around. I put my hand on her arm.

"Did you get sick after all that vodka?"

She nods and I hear her sniffle.

"Did you get in trouble with your parents?"

She nods again, and I can tell she just wants to crumple to the floor. I take her by the arm, close her locker for her and lead her down the hall to the bathroom. The bell rings, but I know Monsieur Levert won't ask any questions when we show up in class a few minutes late. Tracy's swollen eyes will pretty much say it all, and Monsieur Levert is old-school—he would never make a lady discuss her problems in front of others.

Thank god Matt takes Spanish. We can both use a break from that jerk for at least one period.

We go into the bathroom. I check under all the blue stall doors to make sure we're alone. Tracy looks in the mirror, on which someone has painted *Suck this* in fuchsia nail polish. Same handwriting as *Suck it,* which is still on the door of the stall I was hiding in the day Jamie drove me home. At least the nail polish color is different. Slightly.

Tracy is trying to figure out how she's going to fix her runny eye makeup without any makeup remover. I can tell it's stressing her out.

"Why were Regina and Kristin making you drink on Friday?"

What I really want to ask is why she *let* them make her drink. I resolve to rephrase.

Tracy shrugs. "It's just a stupid tradition, initiation. Everybody goes through it."

"But I don't understand why you would let them treat you like that," I say.

"I don't have a choice. If I want to cheer, I have to do things like that."

"For how long?" I ask, kicking at the wet, brown paper towels that have spilled onto the cruddy tiled floor from the overflowing trash bin.

"Maybe for the rest of the year."

"I don't like those girls," I say.

She looks up at me sharply. "You don't like Regina, you

mean. But you don't really know her, or any of the other girls."

I feel my face getting hot. "I know them enough to know that I don't like any of them."

"You don't like Regina because she's with Jamie."

I prop my books on the sink and take my makeup bag out of my backpack. I pretend to look for something in it. I see the sharpener and the blue eyeliner. Tracy, who studies *Teen Vogue* religiously, informed me recently that girls with blue eyes should actually wear brown eyeliner. I wanted to remind her that she's the one who put this makeup bag together for me in the first place, and she should know what color my eyes are at this point, so if I'm wearing blue eyeliner, it's entirely her fault.

Then I remember that all these things in the bag are her hand-me-downs. She probably didn't even stop to think about what color my eyes are. She probably just crammed all the stuff she didn't want anymore in the bag and figured it would be good enough for me.

I'm still ignoring what she said about Jamie and Regina.

"You like him, Rose. Why don't you just admit that, at least to me?"

I often think I can sneak things by Tracy but then she says something that makes me realize she has known what was going on the whole time. It makes me feel kind of bad for underestimating her intelligence, which I seem to do again and again. I mean, Tracy has known me forever. She knows when I have a crush—why would I think I could hide that from her?

"I didn't want to tell you because you don't like him. You think I should go out with Robert and you think Jamie is stupid and too old for me."

She blots under her eyes with a tissue and reapplies her lip gloss before she answers me.

"What I think about Jamie is that he's with someone. But it shouldn't matter what I think, Rose. If you like him, you like him." She turns from the mirror and tilts her head to one side. She's deciding whether to tell me something or not.

"What?" I say, feeling nervous for some inexplicable reason.

"I think he likes you, too."

I know that he doesn't, that he's just "keeping an eye on me" like Peter asked him to. But my heart stops in my chest anyway. "What makes you say that?"

"He left right after you left on Friday. Did he bring you home or something?"

I shake my head, imagining how different my Friday night would have been if Jamie had come to find me. Even if he was just doing it to make sure I was okay.

"Well, it looked like he was going after you, and Regina didn't like that at all. She got really, really mad. In fact, you might want to avoid her for a while."

As big as our high school is, there is no avoiding anyone. Ever. Unless you're Jamie Forta, in which case you can appear and disappear at will.

"She doesn't have to worry, Trace. Jamie doesn't like me. He's just doing Peter a favor."

"What favor?"

"Peter was worried about me starting school this year without him, and he asked Jamie to look out for me."

Tracy stares at me, dumbfounded. "Why would he ask Jamie to do that?"

"Because Jamie's tough, I guess. I don't know."

Tracy shakes her head. "Whatever is going on with Jamie

and you, Rose, it's not because Peter asked him to watch out for you. I saw the way he watched you leave on Friday night."

He watched me leave? With Regina sitting right there on his lap, trying to force him to make out with her?

"How could you have seen anything?" I ask. "Those girls were pouring vodka down your throat."

Tracy rolls her eyes, then takes one more look in the mirror. "Come on. Let's go while I still look like I've been crying so Monsieur Levert won't ask any questions."

"Tracy."

She turns to me.

"I'm really sorry about you and Matt. But I don't think he respects you the way you deserve."

She nods and picks up her books, crossing to the door. I know her well enough to know that she's already figuring out how to win Matt back. And despite the show she put on in health class today, I'm sure I'm not going to like her tactics.

I wish I could just stay in this smelly old bathroom with the unbreakable mirrors and the stall-door graffiti. Because in here, today, right now, my best friend and I are talking again, like we always have. And who knows how much longer that will last.

surreptitious (*adjective*): doing something or behaving sneakily
(*see also:* my mother)

———

9

"ROSE, PLEASE PUT YOUR SEAT BELT ON. YOU NEED TO WEAR it whenever you're in a car, okay? It's the law."

I'm tempted to tell my mother to stop treating me like I'm in elementary school, but I reach over my shoulder and grab the belt without saying anything. We're driving to Morton's, where we will pretend that our first Thanksgiving without my dad—or Peter—is just peachy.

A few weeks ago, she asked me again if I wanted to go to the city for Thanksgiving to see *The Lion King* on Broadway, and I decided it was about time to remind her that we'd already seen it for my birthday. She stared at me as if she were trying to figure out whether I was lying or not, and then said, "Right, I remember now," even though I could tell that she didn't. I don't really know how anyone could forget *The Lion King* on Broadway—even if you hate musicals, which she doesn't, there's no way you could forget actors manipulating huge animal puppets with every muscle they have, decked out in spectacular body paint. I mean, it's unforgettable by design. But somehow it didn't make an impression on my mother. Or she doesn't remember that it did, which ends up being essentially the same thing.

After that conversation, she stopped trying to come up with "fun" ideas for Thanksgiving, which was more than fine with me. I don't need to have fun for Thanksgiving—I just need to get it over with.

Peter called from that girl's house this morning. Mom talked to him, but I got in the shower as soon as the phone rang and I stayed there until I was sure that they'd run out of things to say and hung up. I haven't talked to Peter in almost a month. He emailed me once, trying to be all casual like nothing had happened, but I didn't answer him. I keep waiting for my mother to say something about it, but I don't think she's even noticed that we're not talking.

Mom and I cross the icy parking lot and head toward the squat, brick restaurant with the big plate-glass windows facing Union's main street. Before we even set foot in the place, I smell cooking oil and French fries—Morton's isn't in danger of winning any awards for fine dining. "It's not bad, it's basic," Dad always used to say whenever I would complain about eating there. Then he'd wink and add, "Just don't eat anything that's not thoroughly cooked."

Robert is standing at the host stand when we walk in, dressed in all black with a white waiter's apron around his waist. In his thrift-store wingtips and slicked-back hair, he looks like he stepped out of one of the 1930's photos on the walls that are supposed to make guests feel like the restaurant has been in town for decades instead of about a year and a half.

"Ah, the guests of honor have arrived!" he announces too loudly.

"Hello, Robert," my mother says.

"Mrs. Zarelli, you look lovely, as always," he replies, kissing her hand instead of shaking it, even though that's clearly what she intended for him to do when she offered it. He smiles at me as I roll my eyes. "And Rose, you look ravishing, of course. Right this way, please."

Robert has been waiting tables at Morton's since he turned sixteen a few weeks ago. He's already on probation for allowing friends—or rather, people who became his friends when he got his license and started working at Morton's—to hang out after closing. When I told him that my mom and I had a reservation for Thanksgiving, he arranged his schedule so that he could wait on us. My mother likes Robert—he can make her laugh, which is way more than I can do these days. Not that I try.

After we're seated, Robert asks, "What can I get you ladies to drink?"

"I'll have a glass of the house red," my mother answers.

"Cranberry juice and ginger ale, please," I say.

"I'll be right back." He winks at me as he leaves, making my mother smile.

I keep my eyes focused on the menu. Morton's is quiet, although it's still early. Maybe people are coming later. Or maybe they're having normal Thanksgivings at home with their families, sitting around their dining room tables, serving themselves huge portions of sweet potatoes and turkey and stuffing and gravy. I look at the empty tables with their brown, red and orange crepe-paper-turkey centerpieces, and I want to go home and get back in bed.

"Robert's sweet," my mother says.

"He's annoying," I reply.

My mother looks at me over her menu, one eyebrow raised. "Let's focus on what we're grateful for. You have a friend who arranged his schedule so he could be here for you on Thanksgiving when he could be home with his family."

It's actually not as big a deal as my mother is making it out to be. I'm sure Robert was thrilled to have an excuse not to spend Thanksgiving with his non-family family. He works hard to spend as little time as possible in that house.

"So, Rose, I sensed that you were avoiding Peter when he called this morning. You haven't spoken to him since he told you about his girlfriend, have you?" she says.

Turns out my mother is paying closer attention than I thought.

"Nope," I say.

"Why not?"

"Because he's a jerk," I reply, annoyed that she bothered to ask when the answer is so obvious.

Robert comes back and puts down our drinks, spilling a few drops of cranberry juice on the white tablecloth. "Oops. Sorry, Rosie." He tries to mop it up with the corner of his apron and then gives up, sliding the saltshaker over to cover the stain. "I'll be back in a minute to take your order." He grins.

My mother lifts her glass to take a sip and then stops. "Don't be mad at Peter, honey. Be thankful that he's found someone he cares about enough to spend the holiday with."

Personally, I think he found someone specifically so that he wouldn't have to spend the holiday with *us,* but if I say that, we'll just end up having a conversation about my "negativity."

"How about a toast," she says. "To us. And to your father."

Her glass just hangs there in the air, waiting. I know what I'm supposed to do, but I can't make my hand reach for my drink. I feel weird, like I'm not really in my body. I just stare at her bloodred wine.

"Rose?"

I look from the glass to her puzzled face.

"You don't want to toast?" she asks.

"You can't do that," I say quietly.

"What, honey?"

"You can't just bring him up like that, like we've been talking about him all along."

My mother's face goes white as a sheet and then bright red. I got my blushing problem from her, clearly. She slowly lowers her glass to the table without taking a sip and looks down at her hands. I notice that she's taken off her diamond engagement ring but is still wearing her wedding band. This makes her hands look old, somehow. After a moment, she looks up again.

"I know you're angry, but there's no reason to be cruel. This is happening to me, too."

I'm not trying to be cruel—I'm confused. She hardly ever even says his name, and now we're suddenly supposed to toast him?

Robert arrives. "Have you had a chance to look at the menu, ladies?"

My mother forces a smile for him and shakes her head. "Why don't you just recommend something?"

"Certainly. I would recommend our tasting menu, which will take you on a veritable culinary tour through all the holiday standards." He sounds like he's reciting lines he memorized before his shift started, in order to better play his role of "waiter" today.

"A culinary tour sounds delightful. That's what I'll have," she says, closing her menu and handing it back to Robert.

"And for the young lady?" he asks, turning to me.

"I'll have that, too."

"Excellent choices!" he replies, giving us a quick bow and then departing from the table.

"Is he always like that?" my mother asks, watching him go. I don't answer her. She looks at me for a moment, and I can see that she's trying to figure out how to respond—as a trained therapist or as my mother. "You know, we don't have to talk about your father. Or we can. It's up to you."

"You didn't warn me. You just, out of nowhere… I don't know. Forget it."

"I'm sorry. I didn't mean to upset you," she concedes in her therapy voice.

I hate it when she talks like that. It makes me feel like she's a robot. We both reach for our glasses and drink at the same time. And that's when I see Jamie walk in with a man who looks exactly like him, give or take thirty years.

On the rare occasions when I've seen Jamie in the halls, I've avoided him, too embarrassed to face him ever since Peter told me about their little deal. It's just as well, since apparently Regina has it out for me. But now that I'm looking at him, I can't look away, no matter how much I want to. He catches my eye and smiles.

I'm trying to decide whether I should smile back when his gaze shifts to my mother. His smile fades, and he gets a weird look on his face. Suddenly he's heading straight for our table—or, actually, straight for her.

I can hardly believe my eyes.

When he reaches us, he doesn't even look at me. "Um, Mrs. Zarelli?" he says quietly, sounding unsure about how to address her.

My mother looks up at Jamie with no recognition for a moment. And then she smiles. "Jamie Forta," she says. She stands up and touches his shoulder. "How are you doing?" My gut is telling me that there's something I don't like about this interaction, but my brain hasn't put the pieces together yet.

"I'm okay," he says, nodding. "Sorry. About Mr. Zarelli. And sorry I didn't come to the memorial."

"I completely understand. And thank you for your condolences. Is that your father?" she asks, looking past Jamie at the man who has settled himself at the bar under the big TV—with the biggest glass of beer I've ever seen—without even looking to see where Jamie went.

Jamie nods.

"Is he still a police officer?" The way she says this tells me that there was a time when Jamie's dad may have been in danger of losing his job, and not just because the city was laying off cops.

Jamie nods again and then turns to me. "Hi, Rose. Happy Thanksgiving."

I lift my hand in a lame wave—that's all I can manage. I can't even smile. Jamie was going to come to the memorial this summer? And what does she mean by *I completely understand?*

What the heck is going on here?

Jamie looks from me to my mother and back again, realizing that I have no idea what the story is. But he does nothing to clear up the mystery. "Well, I gotta go. Happy Thanksgiving," he says again, nodding and then heading for the bar.

It's like I've slipped into a parallel universe. My mother sits back down, takes another sip of her wine and looks out the window.

"Mom." She turns to me, takes in my confusion, and says "Yes?" in a tone of voice that I know means *You're not getting any information out of me.* Which, of course, tells me all I need to know.

Jamie, at one point or another, was one of my mother's clients.

No wonder he didn't need directions to my house when he drove me home in September.

"You're blushing, Rose," my mother says, a surprised smile on her face.

I want to be nice to her, I really do, especially today. But I hate everything about this. Why does everyone in my family know Jamie better than I do? And why am I the last to know that they know?

Furious, I get up from the table, my napkin falling to the floor, my chair tipping precariously backward, and I go over to the bar. I can feel my pulse beating under the hot skin on my face. My mother calls after me. I ignore her and reach out to tap Jamie on the shoulder, but I stop short of touching him.

"Can I talk to you for a second?"

Jamie shoots a glance at his father, who doesn't see or hear anything besides the football game on the bar's flat screen. He gets off his stool and leads me toward the coat-check room like he already had a plan in mind for this very moment. Robert stops in front of us, a bread basket in each hand.

"Everything okay, Rose?" he asks, his eyes on Jamie.

"Fine."

"Want me to keep your mother company for a minute?"

"Sure," I say, my fury giving way for one split second to raw shame, shame for leaving my mother sitting by herself on her first Thanksgiving without Dad. But the shame is followed by anger that her grief can make me feel shame.

I exhaust myself.

We step into the coat-check room. "I know why you're pretending to like me," I say before he can even turn around.

Jamie is smart, unlike me. When he doesn't understand what's going on, he keeps his mouth shut and waits. I, however, start talking and can't stop until I've said every thought in my head.

"Because Peter asked you to. And now I know why you knew where my house is. Because you know my mom, not because you drove Peter home one time. You're a liar, Jamie."

There's a flash of anger in Jamie's hazel eyes—I guess he doesn't like being called a liar. At first I'm intimidated by seeing him angry and knowing that I'm the cause, but then I think, *well, too bad—you* are *a liar.* I realize I'm getting a little thrill out of not backing down. He looks at me hard, like he's trying to figure out where I'm going with all this. That makes two of us.

"I don't know your mom. She helped me once."

I wait for more, but apparently that's all he's going to say about that without more prompting.

"You been ignoring me because of your brother?" he asks.

That's part of the reason. The other part is his scary girlfriend and how if any of her minions see me talking to him, I'm likely to get my ass kicked. "I don't like it when people make decisions about me that I don't know about," I say.

"Pete didn't want you to be alone."

"I have friends, you know. I don't need fake ones."

He looks away and slowly reaches his hand into the mass of empty wire hangers dangling from one of the coat racks. They jangle softly in the quiet of the room as he brushes his fingers back and forth across them. For a moment, I lose myself in the sound, and a strange feeling shivers up my spine, as if Jamie were touching me, not the hangers. His touch seems purposeful but gentle, and I can imagine what it would be like to have his hand on my skin. The motion is hypnotic— my eyes practically start to close.

I need to snap out of it. Jamie lied to me, and I shouldn't be thinking about him at all, never mind like this.

"Why did you need my mom?" I force myself to ask. I know it's none of my business, especially since I just told him I don't need his friendship, but I needed to say something before I disintegrated into a puddle at his feet.

He rests both hands on the coat rack that's bolted into the wall and stares at the floor. Then he turns and takes my hand, and I go completely still as warmth begins to radiate up my arm.

"I'm not pretending to like you," he says. My face burns as his words sink in. "I don't do that."

He walks out of the room. I reach for the coat rack to keep myself upright. I need to catch my breath, but for once it's not because I'm angry. I can still feel his hand on mine, and everything is tingling. The feeling spreads across my whole body, like a web across my skin. I couldn't shake it off even if I wanted to, which I don't. I want to stay right where I am for the rest of the day, my eyes half closed, warm from the inside out.

When I finally head back to the table, I see that Jamie's dad is still at the bar, but Jamie is gone. Robert is standing next to my mother. He says something, and she throws her head back and laughs. I realize that I haven't seen my mother laugh since before the day my father decided that their best financial option was for him to pack up his pocket protectors and pencils and head off to Iraq nearly eleven months ago.

I sit back down at the table.

"Robert says you're going to homecoming together. Sounds like we need to start shopping for a dress."

"Yeah," I say. I'm suddenly so tired I can barely keep my eyes open—I feel like I just ran a marathon.

"That's great, honey. I'm glad you're going."

"I'll make sure she has a good time, Mrs. Zarelli," Robert says. *Good luck with that,* I think as he goes to find our meals.

"I didn't realize you were friendly with Jamie Forta," my mother says cautiously. "He's a junior now, isn't he?"

I look her straight in the eyes and shrug, determined not to give her any more information about Jamie than she gave me. She tilts her head and sighs, defeated. Score one for me in my pathetic little game.

Make an effort. Dad would want you to make an effort today.

"I didn't make cross-country," I suddenly blurt out.

She looks startled, a mixture of disappointment and confusion on her face. "I didn't even know you tried out."

"I did. Barely. I sucked."

"Why didn't you tell me beforehand?"

"I didn't tell anyone, Mom," I say.

She starts to say something but changes her mind and nods instead.

"It was my first run since last spring," I offer.

She swirls the last bit of wine around in her glass, studying it intently. I imagine that she's deciding whether to ask me anything else. "How did it feel to run?" she finally says, curiosity winning over caution in what was probably a serious battle in her therapist's brain.

"Like my legs were dead," I say.

My response shocks her. She stares at me as if trying to figure out if my choice of words was accidental or intentional. Robert returns with our "holiday culinary tours"— a plate of turkey, stuffing, mashed potatoes and cranberry sauce from a can—and we start our Thanksgiving in silence.

WINTER

taciturn (*adjective*): not given to talking
(*see also:* Jamie Forta)

———

10

I'M IN THE GYM BATHROOM LOOKING AT MY ZITS IN THE mirror. My "crop" of zits, as Peter would say. I was planning on wearing makeup, but in the trial run earlier, it just made my skin all red and blotchy, and I looked even worse. Mom says I have extremely sensitive skin, just like hers. Thanks, Mom.

My long, brown velvet dress looks stupid, not elegant the way I imagined it would when Mom talked me into it, and it completely flattens out my breasts, the only feature I have that I think someone else might find sexy. My shoes are too big and make my feet look wide. I forgot to put on jewelry. I have my period, and my stomach is all bloated, so the dress doesn't really fit right. In short, I'm ugly. But that's not new information to me.

The door slams open, and the homecoming court—otherwise known as half the cheerleading team—swarms in. I try not to make eye contact with Regina, whose new favorite hobby is to stare me down when we pass in the halls.

The court wears brightly colored tight satin strapless gowns that look like discarded bridesmaids' dresses they stole from their older sisters' closets. They have matching corsages on their wrists that seem to take up half their arms. Their hair is teased and sprayed into elaborate twists and up-dos, and adds at least four or five inches to their heads. I don't have to look in the mirror to know that my brown hair is flat, flat, flat and does nothing interesting at all no matter what I try or whose hairdresser I go to. My hair has always been boring. Just like I've always been ugly.

I hate dances.

"Hey, Rose," says Michelle Vicenza. Her dress is pale pink with rhinestones across the sweetheart neckline. She has gorgeous curly dark hair and big brown eyes, and diamonds in her ears. Michelle is one of those amazing girls who rise above the social hierarchy, oblivious to its rules and regulations. She is friendly to everyone, and everyone—me included—thinks she's a goddess. The rest of the homecoming court is a nightmare.

"Hi, Michelle."

"You look great!" She air-kisses me.

"Oh, uh…" I say, self-consciously shaking my head, feeling like an unwashed potato stuffed into a too-small brown paper bag. "You look beautiful and I love your—"

"Michelle, you got any gloss?" says Regina, talking right over me. "I don't know where mine is."

"I just lent you mine a few minutes ago!" says Susan, wincing in pain as she plunges a pick into the sprayed mass on her head and yanks upward to make it even higher. "What did you do, kiss it all off already? You should let Forta come up for air every once in a while."

I suddenly feel nauseous.

"He got the keg, right?" Susan asks.

"No, he forgot," Regina snaps. "Of course he got the keg. Gloss, 'Chelle?" she demands impatiently.

"Here." Michelle reaches into her matching bag and pulls out some red lip gloss. I suddenly realize I left the vintage black clutch my mom lent me, which is the only cool thing about my outfit, in Robert's car. Not that there's much in it anyway. I was so aggravated by my skin that I gave up trying to look good and, in an act of rebellion, left all aids at home.

"Thanks," says Regina, reaching across me as if I'm not there. When her arm grazes my chest, she scowls, like I somehow came between her and her quest for lip gloss. Regina is the only blonde in the group. Her mean-looking face doesn't seem to fit with the other girls, who look happy and nice, even if they aren't. She's wearing a red satin dress that is suspiciously similar to Michelle's, right down to the rhinestone-studded neckline. Except Regina's rhinestones have been removed, leaving pea-sized dark spots at regular intervals. Maybe there's some unwritten squad rule that your dress can't look like the head cheerleader's or you'll get court-martialed. I suddenly imagine Regina behind bars in cheerleader prison, being forced to make pom-poms by hand. If I weren't so freaked out by my proximity to her, I might actually laugh.

"Who are you here with, Rose?" says Michelle. Regina looks at her like she's talking to the air. Michelle of course pays no attention. Love her.

"Robert McCormack. Do you know him?"

"I don't think so. Is he in your class?"

"Yes. Are you here with Frankie?"

She affectionately rolls her eyes. "Who else?" she says. Frankie and Michelle have been together since she was thirteen. Frankie was homecoming king all four years of high school, even as a freshman. It must have been a bit of a comedown from king of Union High to general manager of Cavallo's. I wonder when it will dawn on Michelle that that is all Frankie will ever do. Maybe Michelle knows already and doesn't care because Frankie is so incredibly hot that most people would never wonder what she was doing with him. But somehow I doubt that. She seems like she might not want her life to be tied to a pizza parlor that's open seven days a week, fourteen hours a day.

When I met Michelle at Peter's graduation party last year, she told me a story about being in shop class with Peter in junior high. Mr. Dray had been called out of class, and Peter decided to entertain everyone, standing up on a table and improvising a song called "Shop Class Blues" to the tune of Elvis's "Blue Suede Shoes." Michelle claimed she laughed so hard she wet her pants and was excused for the rest of the day. I think she had a crush on Peter back then. Sometimes I like to imagine what my life would be like if Michelle had gone out with Peter instead of Frankie. I'd practically be Union High royalty.

"Here, 'Chelle," says Regina, reaching across me again to return the gloss. She takes a few steps back and turns to get a good look at her ass in the mirror, as if it could have changed significantly from the last time she checked it a few seconds ago.

"Did you go to dinner?" asks Michelle.

"We went to Shaun's. Me and Robert, and Tracy and Matt, and Stephanie and Mike—you know, that whole group." Of course she doesn't know, but she nods and smiles anyway. "How was your—"

"Come on, Michelle," squawks Regina, fluttering and jostling at the door with the other girls, who look like a flock of impatient parakeets. "They're waiting."

"All right. Have a good time, Rose," she says. "I'll see you out there."

"Good luck. I'm sure you'll win."

"Of course she'll win," hisses Regina, glaring at me. "Michelle always wins." She flings open the door and I see the guys waiting for the homecoming court, red roses pinned to their lapels. Frankie takes Michelle's hand, and his best friend, Sal, who I recognize from Peter's hockey days, puts his arm around Susan. Regina looks around, shoots a nasty glance at me over her shoulder and says, "Where's Forta? I told him to wait." The door shuts, saving me from being reduced to a pile of ash.

My face is hot. The zit crop throbs. I picture Jamie kissing her at that stupid party, and I have to swallow.

I leave the safety of the bathroom for the snake pit of the gym. It is pitch-black in the corners with bright red-and-blue lights flashing on the hardwood floor. The music is so loud that the chaperones can't stand to be in the room, so they're all standing just outside, talking to each other and peering into the darkness every once in a while to make sure there are no orgies going on. I suspect they all went out to dinner earlier and got drunk. How else could they stand a night like this? I find Robert talking to Mike about the fight he and Stephanie just had about which after-party to go to.

"Robert, can I have the keys?" I say, trying not to see anyone around me. "I left my bag in the car."

"I'll go get it."

"No, that's okay, I could use the air."

"I could use a cigarette."

"You said you wouldn't smoke tonight."

"I know, Rosie, I was just kidding. Come on, let me be chivalrous. I'll go get your bag."

"Robert, please just give me the keys."

"Um…okay." He digs deep into all his pockets, finding his keys in the last one he searches, inside his jacket. "Here. Don't go anywhere. It's my first time out with my stepfather's Lexus, and he'll kill me if I lose it."

"I can't drive yet, remember?"

"Joke, Rosie. That was a joke. Are you okay?"

I ignore him and head toward the back door. Someone clamps a hand on my shoulder. I jump, imagining Regina with her fist cocked back, ready to punch me in the face when I turn around. "You're not supposed to go outside until the dance is over." It seems to be Mr. Cella's lot in life to keep kids from going where they want to go. Reasonless tears spring to my eyes.

"I know, I just…I have to get out." I look up at him, the tears now rolling down my cheeks. In that instant, I learn the unfortunate lesson that some men will give a woman anything in order to stop her from crying, or at the very least, to get her to go cry somewhere else. He looks uncomfortable and awkwardly pats me on the shoulder, waving me in the direction of the door. I wonder what he'd do if I cried in study hall when I want to go talk to Tracy.

As if I have any control over this stupid crying thing.

I push open the heavy metal door to the back parking lot between the school and the track, and the cold December air rushes into my lungs. I run to the car, and as I slide behind the steering wheel, I step on my bag, which has somehow found its way to the floor. Something crunches. I can't figure out what it could be, until I remember my mom lending me her compact so I could check for food in my teeth after dinner. I kick off my shoes and slouch down, my head against the headrest. I see two people leaning on a car nearby, kissing, backlit by the lights of the school. They look perfect.

There's a knock at the passenger-side window. Jamie raises

his hand. I blink at him, wondering if I'm seeing things. He knocks again. I realize he wants me to let him in. He gets one boot in the car before I figure out that I should let go of the door. I turn and look out the rear window to see if anyone followed him, but there's no one there.

"What are you doing here?" I whisper, as if Regina could hear me over the blasting music from all the way inside the gym.

"Want me to go?"

"No, I just—no."

We sit. We stare out the windshield. I'm about to start talking, and then I decide that I'm not going to be the first one. He came out here, he can do the talking.

"So you think I'm a liar, huh?" he asks.

"I don't really think that."

"Still mad about the Peter thing?"

I think for a minute. "I'm more mad at Peter than at you." He doesn't say anything. So much for me making him do the talking. "Having a good time?" I finally muster.

"Not really."

"Did you go to dinner before?"

"Fitzpatrick's."

"Was it good?"

He shrugs, reaching into his pocket and pulling out a piece of paper folded in quarters. I watch as he opens it. It's a grocery list. He refolds it and puts it back in his pocket.

"Why aren't you having a good time?" I ask.

"Same reason you aren't."

"I never said I wasn't having a good time," I counter, proud of myself.

"So why are you out here?"

"I needed a break."

"Me, too," he says.

I can see his breath. He doesn't breathe very often. I inhale and exhale three times for every breath he takes.

"Why did you need a break?"

"Regina."

I make an unattractive snorting sound and instantly regret it on so many levels. He says nothing. "She's mean," comes out of my mouth.

"To you?"

"To everyone," I say. "Are you guys really going out?"

He shrugs, and his starched shirt moves in one stiff piece up to his ears and back down. He has on a black tie, a black jacket, black pants, construction boots.

"I've never seen you dressed up. You look really nice."

He stares out the passenger-side window. "So do you."

"No, I don't. My dress looks like something I would have worn to my sixth-grade graduation. And my hair is a disaster. It doesn't do anything."

He looks at my hair for what feels like a long time. "What do you want your hair to do?"

"Curl. Poof up. Anything but hang straight in my face."

"Why, so you can look like everyone else?" he says.

Maybe he has a point.

He reaches forward to fiddle with the latch on the glove compartment. I wonder what Robert would say if he knew I was sitting in his stepfather's car with Jamie Forta when I'm supposed to be dancing with him in the gym. Well, I know what he'd say, actually. He'd say, "I told you so." As I'm thinking about this, the glove compartment door falls open and a plastic bag slides to the floor. Jamie reaches for it and grabs the wrong end, dumping out the contents. He leans down to pick them up and hesitates. Then he puts them in the bag in the darkness of the floor well and sits up, shoving the bag back into the glove compartment and latching it shut. He puts his hands in his pockets and exhales. His breath hangs in the air between us.

"What was that?" I ask.

"Don't know."

"You didn't see?"

"Not really."

"How could you put it back in the bag without seeing it?"

Something about the expression on his face makes me reach past him to open the glove compartment. He carefully studies the car parked next to us as I take the crinkly bag out and find two boxes of condoms. Two.

"Those for you?" he asks.

"No!" I wrap the bag over itself a few times and jam it back into the glove compartment as if it were burning my hands.

"Whose car is this?"

"Robert's."

"Aren't you here with him?"

"Yes, but—"

"But they're not for you?"

"Robert and I aren't even going out!"

"Guess he's thinking tonight's gonna be his lucky night."

"Well, he's not getting lucky with me. He's just a friend."

"Uh-huh."

"Not like you and Regina Deladdo." I spit her name out with such a vengeance it surprises us both.

"What do you got against her?"

"She hates me. She stares me down in the halls."

"So, what did you do to her? You musta done something."

The answer to that question is, I was followed by her boyfriend. But I don't feel like saying that. Jamie opens the glove compartment again and takes the bag out. He looks inside and smiles. "You know how many times you gotta have sex to go through two boxes of condoms?" I realize that

I don't actually know anything technical or practical about condoms. Ms. Maso would be very disappointed in me. "If a guy is takin' you to a dance and you find two unopened, new boxes of Trojans in his glove compartment, you can bet they're for you."

"Well, I don't want them, so you can put them back."

"What I'm sayin' is, he likes you."

"I don't like him."

"So why are you with him?"

"Why are you with her?"

"Favor for a friend."

"Same with me." Did he just say that Regina is his friend? Is that what he meant? I'm suddenly exhausted. I want my sweatpants. "Why does he think that…that something like *that* could happen between us?"

"He's a guy."

"I don't even want to know what that means."

"Guys are always prepared. In case they get lucky."

"Why do guys get so obsessed with sex? It's dumb."

"You haven't done it yet." How does he know that? I'm so irritated with Jamie's ability to make me blush that it almost overrides my embarrassment. I memorize the grooves on the steering wheel. "I embarrassed you," he says.

I shake my head. When he reaches for the door, I panic and ask the first question that comes into my mind. "Are you going to get 'lucky' tonight, Jamie?"

And then something miraculous happens. He laughs. It's the first time I've heard his laugh—it's warm and rich, and I want to wrap myself up in it—but I'm too busy being jealous to fully appreciate it.

"That depends," he says.

"On what?"

"What you consider lucky."

"Sex. With her. Regina," I say, annoyed by his dumb question.

"No."

"Then you're not going to get lucky."

"Not with her."

"You're going to have sex with someone else?" I say, furious and clueless.

"No."

"So how are you going to get lucky?"

The next minute happens in slow motion. Jamie Forta turns to me, puts his warm hand on my neck, and pulls me toward him. It dawns on me that he is about to kiss me, and I panic because I've never kissed an older man—I've never kissed anyone for real, only while playing stupid games at junior high school parties—and he surely must know everything there is to know because he's wiser and he's a bad boy and he gets around and I'm just a silly girl and none of that matters because his lips are on mine and it's so easy I can hardly believe I worried I wouldn't know what to do. His thumb strokes my cheekbone while his fingers clasp the back of my neck. His other hand is in my flat and boring hair, pulling down lightly, causing my head to tilt back. His tongue traces the outline of my lips and finds its way inside my mouth. He's gentle and moves slowly, but he has a firm hold on my hair, and he's increasing the force of the pull, exposing my throat. His lips disappear from mine, and I feel them a second later in the hollow between my collarbones. He finds his way up the side of my neck, biting me just a little, moving lightly back and forth, like he's searching for a special spot. When he finds it, I make a small sound I've never heard myself make before, like a gasp. He traces his tongue in slow circles around that spot. I realize my hands are just lying in my lap, doing nothing. I concentrate on lifting my arm and reaching for his face, but he catches my hand and holds it tightly at the wrist. His lips leave the spot and find their way back to my mouth, which is waiting, hoping for his return. He plants a gentle kiss on my lower lip and then whispers in my ear, "I just got lucky, Rose."

He's gone before I've opened my eyes. If it weren't for the rearview mirror, I'd think I imagined the entire thing. As I try to remember how to breathe, I watch to see if he looks back, but he heads straight for the door as if he hadn't just given me what I'm sure is the best first kiss in the history of humankind.

As he goes back inside, Robert comes out, his hand raised in greeting. Jamie nods slightly as they pass each other. Robert watches Jamie go and then looks out toward the car. I can barely move. The last thing I want to do is talk to Robert right now. I want to sit here and relive what just happened, over and over again, and try to relearn how to inhale.

But then I remember the glove compartment and I decide to head Robert off at the pass. I get one foot out the door and realize I forgot to put my shoes back on.

"Find your bag?"

"Yes."

"What took you so long?"

"I was sitting in the car," I say, struggling to get my shoes on, not looking at him.

"You're not having a good time."

"Robert, why are there two boxes of condoms in your glove compartment?"

He blanches, shocked. Then the shock turns to anger, and the blood rushes back into his face. "Why are you snooping around in my car?"

"I wasn't snooping. I was looking for a tissue. And the bag fell on the floor. And they fell out. Why do you have them?"

"Just in case."

"Just in case what?"

"You know, just in case...we..." He trails off. I leave him twisting in the wind for a few seconds before I let him have it.

"Are you crazy, Robert?" I slam the car door shut.

"Well, I didn't know what you wanted to do! How should I know? What if you wanted to and I didn't have anything?"

"You're not even my boyfriend!"

"Fine! Just forget it."

"Is that why you asked me to come to this stupid dance with you?"

"I just wanted you to be my date."

"You could have told me you were expecting me to have sex with you!"

"Rose, I wasn't expecting anything! Just forget they're there. They don't matter, okay?" We stand there in the cold, me staring at him, him staring at his shoes. "I'm sorry, Rose."

"Let's go in," I say. We start back to the gym, both of us shivering.

"Want my jacket?"

"It's zero degrees out here, Robert. Keep it for yourself."

"I don't want you to be cold."

"We're almost there."

"Will you dance with me?"

"I don't really feel like it."

He reaches to open the door and stops with his hand on the handle. "Rose?"

"What?" My irritation is always right there, ready to surface. I know that my impatience with him is in direct proportion to his patience with me, but there doesn't seem to be anything I can do about that.

"Were you out here with Forta?"

My neck feels hot and slick where Jamie kissed me, and my heart is still beating really fast. "What?"

"He passed me while I was on the way out. What was he doing out here?"

"How should I know?"

"Did you come out here to be with him?"

"No," I say, telling the truth.

"Well, did he come out here to be with you?"

"How would I know that, Robert?" I say, reaching for the other handle and pulling open the door.

The gym is hot, the windows dripping with condensation. Bodies stumble around in the darkness of the dance floor, and I see a few teachers in the corner, inhibitions nowhere to be seen.

Tracy and Stephanie are huddled together, probably conferring about whether Stephanie should break up with Mike tonight, just to make a point. Michelle, Regina and the rest of the homecoming court, having just been crowned, are posing for pictures for the local newspaper. Michelle looks radiant, and Frankie, standing on the edge of the crowd, keeping an eye on this year's homecoming king, looks bored. I wonder if Frankie misses wearing the crown.

Between flashbulbs, Regina bitches at Frankie to find Jamie. But Frankie has no intention of going anywhere while Michelle is standing next to her king, Mr. All-American Quarterback Richie Hamilton, who has had too much to drink and is enjoying the feel of Michelle's arm in his. When he starts to get a little too handsy, Frankie steps into the frame and tells the photographer that he's taken enough photos. The photographer smiles patiently and suggests a few photos of the former homecoming couple. Frankie and Richie stare at each other until Richie calls him a *guido,* and Frankie starts for him but is held back by something Michelle says. Richie returns to his football frat boys who have already gathered to stoke the fire. Michelle smiles anxiously for the camera as the footballers sulk and lurk, as Frankie and his pals decide who is going to take which jock, as Regina screeches about Jamie.

I am tempted to go up to Regina and tell her that Jamie just kissed me in a way that I am almost certain he will never kiss her, but I know that if I don't want to cause an international incident, I should keep my mouth shut. In an uncharacteristically bold move, Robert, who has silently been watching the homecoming court next to me, takes my hand and leads me out on the floor. I'm too lost to protest.

notorious (*adjective*): widely known in an unfavorable way
(*see also, for the third time:* me)

———

11

I CAN'T BELIEVE THE COPS HAVEN'T SHOWN UP YET. ABOUT a hundred of us are crammed into two rooms at the gross Amore Motel in West Union, the next town over, and MGMT is blasting out the windows of a car in the parking lot because nobody remembered to bring an iPod dock. The guy who's playing Parking Lot DJ is arguing with a trombone player I recognize from orchestra about whether this is the right musical choice for the moment or not. Apparently Orchestra Guy would prefer the Yeah Yeah Yeahs, while a girl I've never seen before is trying to make a case for Florence + The Machine. I agree with the girl.

Robert and I have ended up at the seniors' after-party because that's where Tracy, Matt and Mike wanted to go, and they were in our car. Stephanie was outvoted because Robert and I didn't vote. We were too busy not talking in the front seat. Stephanie wanted to go to the underclassmen party, and I'm starting to see her point. So far, after a tour of the two rooms and a perusal of the parking lot from the second-floor balcony, the only person I know even remotely is Orchestra Guy, and he just got in his car and drove away without his date, presumably because he was not pleased with the music selection, or with her speaking up in favor of Florence + The Machine rather than seconding his vote for the Yeah Yeah Yeahs. I figured out she was his date when she started chasing after his car and screaming, "You dick! Are you really going to leave me at this shitty motel with these people?!"

I get it. I really do.

When Stephanie, who is drunker than I've ever seen her and still drinking, complains that we don't know anyone here, Tracy tells her that the squad will be here any minute—like that's supposed to make us all feel better—and that they've got a surprise for everyone.

Whatever their surprise is, I can pretty much guarantee that I don't want it.

As Tracy mysteriously excuses herself with great self-importance, I contemplate asking Robert to take me home, but I really don't want to be alone in the car with him and the condoms. It's not like I think they're going to jump out of the glove compartment and do something, but I just don't want to be around them any more than I have to. I've only got a half hour left before my curfew anyway. I can stand anything for half an hour, I think.

Famous last words.

What I really want is to go home, take off this ugly dress, and lie in bed thinking about Jamie.

Who kissed me.

Six months ago, I thought nothing good would ever happen again. But now...this.

It was perfect.

I haven't kissed anybody before, so I might not know what

I'm talking about when I say that what happened with Jamie was perfect, but I can't imagine how it could have been any better. His hands were gentle but they felt strong—I knew they would feel like that. I knew it the first day I looked at them, and he had that smudge of blue ink on his thumb. And he has perfect lips. I wanted them to stay on my neck forever.

But what does it mean, that he kissed me? Am I his girl-friend? Is he just cheating on Regina with me? Is Regina going to come after me?

Is it okay for me to feel happy about something?

"Are you all right, Rose? Your face is flushed, like you have a fever or something," Robert says. I don't know when he ended up standing next to me, leaning against the balcony railing on the second floor of the motel, looking out over the parking lot. It takes a few seconds for me to come back from wherever I was.

"It's December. It's cold out here," I say, pulling my down coat tighter around me. Everyone else seems to have dress coats on. I forgot about that part of the outfit. As usual, I didn't read my *Lucky* magazine this month—Tracy forced me to get a subscription—and so have no idea what girls wear over their dresses when they go out to, say, a dance. If Tracy hadn't gotten drunk before we even got to dinner, I'm sure I would have heard about it.

"Are you still mad at me?" Robert asks quietly.

He looks so upset that I feel like I've been torturing him. Actually, I know I've been torturing him.

"I just don't understand. We're not even going out."

"I know."

"So why do you act like we are? Why do you tell people we are when I ask you not to?"

He shrugs. "I guess because I wish it were true. And some-times it seems like you do, too. Like this summer."

I know what he's talking about, and he's totally right—I can't deny it. Right after my dad's funeral in June, we went to the beach with Tracy, Matt, Stephanie and Mike, and I flirted with Robert. I did it because I knew he'd flirt back. It made me feel good to hear that I looked cute in my new pool-blue bathing suit, and I liked having someone put lotion on my back and act like it was the coolest thing he'd gotten to do all year.

But deep down, I knew I was being unfair. I didn't have any intention of going out with him, and I shouldn't have been flirting. I guess I didn't want to be the girl with a dead dad and no boyfriend. Tracy had Matt, Matt had just introduced Stephanie and Mike, and I was feeling left out. So I used Robert. Which was kind of an awful thing to do. But Robert had been so nice since my dad died, and he took care of me at the funeral, and he was…there. I was feeling bad and it was easy to treat him like that.

I used to think that Robert *let* me use him in those situations, which made it his fault and meant that I wasn't responsible. But now I think that he doesn't exactly know I'm using him. He's just hoping that I've finally seen the light.

Some girls do this kind of thing all the time, but I think it's stupid and mean. I wouldn't want someone to do it to me.

Sometimes I'm not too proud of the way I act.

The sound of squealing tires saves me from having to hear Robert go into detail about how confusing I can be. A big SUV pulls into the parking lot, and cheerleaders pile out of it like it's some sort of weird clown car. They are no longer wearing their homecoming dresses—they've changed into their uniforms—and they are getting into some sort of formation in the parking lot, shivering and jumping in place in the below-freezing weather. I notice that the whole team is here, except Michelle. She probably decided that it would be wise to keep Frankie and Richie as far away from each other as possible. Although I haven't seen Richie anywhere, so maybe he and Frankie are beating the crap out of each other in the school parking lot, and Michelle is trying to pry them apart.

Michelle's absence probably means that someone is about to be humiliated. Tracy told me that Michelle doesn't participate in initiation because she doesn't believe in it. But even the all-powerful Michelle can't stop it from happening—it's a tradition with a long history that's just too delicious for some people to resist.

Regina is strutting around, barking directions. Every once in a while, she looks up at the balcony, scanning the crowd for someone. Probably Jamie, who I have to admit I've been looking for, too. But when her eyes land on me, she stares for a few seconds and then turns away as if she found what she was looking for.

"Could you turn that off?" Susan yells to Parking Lot DJ guy, waving frantically to get his attention. "We need our own music for this!"

When he ignores her, Regina stomps over and tries a different tack—screaming at him. He screams back for a minute and then realizes the futility of trying to outscream a witch. He jumps in his car and takes off, yelling some obscenity out the window that no one can hear because he's now blasting Takka Takka, a band I'm sure that no one at this motel has ever heard of besides me.

Maybe that means I should leave, too.

There's a strange moment of silence while the cheerleaders stand in formation in the parking lot, and nothing happens. And then I hear a count-off, and "Single Ladies" blares out of the SUV. The girls start gyrating and the crowd goes crazy.

"Are they doing a dance routine?" asks Robert, incredulous.

They start to do their own version of Beyoncé's video, minus the cool body suits and talent. They're dancing with pom-poms and short skirts, which makes it seem like a *Saturday Night Live* skit. And then suddenly Kristin and Tracy bound into the middle of the group and become the lead dancers. The other girls form a line behind them and start clapping and chanting. For a second, I don't understand what they're saying. And then it becomes painfully clear.

"Strip! Strip! Strip!"

At this point, it seems like our whole high school is watching from the motel's balcony, picking up the chant. Matt is standing nearby with Mike, clearly enjoying his girlfriend's public humiliation. Although, to be honest, his girlfriend seems to be enjoying her public humiliation, too. I'm puzzling over whether Tracy was wearing her uniform under her homecoming dress when, with one swift motion, Tracy and Kristin yank their tops off and throw them up at the balcony, directly at Richie Hamilton, who has just arrived and doesn't seem to have been beaten up by Frankie. The boys lose their minds as Tracy and Kristin continue the dance in their bras in zero-degree weather. When the chanting doesn't stop, I turn away.

"I can't watch anymore. This is pathetic," I say, expecting Robert to agree with me, but he stares, enraptured. What is it about cheerleaders and high school boys? Even the boys who claim to think they're idiots will still watch them strip, drunk, in a sleazy motel parking lot.

I have a lot to learn about high school boys as a species.

I go into one of the rooms, looking for my mom's clutch. I'm going home, whether Robert is taking me or not. I find the bag, and I'm about to leave when I hear a noise in the bathroom. It sounds like someone groaning. I push the door open a little, and it hits something in the dark. I push a little harder. When I get it open wide enough to stick my head in, I flick on the light and I can see that Stephanie is passed out on the floor in a puddle of vomit.

Great. Of course I had to be the one to find her. Now I'll have to do something responsible.

"Stephanie?" I say, bending over her and trying not to inhale the smell. I shake her by the shoulder, but she doesn't respond. "Steph!" I yell, but I still get nothing. I get closer and realize that she is the color of pea soup. I also realize that she's not breathing.

Is that possible? I stare at her, desperately hoping to see some movement that indicates breathing.

Nothing.

I run back into the room and grab the phone. I pause for just a second, realizing that I'm about to blow the whistle on my entire school. I know it's the right thing to do—I'm not going to be the person who let Stephanie Trainer die on the floor while everyone was getting off on an under-age striptease—but I just need this one second to gather my strength before I destroy myself and sink even lower in the caste system of Union High.

I call 911.

"Operator here. What's your emergency?"

"Hi, um, I'm at a party at the Amore Motel and my friend is passed out in the bathroom. I don't think she's breathing. We need an ambulance."

"What's your name, please, miss?"

"My name? Do you really need that?"

"Your name, please?"

I knew it would come to this, but hearing her ask really drives the point home. I might as well move to another state right now, tonight. I am never, ever going to live this down.

I take a deep breath. "Rose Zarelli."

"An ambulance is on the way, Rose. What room are you in?"

"Thirty-three."

"Do you know CPR?"

"Yes. Um, I mean, I think so. We just learned it in health class."

"Okay. If your friend isn't breathing, administer CPR until the EMTs arrive, okay? You could save her life."

I hang up the phone and run back into the bathroom. Stephanie is completely covered in vomit. I'm not generally a squeamish person—I don't get freaked out by blood. But there are two things that I have a hard time with: mucus and vomit. Mucus because of the consistency, vomit because of the smell.

I kneel down next to her, trying not to gag. Can I really do this? Can I put my mouth over hers? Will she die if I don't?

As I'm trying to picture the health class CPR dummy and remember whether I'm supposed to clear her airway or tilt her head back first, Stephanie rolls over and throws up again, right on my knees. I guess she's breathing after all.

"Steph? Can you hear me?"

She groggily opens her eyes and tries to speak, but gibberish comes out. The only word I catch is "Trace." For a second, I'm so relieved that she's alive that I'm not grossed out by the puke on me, and I forget about the fact that I just called 911. And then I hear the sirens, followed by someone on the balcony yelling, "Cops!"

Everyone scrambles back into the rooms to get their stuff and get the hell out. But people are too drunk to move fast, and no one makes it out before the cops and ambulance arrive, except, of course, for the cheerleaders, who were already next to their car. I can hear them screaming at the sound of the sirens, and I just know they're piling back into their clown car and taking off, leaving everyone else behind to fend for themselves. And I'm sure that Tracy is with them.

Would she still go with them if she had any idea what was going on up here?

I peek out into the room just as an EMT guy comes barreling through the door of room thirty-three, followed closely by a pair of cops. He pushes through the crowd of people who ran into the room when they heard the sirens, and the cops block the door so no one can leave. I duck back into the bathroom, wishing this night would either end or go backward in time, before all the Beyoncé wannabes and vomit, so I could kiss Jamie again. Except this time, I wouldn't let him out of the car, and we wouldn't go back to the gym. We'd leave the dance and go…somewhere.

"Rose Zarelli?" asks an EMT from the bathroom doorway.

I raise my hand like I'm in class or something.

"You the one who called this in?" He comes into the bathroom holding a red plastic box by the handle that says Emergency on it in big white letters. He has curly brown hair and blue eyes, and looks vaguely familiar to me.

I nod and get out of his way. I can hear people in the room whispering to each other already. The cops start to take down everyone's names, threatening to haul them in for underage drinking if they don't cooperate.

"Rose? Rosie?" a panicked Robert yells from the room. I don't answer him.

The EMT bends down and checks Stephanie, and then radios to his partner that her breathing is irregular and they'd better take her in for alcohol poisoning. The partner says he'll be up in a minute, and Stephanie vomits again. The smell makes me woozy, and I'm wondering if we should all be moving a little faster to get Stephanie to the hospital, but the EMT just casually turns her on her side so she won't choke.

"You any relation to Peter Zarelli?" he asks, one hand on Stephanie's cheek, holding her head to the floor. He looks like he's done this at least a million times.

At this point, I'm so used to people asking me that question that it barely fazes me, despite the weird context. "Yeah. He's my brother. He's away at college."

"Huh. Small world. I used to play hockey with Peter. He was a junior when I was a senior. I skated over his hand by accident once. I think he had to get stitches."

I read his name tag, which says R. Passeo. "Bobby?"

He looks at me, startled. "Uh-oh. Am I legendary at your house or something?"

"No. It's just funny because, um, somebody told me a while ago that he was the one who drove Peter home after that happened." I'm tempted to ask him if he knows Jamie, but then I remember that fifty people are out there in the bedroom, listening to my conversation with this guy. Fifty people who are probably already plotting their revenge against me. I keep my mouth shut. Stephanie tries to raise her head, but Bobby tells her not to move, to just relax, that she's going to be fine. She opens her mouth to say something, but only spit bubbles come out. I reach for a towel and start trying to get some of the puke off me.

"Little young to be drinking," he says to me.

"It's homecoming." I shrug. "You remember, right?"

"Yeah. It seems like a long time ago, though, all that partying. You okay? How much have you had?" he asks.

"Me? None."

"None?" he says, skeptically.

"*Rosie?*" Robert calls again, his voice closer.

Bobby looks at me, expecting me to answer, but I don't. "Is that your boyfriend out there?" he finally asks.

I shake my head. "Just my ride home. It's past my curfew."

"The cops are confiscating keys and calling parents, so I don't think he's going to be driving you anywhere. Why don't you go tell them what happened so they can file a report." Bobby leans in and says quietly, "Talk to the older guy. He's nicer. And don't worry about your friend. We'll take good care of her. What's her name?"

"Stephanie Trainer," I say, gingerly picking up her bag from the vomit-covered floor and wiping it off with the towel, which is useless because now the towel is also completely vomit-covered. I gag as I hand the bag to Bobby, but he doesn't appear to be grossed out at all. He's seen a lot worse, I guess.

"The cops will probably take you home without calling your parents— Uuh, your mom. Think of it as a little reward for being the good citizen tonight," he says.

Whistle-blower is more like it.

When I walk into the room, everyone falls silent, even Robert, who I now see was being held back from coming into the bathroom by a cop with gray hair who looks like he's about two seconds away from retirement. My classmates all stare at me as if they'd just learned that I was a serial killer who had murdered each and every member of their families.

"Are you Rose?" asks the older cop. When I nod, he lets go of Robert and gestures for me to follow him out of the room past the younger, mean-looking cop, who is holding a cardboard box that he's filling with all the alcohol he can find. Some of the guys are watching him with tears in their eyes—they worked very hard, probably calling in a lot of favors, to score all those bottles for tonight.

I'm so dead.

"I'm Officer Webster. Grab your things," he says, slapping his nightstick in his hand, his eyes on the grief-stricken boys. I hold up my bag, showing him that I already have my things.

He steps out of the way so I can walk in front of him, and we head out of the room and across the balcony to the staircase.

It's like walking a gauntlet. Richie Hamilton watches me as if he can't quite grasp what's happening. I hear somebody behind him say, "Nice work, Rose." And when we walk past Matt and Mike, Matt snarls at me, "What the hell did you do?"

Officer Webster's nightstick goes "thwack" against his palm, and Matt shrinks back a little, which I thoroughly enjoy. It might be the last moment of enjoyment I will ever experience in my teenage life. I ignore Matt and look at Mike.

"Stephanie's in there, Mike. She almost died." I have no idea if she really almost died or not, but I feel like saying it anyway. "You might want to go check on her before they take her to the hospital. In fact, maybe you should go to the hospital with her. That would be the nice thing to do. Since you're her *date*," I say, with extra emphasis on the word "date." He looks a little ashamed as he heads toward the room, and my opinion of him improves. Slightly. As I go down the staircase, I hear Matt say, "You just screwed this whole night up for everybody, you know that?"

When we get to the bottom of the stairs, the cop leads me across the parking lot to his car. Someone on the balcony yells, "Cuff her!" and they all start clapping. I feel my face turning red, and I don't turn around. "Where do you live?" he asks.

"Brook Road, in Union."

He opens the back door to the cruiser and says, "Get in. I'll drive you home."

The thought of arriving home late for curfew in a cop car with flashing emergency lights makes me feel sick. Although I might still prefer it to riding home with Robert and his

condom collection. The jury is still out on that one. But I
know I don't want my mother to look out the window and
see me getting out of a police cruiser.

"Would it be possible to wait for one of my friends to
drive me home?" I ask, hoping against hope.

The officer looks at me and then up at my jeering classmates. He sighs a very deep, bone-weary sigh.

"Rose, trust me when I tell you that you don't want to
stick around here. I don't think your friends are too happy
with you," he says, shaking his head as if he can't believe
what I did any more than my classmates can. "Monday is
not going to be easy for you." He looks up at the balcony
and waves his nightstick, getting them to shut up for a few
seconds. "Go on, get in. Watch your head."

I duck into the back of the car, my hands clasped in front
of me as if Officer Webster had actually slapped on hand-
cuffs. He gets in the front and picks up the radio to tell the
station where he's going. Before he starts the car, he turns
around and says to me through the metal gate that's supposed
to keep me from doing anything bad to him, "Did you at
least have a good time before your friend almost drank herself to death?"

I don't know what the appropriate response is here. Maybe,
*No, Officer, I had an awful time because my date brought condoms,
thinking that I was going to have sex with him.* Or perhaps, *I can't
remember anything that happened before I dialed 911 and committed social suicide, Officer.* And then there's always, *Yes, Officer,
I had an incredible time because somebody else's boyfriend kissed
me, and it was the best first kiss anyone could ever ask for, and even
though I have no idea if we will ever kiss again, or if his girlfriend
is going to try to smother me with her gold-and-black pom-poms,
it was all worth it.*

As we drive back to Union, I wonder once again if this

is really the way high school is supposed to be. It seems like everyone around me is having a great time drinking, dating, having sex and almost getting arrested. But somehow I always seem to be on the wrong side of the equation. Like, I had my first kiss tonight, and it was amazing, but isn't your first kiss supposed to be with your boyfriend—or someone who is free to *be* your boyfriend? And aren't you supposed to be ecstatic after your first kiss, not worried that the guy's girlfriend is going to beat the crap out of you? Aren't you supposed to be reveling in it, not calling 911 because you think your friend is dead?

Maybe it's me. Maybe I don't know how to have fun. Tracy always says I need to loosen up. But I don't want to take my clothes off in front of half the school, and I don't want to have a funnel full of vodka jammed down my throat. I don't want demonic cheerleaders making me do awful things, and I don't want a jock boyfriend who pressures me into having sex and might be cheating on me.

None of that is fun, as far as I'm concerned. It seems more like the ninth circle of hell than ninth grade. But what do I know?

quagmire (*noun*): a predicament; a bad situation
(*see also:* arriving home in a police car)

———

12

AS I HEAD UP THE FRONT WALK, LIGHT FROM THE TV flickers through the window onto the frozen lawn. The effect would be pretty if it didn't mean that my mother is waiting up for me. Of course she is. That's the kind of luck I have.

She pulls the curtain to the side and looks out the window just in time to see the officer leaving in his cruiser. The front door flies opens as I reach for the handle, and I expect her to be standing there, having run from the TV room to the door at record speed. But it's not her. My heart does a weird skip-stop thing, missing a few beats, like I'm suspended in that moment between tripping over something and falling to the ground.

Dad?

No, idiot. It's Peter, your brother, who didn't bother to show up for Thanksgiving, apparently putting in a rare holiday appearance in honor of Christmas.

Peter doesn't really look like Dad at all, except for his hair.

But apparently when he's backlit in a doorway and his face is in shadow, he's a dead ringer.

Bad choice of words. I seem to do that a lot.

"You okay?" he asks, looking really worried. I'm guessing I look like I've seen a ghost.

"Did you just get out of a police car?" my mother says, her voice shrill and grating, like a dentist's drill on high speed. "It's forty-five minutes past your curfew. What is going on? Where the hell have you been?"

"Hurry up, get in here—it's freezing," Peter says, ignoring Mom and helping me take off my coat.

"You sit down right now and explain," she demands, grabbing me by the arm and shoving me onto the couch so hard that my head makes contact with the wall. Peter is so surprised by her minor act of violence that he forgets to finish closing the door.

"Did something happen? Are you hurt? Is Robert hurt? Was there an accident?" She's standing in front of me, yelling into my face. In a strange way, I feel like she's looking at me for the first time in months. Well, she's looking at me like she's never seen me before, but at least she's *seeing* me.

Peter is suddenly between us, facing her, my coat still in his hands, cold December air pouring in through the partially open front door.

"Mom, you're being crazy. Let her answer one question at a time."

My mother puts her hands on her hips and stares at the ceiling, shaking her head. Peter slowly turns toward me without taking his eyes off her. He actually looks a little freaked out. I guess my beloved brother expected to come home to a house that was exactly like it used to be before he left— minus Dad, of course. Well, sorry to disappoint you, Peter, but life here in good old Union did not freeze in time the second you departed for college, and nothing is like it was before you left. Your mother and sister have been replaced by aliens that have no common language and no clue how to talk to each other.

"Rose? You have three seconds to start explaining yourself," she says to the ceiling.

"I'm fine, Mom. Everyone's fine. Stephanie just drank too much—"

"She drank? There was alcohol?" my mother says, her hands flying up into the air.

"Mom! Stop!" Peter demands. My mother goes quiet again but she's pacing now. When did Peter start talking to Mom like that? And when can I start doing it? "What the hell happened, Rose?" he asks.

I debate whether I should tell the truth or not but realize there's absolutely no point in lying. The whole town will know what happened by morning. "Stephanie got sick and I was worried, so I called 911. I thought she was dying. The EMTs and the cops came and broke up the party—"

"I thought you said you were going to Tracy's after the dance!"

"We were supposed to go there, but we ended up at the Amore Hotel instead—"

"What do you mean, 'We ended up at the Amore Hotel'? You don't just end up at a sleazy hotel at age fourteen! Do you realize you were supposed to be home close to an hour ago?" my mother yells. I'm about to scream back at her when her furious expression melts off her face, and she bursts into tears.

Peter and I look at each other, stunned. Something weird is happening here—it's like we're watching our mother wake up from a six-month coma.

And then I realize: that's exactly what we're watching.

She's been in shock since she got the call the day after Peter's graduation party.

The call came out of the blue, which I guess it probably always does. Even if someone you love is in a war, you don't really think that they're going to die. You know it's a possibility, but you don't believe that someday, two nicely dressed soldiers are going to show up at *your* door and tell *you* that the person you love is dead.

Not that that's how it happens for contractors' families.

Those nicely dressed soldiers that show up at front doors, bearing bad news in all those war movies only visit soldiers' families. Apparently contractors' families just get a phone call. I still have no idea what the person on the other end of the line said to my mother that day. For all I know, they said, "Your husband is dead. Sorry," and hung up. It wouldn't surprise me—people don't care about contractors' contributions to the war. Or maybe it's not even that people don't care—they just don't know. They don't know that there are all these non-soldier people over there trying to do normal jobs like build things and drive trucks and deliver supplies in the middle of a war zone, even though they don't know the first thing about how to survive there.

Anyway, when the call came, Mom answered the phone, went into shock and has been there ever since. Until the terror of losing another one of us snapped her right out of it.

"Mom," Peter says quietly, taking her by the shoulders. "Sit." He pushes her gently into a chair. "Rose is fine. She's right here. Nothing happened to her. See?" He gestures toward me. "She's fine."

My mother glances at me, taking me in from head to toe like she's looking for injuries. Then she takes a few deep breaths and wipes her eyes. She's starting to look embarrassed already, as if she shouldn't have cried in front of us. "Where is Stephanie?"

"The EMTs took her to the hospital."

"And Robert?"

"I don't know, probably at home."

"Why don't you know where he is, Rose?" she asks, her tone implying that once again, I've mistreated Robert. This pisses me off.

"Because I wasn't allowed to stay long enough to see what happened to him. The police officer wanted to get me out of there before everyone tried to kill me."

"Why would they want to do that?"

"For calling the cops, who confiscated all their alcohol," Peter answers, guessing correctly.

"Were you drinking?" she asks.

"No."

"You weren't drinking," she says skeptically.

"Why even ask me if you're not going to believe what I tell you?" I snap.

She stands up from her chair and points a finger in my face. "You are grounded," she says, deadly calm, all trace of tears gone from her voice.

"What? Why? For calling 911?"

"For scaring me by being more than an hour late for your curfew—"

"I was only forty-five minutes late!" I say, rage starting to boil up from the pit of my stomach. As my temperature rises and my common sense takes its leave, a thought calmly pops into my head: I don't have panic attacks—what I have are rage attacks.

"—and for lying to me about where you were going after the dance."

"I didn't—"

"We'll discuss the specifics in the morning," she says, her therapy voice back in place, the cracks in her facade firmly sealed up again.

"Mom, that's not fair. Rose did exactly what you would have—" starts Peter. I cut him off by grabbing the first thing I see and chucking it at the wall, effectively destroying any case Peter was about to make about me behaving responsibly. Peter and my mom duck as holiday M&Ms go flying and a candy dish shatters to the left of a bare Christmas tree that is leaning against a wall in a bucketfull of water. The sound of the glass breaking and the M&Ms clattering to the floor is unbelievably satisfying.

"Enough. This is my house. You are my children. I make the decisions." She slams the front door closed, locks it and goes upstairs. The house is quiet again.

I turn to Peter, who is looking at me like I'm a stranger. I guess we've both had moments tonight when we didn't recognize each other.

"Jesus, Rose, when did you start throwing shit?" He goes into the kitchen and comes back with a dustpan.

"I'll do that," I say, embarrassment slowly filtering into my veins, taming the rage.

"Uh, no. No, you won't. You just sit there and calm the fuck down." I drop back onto the couch. He cleans in silence for a full minute before he says, "Mom told me you were pissed off at the world, but I didn't realize you were acting like a two-year-old."

"Yeah, well, maybe if you'd come home for Thanksgiving, you would have seen it for yourself."

Peter sweeps up the last of the mess and turns to face me. "Get over it, Rose. I'm here now."

"And I'm supposed to be grateful for that?"

"Grateful? No. But you could be happy about it— *I'm* happy to finally see *you*."

I have no idea what to say to this. I'm not "happy" to see him or "happy" that he's home, except for the fact that I've been looking forward to telling him off for abandoning us at Thanksgiving.

"I miss listening to you whine on Saturdays about the social injustices of high school," he says as if he graduated years ago and couldn't possibly remember what it's like now that he's in college. "Oh, yeah, and thanks for answering my email," he says sarcastically.

"You're an asshole, Peter," is how I choose to respond.

I have never, in my entire life, spoken to my brother this way. And it shows on his face.

"I'm a *what?*" he asks, sounding way more hurt and shocked than mad. I hate to admit that his stunned expression takes some of the wind out of my sails. I'm such a sucker.

"You heard me," I say with a lot less confidence than I had a few seconds ago.

"I just saved your ass—you realize that, don't you?"

"How did you save my ass? I'm grounded!"

"No, you're not. She just felt like she had to say that, but she knows you did the right thing."

"That's not what it sounded like to me," I say.

"All right, Rose, just tell me what the fuck is wrong with you. Let's get this out of the way so we can do this holiday shit and I can go back to school."

He puts the dustpan on the floor and sits in a chair across from me.

"Are you really going to act like you don't know what's wrong?"

"Thanksgiving, right?"

I just stare at him. As I look, I see that his anger is under-

cut by something that lurks just beneath the surface, something that might be embarrassment or shame. I feel relieved
to see it there.

"I didn't want to be here, Rose."

"Yeah, I know. Well, you should have anyway. Dad would
have wanted you to."

"What Dad wants doesn't matter anymore," Peter says.
"He's dead, remember?"

I want to pick up the dustpan at his feet and dump the
dirty M&Ms and glass shards over his head. "Why do you
say things like that?"

"Because it's true—he's not here anymore, so what he
thinks or wants doesn't matter. It's just a fact of reality. I'm
not trying to be—"

"You're mad at him." I didn't know that I knew this until
it came out of my mouth, but suddenly, there it is as if I'd
known it all along. It seems so obvious now.

"I'm not mad at him."

"You talk about him like he just…like he did something
just to piss you off."

"Well, he did take a job in fucking Iraq in the middle of
a war, Rose."

"Yeah, and you kept applying to the most expensive col-
leges in the country even after he lost his job. So whose fault
is it that he felt like he had to go there?"

As soon as the question comes out, I regret it. I regret it
more than I've ever regretted anything in my life, because I
don't mean it. I really don't.

So why did I say that? Just to hurt him? When did I start
doing things like that?

"Sorry. I'm sorry, Peter, I didn't…that's not…"

He stares into the dustpan at his feet, then he reaches down and picks it up, holding it out to me, the shattered glass making the candy glitter in the light.

"M&M?" he offers.

I look at the shards and give half a second's thought to taking one. Eating glass would solve a lot of problems for me right now. It would help me to feel less bad about what I just did to Peter, and it would probably land me in the hospital and keep me from having to go back to school on Monday. I reach out to take one, half joking, but he pulls the dustpan away.

"You know I only applied to all those schools because he wanted me to. After he lost his job, he just kept saying they'd figure it out, that he didn't want me to graduate with loans."

"I know. I remember."

"But thanks for the guilt trip, though," Peter says as he stands up and carries the dustpan into the kitchen. When he comes back, he sits on the couch next to me, facing the sad Christmas tree, which is still tied up in twine. I have no idea when Mom bought it or how long it's been there.

"Look, you did the right thing, if you really thought Stephanie could die."

"Tell that to the crazy woman upstairs," I say.

"Mom's a total mess, huh."

"At least we know she's still human," I answer. "That freak-out was the first time she hasn't seemed like a robot since Dad died."

"Can you blame her?"

"Kinda. She's a shrink. Don't shrinks know how to deal with this stuff?"

"I guess it's different when it's your own family," he says. "Amanda's dad's a shrink and he's a fucking nut job."

"Who's Amanda?" I ask without thinking.

"My girlfriend," he says, surprised. "Mom didn't tell you her name?"

I shake my head. Peter takes a moment to consider this, and I sort of enjoy watching him realize that he is not a regular topic of conversation in the house. Of course, the reality is, there would have to be regular conversation for there to be regular *topics* of conversation.

"Amanda's cool, Rosie. You'll like her."

I know that Peter stood up for me tonight and tried to get me out of trouble, but I'm still not ready to forgive him. And I don't care how "cool" this girl is. As far as I'm concerned, she doesn't exist until she shows up here and explains what could possibly have been so important that she had to take my brother away from his family on our first Thanksgiving without Dad. If she offers me a satisfactory explanation—and only if—I'll consider liking her.

"So what really happened tonight?" Peter asks, as if sensing that the subject should be changed and quickly.

Just a few months ago, I would have told Peter about Jamie without thinking twice. But everything is different now. Peter doesn't automatically get to know things about me. Besides, I finally have a piece of Jamie that's just mine—not Peter's, not Mom's—and I don't feel like sharing it. Not with anyone.

"It happened just like I said. Oh, except the EMT who came to take care of Stephanie was Bobby Passeo. He still feels bad about your hand, by the way."

Peter lets out a laugh—it's more of a chuckle, really—that I've never heard before. It sounds like he's purposely laughing in a new, different way. "Bobby Passeo is an EMT? I thought for sure he'd be drinking tallboys in the school parking lot until he was fifty."

"Well, he's now a contributing member of society, taking care of vomiting students at high school dances."

"Go figure." Peter yawns. "I thought he'd joined the army or something."

I try to picture Bobby Passeo in an army uniform. Instead, the twenty-one-year-old sergeant I found online—the one with the memorial website—comes into my head.

"Have you ever searched online for Dad?" The question slips out of my mouth as if it had been waiting for a chance to escape. In my peripheral vision, I see Peter's head turn quickly.

"What did you find?" he asks in a low voice, as if I'm about to reveal that I learned on Google that our father had a second family somewhere, or that he was a Russian spy on the FBI's most-wanted list.

"Nothing, really, just…did you ever think about the other people who died with him?"

"At first, when the names were released. But not since then, not really."

"Well, Dad's name shows up on these websites—I guess they're called memorial websites. Family members and friends of the people who died build these sites and they post, um, pictures, and emails and things like that. And these people listed the names of everyone who died in the explosion, so if you Google Dad, these other people's sites come up."

I'm so nervous telling Peter about this that I can't look at him—I have no idea why. I can feel that he's still staring at me, but I keep my eyes glued to the top of the bare Christmas tree, where our ancient, moth-eaten, "family-heirloom" angel ornament should be sitting.

"Are you going to build a site for Dad?" he asks.

It's weird to me that he thinks I might do something like that on my own—and then I realize it's weird that it didn't occur to me to do it on my own. Was I waiting for someone's permission? I hate when I'm a coward about things.

I shrug. "I don't know. I might."

"Well, if you do, don't put my name or face on it." He stands up. "I'm going to sleep. You coming upstairs?"

"In a minute," I answer, trying to keep my voice as normal as possible even though I'm floored by Peter's response, by the anger behind his words. I know I shouldn't be surprised, given what I just figured out, but I am anyway.

"You're not going to break anything else, are you?"

"Like what? Christmas ornaments?" I say sarcastically, looking at the bare tree. "She didn't even bother to decorate that thing."

"I just brought that tree home tonight, Rosie," he says. "Mom shouldn't have to do everything by herself. Stop being a fucking brat."

I want to tell him that I'm not the only one acting like a brat, but in the spirit of Christmas I just say, grudgingly, "It smells nice."

"Maybe we can all decorate it tomorrow."

I don't have any intention of doing anything with my mom tomorrow. My plan, as it stands now, is to spend the rest of the weekend in my room, protesting being grounded for the first time in my life and plotting my strategy for getting through the remaining two days of school before Christmas break without having both my legs broken as retribution for being a buzz-kill.

"Don't stay up too late," he says, sounding annoyingly parental.

"Don't you have to go text your girlfriend or something?" I ask.

"You're welcome, Rosie—glad I could help you out tonight," Peter replies as he goes upstairs.

When I can no longer hear Peter moving around in his old room, I curl up in the corner of the couch, looking out the living room window at the colored lights glowing on the huge Christmas tree in the Parsons' house across the street. I can't stand the thought of going up to my room, so I sit. I wonder why Jamie didn't show up at the hotel, and why Regina looked at me that way when I was standing on the balcony. I wonder whether my mother will come to her senses tomorrow and realize that I did exactly what she would have wanted me to do tonight when I called 911. And I wonder just how awful Christmas day is going to be without my dad, and whether he's in heaven or the cosmos or whatever, trying to figure out why no one in his family has bothered to build him a memorial website.

The Parsons' Christmas lights fade as the sky turns pink. The color calms me and my eyes close. Finally.

coerce (*verb*): to convince using threats
(*see also:* another specialty of Regina's)

———

13

THE VOLLEYBALL IS HURTLING STRAIGHT AT MY FACE, BUT I am powerless to do anything about it. My hands go up too high and wide, and the ball passes right through my arms and hits me on the forehead for what feels like the fifteenth time.

Mr. Cella's shrill whistle blows.

"Don't make me tell you again, people. Stop trying to hit your classmate! It's not her fault you were all too dumb to know when to quit."

I appreciate Mr. Cella's attempt to defend me, but really, the only person who truly didn't know when to quit on Saturday night was Stephanie, who ended up with nothing more than a hangover on Sunday and is now standing on the other side of the net on Monday morning, trying not to make eye contact with anyone, least of all me. She knows that out of everyone who was at the Amore Motel that night, I'm the one who had to pay the most for her mistake, and I'll probably continue to pay for it for a long time to come.

I already feel like everyone in school has taken a shot at me, and it's only second period.

Two days left before Christmas break. Two days. I don't know if I can make it.

Why couldn't it have been a health-class Monday? We could have been listening to Ms. Maso tell us about the dangers of drinking, and she'd be singing my praises for being responsible and telling people that they should be thanking me instead of cursing me in the halls. Instead, it's a gym Monday. I never in a million years thought I'd rather be in health than gym. I used to love gym.

Volleyball provides my classmates with the perfect opportunity to repay me for getting them all in trouble. The great irony is that Stephanie got off easy—her mother still feels too guilty about the divorce to do anything drastic. My mother, however, has grounded me for two weeks without phone or email privileges, and put me on "probation" indefinitely. This is her way of expressing that she's proud of me for calling 911 but mad at me for being at the hotel in the first place. She claims I'm grounded more for lying than for staying at a party with alcohol.

The bottom line is, I probably won't be invited to any parties in the near future, so being grounded doesn't really matter anyway. I'll just spend Christmas break in my room, studying for the PSATs.

Mr. Cella's whistle shrieks again. "All right, let's go, let's go!"

I see Richie handing Matt the ball on the other side of the net. Richie gives him a few instructions that I am sure have something to do with velocity and some specific area of my body. Matt nods seriously, as if he'd been given an extremely important mission, and winds up to serve. And then, miraculously, a voice floats across the gym.

"Rose Zarelli to the main office, please. Rose Zarelli, main office, please."

A chorus of "Oooooooh" erupts, along with raucous laughter.

"You better get down there in case somebody needs you to call an ambulance," yells Matt from across the net. He high-fives Richie. I don't know when Matt and Richie became friends, but I do know that it's not a good sign. Matt doesn't need encouragement to be any more of a jock-hole than he already is.

Robert angrily tells everyone to shut up. Only a few people listen. He looks at me and nods, as if to give me some sort of reassurance that everything is going to be okay, but quite frankly, I know that nothing is going to be okay. Robert got lucky—his stepparents didn't care about his being at the hotel. As long as the Lexus was fine, they were fine. At least that's what he said in one of the million emails he sent me over the weekend that I didn't answer.

"All right, all right, enough harassment, okay? Rose, go get changed." As I pass Mr. Cella, trying to ignore the jeers, he says quietly, "Stay in the office until the end of the period."

When a teacher feels so sorry for you that he tells you to skip the rest of his class, you know you're in serious trouble. I run to the girls' locker room, relieved that at least I'll get to change by myself for once.

And then, the unthinkable happens.

I bump smack into Regina. Literally. My shoulder hits her chest as I'm turning the corner in the locker room. The only thing that's missing from the scene is a screeching horror-movie soundtrack.

She looks as surprised to see me as I am to see her, and she stuffs something in her bag quickly. She seems almost nervous for a second, and I realize that it's weird that she's here right now—she doesn't have gym this period. I start to go around her, and that's when she strikes with killer speed, grabbing my arm hard enough to leave bruises.

"I don't know what it is you think you're doing, but I better not ever catch you anywhere near my boyfriend again. I don't even want you looking at him, you got that?"

"You have a boyfriend?" I ask, trying to be all cool and nonchalant, like she isn't digging her super-red talons into the flesh of my arm.

"Don't even pretend you don't know what I'm talking about. I saw him follow you up the stairs at Tracy's, and I saw him follow you outside at homecoming."

I contemplate pointing out that *he* followed *me,* and that I don't really have control over whether somebody follows me somewhere. But I decide to keep my mouth shut.

"If I see you near him again, I will kick your ass and get your little friend thrown off the squad. You hear me?"

I've seen those cheerleading movies—Tracy made me watch them over the summer—but I had no idea that they were true to life. Not only are some of these girls complete and total witches, but they honestly think that the world revolves around them, that they are at the top of the social hierarchy. They may have been at one point, like in the last century sometime, but not anymore. Now they seem like something left over from another era, like when Title IX was actually more than the name of a women's sports clothing company. I'd laugh right in her mean face if my arm didn't hurt so much. And if I didn't think she'd come up with some evil plan to get Tracy booted off the team before I could even change out of my gym uniform. Tracy would never forgive me. Never.

If I thought I despised the Union High cheerleaders before, I had no idea what the meaning of the word *despise* is.

I look Regina straight in the eye and say, "Let go of my arm. Now."

The door slams open behind us as Coach Morley comes in to get ready for her next class. We both freeze, and Morley goes into the fitness office without noticing us, writing something on her clipboard as she walks. Regina lets go of my arm, and though I'd like to think it's because I told her to, I know it's because she doesn't want to deal with Morley.

"I'll make your life a living hell if you come near Jamie again," she whispers to me, sticking a manicured claw in my face before turning to leave. "I don't care if your damn dad is dead."

The rage hits me so quickly I almost have no say over my actions. It takes everything I have not to grab her by the hair and yank her backward as she stalks out of the locker room. My chest is tight, and I can't get any air. The blood is rushing to my face. I hear my pulse in my head, and it's racing like crazy. *Breathe,* I tell myself. *She's not worth it. She's not worth anything. Breathe.*

In some ways, I have to hand it to her—she's good. The last thing I ever expected was for her to say something about my father. I'm surprised she even knows about him. She's so obsessed with herself that I didn't think she had room in her tiny little head for knowledge about anyone else.

Breathe.

I take another second to collect myself, then I round the corner to my locker. Usually I have trouble finding it because I never bother to memorize the number of the one I've chosen for that day, and almost all of us use the same kind of lock. But today it's easy for me to find my locker because the words "Suck it, Stupid 911 Bitch" are painted on it in fuchsia nail polish.

At least now I know who the school's nail-polish graffiti artist is.

I hear a little gasp behind me. I turn and see Morley standing there, her mouth agape.

"Rose, are you responsible for this?"

I shake my head.

"Is that your locker?" she asks.

I nod.

"It smells like it's still drying," she says, coming closer for inspection. "Who did this?"

I'd love to get Regina in big fat trouble for defacing school property. Nothing would make me happier. I could just open my mouth right now and get her suspended, and possibly even thrown off cheerleading. Who would she be if she couldn't prance around and bully people with her pom-poms? Would she have any friends left? Would she still have Jamie?

As tempting as it is, I don't want to jeopardize Tracy's standing on her beloved squad, and I can't do anything else to draw attention to myself. I already have a reputation for being a tattletale after this weekend, and nobody likes a tattletale—we all had that lesson drilled into our heads from the first time someone dumped sand on us in the sandbox.

"I don't know who did it, Coach Morley," I say, even though it nearly kills me.

The first person I see when I get to the main office is Tracy, who wasn't in study hall or gym this morning. She's curled up in a chair in the corner, crying underneath multiple red-and-green Christmas garlands that are dipping down into the room from the ceiling. Tracy is crying like something really terrible has happened, but I've seen her cry like this when she can't get her hair the way she wants it. I sit down next to her and pull her into a big hug.

"Trace, what's wrong? What happened?"

She cries even harder and can't answer me. I just sit there with my arms around her, waiting until she can talk. When she finally catches her breath, she says only one word.

"YouTube."

"What?" I ask, baffled.

"Ms. Gerren? Would you come in here please?" asks the principal, Mrs. Chen, from her office doorway. She's wearing a green pantsuit and a red headband topped with glittery reindeer antlers. "Actually, Ms. Zarelli, why don't you come, too. You can provide some moral support for your friend here."

Despite the way she's dressed, terror strikes as I look up at our principal, who I've never even met before. The only principals I've met were giving me awards or diplomas. This disciplinary thing is a first for me, especially since I'm not sure what I'm being disciplined for.

We walk into Mrs. Chen's office. It looks like a Christmas emporium. The fake-wood paneling on the walls, which is stained from ceiling leaks, is draped in holiday bunting. There are poinsettias everywhere and a talking, dancing Santa on the windowsill. The only non-Christmasy thing in the office, aside from the token menorah next to the Santa, is the industrial orange carpeting.

"Please, ladies, have a seat," she says as she reaches back to shut off the "Ho ho ho!" Santa behind her.

We sit in the uncomfortable wooden chairs in front of her desk. They're too big, so we either have to slide all the way back and have our legs sticking straight out in front of us like kindergartners, or we have to sit on the very edge of the chair as if we're about to bolt at any second. Tracy is still sniffling. Mrs. Chen offers her the big box of tissues sitting on her desk, which Tracy accepts with a whispered "Thank you." There is a jar of red and green Hershey's Kisses on her desk, but she doesn't offer us any of those, probably because she doesn't bother offering candy to students she's about to expel.

"First of all, Rose, I'd like to offer you my condolences, since I didn't get to talk to you at the funeral. I met your father several times at hockey games. He was a lovely man. I'd also like to thank you for your courageous act on Saturday night," she continues, "which, from what I understand, may have saved Stephanie's life."

I don't know how to respond. I've been getting my butt kicked all morning for that "courageous act," and I'm not exactly proud of what I did. "I didn't save her life. She woke up right after I called for the ambulance."

"Well, who knows what would have happened to her if someone less responsible had found her. I know it took courage to pick up that phone, so thank you for that."

"Okay," I say, knowing that isn't an appropriate response but not exactly willing to accept her thank-you.

"The janitors are already working on removing the nail polish from the gym locker as well as your hall locker."

"It was on my hall locker, too?" I had no idea Regina was so observant. Or resourceful.

Tracy stops sniffling for a second and looks from me to Mrs. Chen and back, puzzled.

Mrs. Chen nods. "That's why I called you down here. Do you have any idea who might have done that?"

"Someone who wears ugly hot-pink nail polish," is as close as I can come to giving up Regina.

"Well, that narrows it down, doesn't it?" Mrs. Chen says. Was that a joke? Does our principal have a sense of humor?

"Now. Ms. Gerren, would you like to tell your friend why you're here, which will explain why I invited her in to provide some moral support for you?"

I do not like the sound of this at all. She's said the word "moral" too many times. Have I suddenly become some kind of ethical role model just because I didn't want Stephanie to die on Saturday night?

Tracy sniffles a bit more and then takes a deep breath. "The 'Single Ladies' dance is on YouTube," she says.

I don't know why she's telling me something I already know—she's made me watch that Beyoncé video with her on YouTube a million times. And then it comes to me in a rush. In all the drama and trauma of Saturday night, I'd forgotten the "Single Ladies" striptease that Kristin and Tracy did in the parking lot for the benefit of everyone at the motel.

"Really?"

Tracy looks at me, misery in her eyes. "All of it."

I actually don't know what that means, since I didn't stick around for the whole thing. In my mind I try to reconstruct who was there, who would have been mean enough to record it and put it on YouTube, but the possibilities are endless. For all I know, having it posted on YouTube is just a part of her stupid, endless initiation.

"Ms. Gerren, this is not conduct becoming of a young lady or a student of Union High School. You are aware of this, yes?" Mrs. Chen asks.

"But, Mrs. Chen, it's initiation. If I want to be a cheerleader, I have to do whatever the older girls tell me to do. I don't have a choice."

"That's exactly what Kristin said. And as I told her, there's always a choice. You may not like the options, but there's always a choice. Ms. Zarelli, you seem like you have a good head on your shoulders. How do you advise your friend to handle this situation?"

What I want to say is, Tracy should just quit the stupid team. But beyond that, I'm out of ideas and not interested in being the principal's pet. Even though I do like her reindeer-antler headband, which adds a surreal element to this whole conversation. I just shrug.

Mrs. Chen looks disappointed, as if she expected me to whip out a PowerPoint presentation outlining the many ways that Tracy could rise up and rebel against cheerleaders who use their powers for evil instead of good.

"Here's what we're going to do," she says. "I'm going to have a little sit-down with the captains of the athletic teams to discuss these so-called 'initiation routines.' Initiation will be banned from Union High, and any student found guilty of perpetrating or participating will be suspended or expelled, depending on the severity of the situation."

I'm not a lawyer, but I'm pretty confident that there are plenty of ways for students to get around this new rule, such as no longer using the word *initiation*. But I don't say anything, primarily because I don't want to be late for French, and the bell is about to ring.

"Ms. Gerren, we've called your parents to inform them of the situation, and the video is being removed from YouTube. You and Kristin will be allowed to stay on the cheerleading team, but you are suspended for the next three games—unless you'd like to tell me right now who forced you into dancing in your underwear on Saturday night in the freezing cold."

Tracy stares at the orange carpeting and doesn't answer.

"I'll take that as a 'no.' If there are any further incidents, you will be instantly removed from the squad. Is that clear?"

Tracy nods, and the principal dismisses us. We get to the door before Mrs. Chen adds, "Oh, Rose, I'd like you to keep me posted on any further harassment you experience. There are only two days left before break, of course, but it's possible it could continue outside of school in some form."

I can feel the look of horror on my face—it hadn't occurred to me that this might keep going outside of school, especially since it's peace-on-earth time. Mrs. Chen smiles sympathetically at me. "Get my email address from the secretary on the way out, okay? Don't worry. This should all blow over soon."

Sure, if you define *soon* as *never*.

quarantine (*verb*): to isolate or cut off from interaction
(*see also:* Christmas at the Zarellis')

————

14

ON CHRISTMAS, WE DON'T EXACTLY RUSH TO OPEN OUR presents. My mother sits at the kitchen table reading the *New York Times* like it's any other day while I uncharacteristically muster up every ounce of holiday spirit I can find and attempt to make Christmas pancakes with reindeer cookie cutters. Peter sits at the island near the stove, alternately trying to make conversation with me and making his weird new chuckling sound as he reads texts from his girlfriend. I can tell he wants me to ask what she's texting him, so I don't.

Finally, in the afternoon, when we can't put it off anymore, the three of us go to the living room and sit down by the tree, which has a grand total of four ornaments hanging from its branches, no thanks to me. At least Peter draped some white lights on it so it doesn't look completely pathetic.

There are just a few presents, but that's enough, considering this whole thing feels like a fraud anyway.

Peter makes the biggest effort, filling in for Dad, who used to be the master of ceremonies. He reaches under the tree and pulls out each present with great fanfare. My mom watches him with a look on her face that's half misery, half pride. I open my presents as quickly as possible—a sweater, a new iPod, a book—and then I stand up, ready to make my escape back upstairs.

"Hold up, Rosie, there's another one for you," says Peter as he practically crawls under the tree to grab the last present. He pulls out a small velvet jewelry box with a card attached.

"Oh! That came for you yesterday, special delivery," says my mother. The way she's smiling tells me that while she didn't get it for me, she knows who did. I open the card. It says, "Rosie, I'm really sorry about the thing at homecoming. I hope your first Christmas without your dad goes okay. Love, Robert."

The box holds a pretty silver pendant engraved with an "R." I wonder if it stands for Rose or Robert.

"What is it?" Peter asks.

"It's from Robert," my mother answers, still smiling.

"A necklace," I say flatly.

"You sound really thrilled about it," Peter says.

I shake my head, not willing to explain that Robert's Christmas gift is actually an apology for assuming that I was going to have lots and lots of sex with him at homecoming. If I told my mother that, I'd probably be grounded for all eternity, not just for Christmas break.

"Can we see it?" she asks.

I take the pendant out of the box and hold it up.

"It's beautiful," my mother says with way too much enthusiasm. "Why don't you put it on?"

I shake my head again and put it back in the box.

"You can email him to thank him, if you'd like."

"I thought I wasn't allowed to use my email," I reply.

"I'm willing to make an exception in this case," she says

as she starts to gather the wrapping paper off the floor. "It's a lovely gift and you should thank him. You can use the computer in the kitchen."

As much as I'd like to get on my email right now, Condom Boy's thank-you can wait.

"What's the deal with Robert these days?"

"Robert has developed a bit of a crush on your sister."

"Mom, Robert has liked me since the sixth grade, which Peter already knows. Where have you been?" I snap.

"Rose," Peter says, his voice full of warning.

I'm just about to tell Peter to shut up when the doorbell rings. We pause, looking at each other as if we've forgotten what to do about a ringing doorbell. Even though it's nearly four o'clock, Peter and I are still in our pajamas, and Mom doesn't look much better in her sweatpants. She gets up, tries to fix her hair in the coat closet mirror, then gives up and opens the door.

Tracy and Stephanie each hold a plate wrapped in foil with a red-and-green bow on top, snow landing on their winter hats, looking like a holiday postcard or a Gap ad. My mother does her best to greet them with appropriate cheer, but she looks like she might throw up. I know that, even though it's snowy and cold, she has been transported right back to the summer—when people showed up at our door every hour with casserole dishes—because I have, too. I feel sorry for her, which, as usual, first makes me mad at her and then mad at myself.

"Merry Christmas, Mrs. Zarelli," says Tracy. "Stephanie and I made cookies."

"That's so nice, girls. Come in."

"Sorry to bother you, Mrs. Zarelli, but I want to apologize for, um, getting sick at homecoming." By the way Stephanie just plunges in before she's even made it across the threshold, I can tell she's been nervous about apologizing and has practiced her speech, probably coached by Tracy. Stephanie looks at the floor as she talks, and the tips of her ears turn as red as her hair. "And I'm also so sorry for putting Rose in that situation. I feel real bad about it. I mean, Rose and I have talked but I just wanted to...you know."

"Thank you, Stephanie. I hope you've learned a lesson about drinking?"

"Mom, it's Christmas—stop lecturing," says Peter, getting up from the floor.

At the sight of Peter, Tracy lights up brighter than the Parsons' Christmas tree, which is glowing like a beacon through their living room window across the street, putting ours to shame. "Trace, congratulations on your YouTube debut," he says, giving her a hug. Tracy blushes like crazy but looks way more thrilled than mortified, which I find kind of disturbing.

"It was good," says Stephanie, always the supportive friend, twirling a strand of her red hair around her finger. "Tracy can really dance, you know."

"Tracy, you have a video on YouTube?" my mother asks, clueless.

"Um, well—"

"What kind of cookies did you bring?" I interrupt.

Tracy shoots me a grateful glance as she takes the foil off to reveal a plate piled high with ginger snaps, butter cookies, chocolate-chip cookies, fig bars and candy-cane brownies.

"Wow, you really went to town," Peter says.

Tracy grins. "We've been baking all day."

"We made your favorite, Rose," says Stephanie, pointing to the chocolate-chip cookies.

"My mom wants to know if you want to come have dinner with us," Tracy says, looking at Peter. "All three of you," she adds for good measure, in case we thought the invitation was just for Peter. Which, judging by the look on her face as she gazes at him, would be Tracy's first choice.

I'd give just about anything to go over to Tracy's house for Christmas dinner, but I can tell that my mom has had all she can take today and we aren't going anywhere.

"No, Tracy, we wouldn't want to intrude. And we're just about to eat, too. But thank you for the lovely invitation, and please thank your mom for us."

My mom takes the plates from them. As she hands them to Peter and asks him to bring them in the kitchen, Tracy leans in and whispers, "Did you tell him yet?"

"I'm going to walk them out," I say as nonchalantly as I can.

My mother looks at me sternly. "Two minutes."

Apparently she's happy to change the rules of my being grounded if it involves emailing Robert, but not if it involves talking to my girlfriends. Interesting.

I grab my down jacket as Peter comes back from the kitchen. Tracy takes her sweet time saying goodbye to him and giving him an extra special, long-form hug. I roll my eyes at Stephanie, who giggles as Peter sort of has to peel Tracy's arms off his neck and assure her that yes, he'll come by her house and say hello before he goes back to school. Finally the three of us step out into the snow.

"Well?" Tracy asks. "Did you tell him?"

"No."

"You should. Peter can help you figure out what to do."

"There's nothing to do, Trace. I just have to wait it out. Mrs. Chen is probably right—it'll blow over after break."

"What if it doesn't? What if the nickname '911 Bitch' sticks with you for the rest of high school?"

I've thought about this a lot over the past few days and I keep coming to the same conclusion: If I tell on Regina, there's no doubt she'll get revenge. And it'll probably be a lot worse than just nail polish on my locker. It will involve rearranging my face, getting Tracy thrown off cheerleading and ensuring that I never lay eyes on Jamie again—not necessarily in that order.

"Who do you think did it, Rosie?" Stephanie asks.

"I have no idea," I lie. "So what did you get for Christmas?" I ask, hoping this will be a good distraction for at least a minute or two.

"Matt got me these earrings," Tracy answers, lifting her hair so I can see. The earrings are actually very pretty. I try to hide my surprise, ignoring the image in my head of Matt buying a present for Tracy and a present for Lena at the same store, too lazy to go to more than one place.

"And Mike got me this," Stephanie beams, displaying a gigantic plastic bangle that I can tell Tracy wouldn't be caught dead in. To her credit, she doesn't say anything snarky about it, nodding in approval as Stephanie shows it to her for what is probably the millionth time. "Did you get good stuff, Rose?"

"The usual. I mean, it's all nice," I say, trying not seem ungrateful. "Peter got me an iPod Touch."

"He should have gotten you an iPhone, so you can be in the twenty-first century with the rest of us. I'll talk to him about it," Tracy says, as if Peter calls her to ask for gift-giving advice on a regular basis.

"So, um, how are y'all today?" Stephanie asks, shuffling a foot back and forth over a ridge of dirty ice on the snowy sidewalk.

"It's almost over."

"To be honest, Rose, you and your mom and Peter look kind of miserable," says Tracy. "Even though I can tell Peter's trying not to."

"It's just…hard," I say. That's not what I mean, but I

know that that's what people say. Clichés are useful in situations like this, not just for the people who are offering condolences, but for the people who have to respond, too. But once all the clichés have been used, most people have no idea what to say to make someone feel better. I can't really blame them—I don't know what to say to make me feel better, either.

We stand there in the kind of awkward silence that I've gotten used to since the summer. Although, the fact that it's happening with my best friends kicks the awkwardness up a few notches.

"I have to go. My two minutes are up," I say.

"Rose, I'm real sorry that you got in trouble because of me," Stephanie mumbles, tucking her left foot behind her right ankle as if she has an itch there.

"I know, Steph, it's okay. It doesn't matter anyway."

"You know, people might be mad at you, but you were smart to do what you did," Stephanie says. "I think your dad would have been proud of you for, you know, taking care of me."

One of the things that I love about Stephanie is that if something like what she just said comes into her head, she'll say it out loud. She's shy in some ways, but if she thinks somebody needs to hear something, she says it even if it's scary to say.

But that doesn't mean I know how to respond. And to be honest, I don't even know if what she said is true. So I just say goodbye and start up the front walk, wondering if maybe I've just been rude. I stop and turn to say something else, maybe something funny, but nothing comes out, so I just watch them—arms linked, slipping and sliding down the icy street together—as snowflakes gently fall on my face.

* * *

"What's the last happy memory you have from before Dad died?"

Peter thinks about it as I scrub a pot caked with fat and grease from the burnt roast, and he finishes drying a clean pan.

"My graduation party." He puts the pan back in the cabinet.

"That was fun," I say, feeling like a traitor for condoning his choice of a memory that does not actually include Dad, when of course I was fishing for one that does.

We're both quiet as we think about that day. Less than twelve hours later, everything fell apart. We were all still in bed when the phone rang. Peter knew something was wrong before I did—his room is closer to Mom's than mine, and he could hear her through the wall. She hung up the phone and knocked on our doors. We both came out into the hallway, and she said, "There's been an explosion." She didn't have to say anything else.

"What about since he died?" Peter asks. I almost laugh at the idea that anything could make me happy these days, and then I remember sitting in the car with Jamie at homecoming. I'm still not sure I want to tell Peter, but I must have a weird look on my face because he says, "Does it have anything to do with Robert and that necklace?"

"No. Robert is a pain," I say as I hand him the clean, wet pot.

"So he still likes you?"

"Yup."

"But you don't like him."

"Not like that."

"Who *do* you like?" he asks in that annoyingly parental

tone of voice that he's now used too many times this holiday season for my tastes.

"You sound all old," I tell him, hoping to change the subject. "Adult, or something. I don't like it."

"Something's going on with you. What is it?"

Everything is going on with me. Where to start? "Well,
let's see. My new nickname is '911 Bitch,' according to the
graffiti that's all over the school."

Peter stops drying and looks at me. "Seriously?"

"Yup."

"Do you know who it is?"

"Yup."

"Who?"

"Promise you won't tell anyone? Ever?"

"Okay."

"Regina. Deladdo."

"Because of what happened at homecoming?"

"No, that just gave her an excuse to harass me."

Peter puts the pot and dish towel down on the counter
and leans against it, facing me at the sink. "So what's her
problem?"

Should I take Tracy's advice and tell Peter? Maybe he *can*
help me. Or is it stupid to think that anyone can help me
with this?

"She thinks something's going on with me and Jamie."

"Oh, shit. That's totally my fault. I'm sorry. I didn't think
that when I asked him to—"

"It's not your fault. She's sort of right. There is something
going on. I just don't know what."

Peter pauses for a second. "What? Jamie? Rose, he's too..."
He trails off, realizing I'm about to tell him yet again that
he sounds like an annoying adult.

"It's not really like that. I mean, we kissed once," I say,

waiting for his reaction. His eyebrows practically hit his hairline. "But Regina thinks it's more than that and she said if she saw me near him, she'd kick my ass and figure out how to get Tracy thrown off cheerleading. And if Tracy gets thrown off that stupid team because of me, she'll never speak to me again."

"Are you...into Jamie? I mean, more than just a crush?"

I don't know if I should answer that. I know I'm not supposed to like him—he's older, he doesn't really fit into any category, he's going out with Regina—but obviously I do. Although it doesn't matter that I like him because that kiss was probably just a gigantic fluke. "He's just being nice to me because you asked him to."

"I sure as hell didn't ask him to kiss you, Rose."

I can't help the smile that steals across my face.

He looks at me hard for a minute. "Whatever is going on, it doesn't have anything to do with me anymore, that's for sure." He picks up the pot again. "Dad would fucking freak, you know. He was there when Forta got thrown off the hockey team for nailing Anthony Parrina. Dad knew what a badass Jamie could be."

"I thought we weren't supposed to care what Dad wanted anymore," I say quietly. Peter's silence tells me I won the point, but I know he's not going to admit it. "Maybe Dad would like that I'm with someone who can watch out for me in a certain way. I mean, isn't that why you asked him to be my watchdog or whatever?"

"I guess. But if I hadn't, Regina Deladdo wouldn't be talking shit about you right now."

Maybe. But if he'd never asked Jamie to look out for me, then Jamie never would have kissed me at homecoming. And as we've just established, that is the only good thing that has happened to me in the past six months.

"Listen, if Forta does anything—and I mean anything—"

I shut the running water off and hold up my hand. "Stop trying to be Dad, Peter."

This catches us both off guard. I didn't realize that that's what he was trying to do until the words came out of my mouth. And by the look on his face, I can tell that he didn't, either. He grabs another wet pot from the drain board.

"Just be careful," he says. "I don't want you to get hurt. Forta can be a good guy, but Regina sounds fucking certifiable. Is this thing with Forta worth the trouble?"

The question strikes me as funny, as if I have any say whatsoever in this whole Jamie thing, as if I get to define what is or isn't happening between us. All I know is, he gave me one perfect kiss and then disappeared. The way my luck goes these days, that's probably the last I'll ever see of him.

After Peter and Mom are asleep, I crawl into bed with my laptop and visit the twenty-one-year-old sergeant's website. As soon as the page loads, Christmas music starts blasting from the tiny speakers on my computer, and I quickly hit the mute button on my keyboard so I don't wake anyone up. The sergeant's graduation photo is wreathed in holiday garlands, and as I move my cursor, a tiny angel with a halo and wings flies across the page, mimicking the movements of my finger on the track pad. The other two photos that were on the home page before are gone now, and there is something new since the last time I visited—a box that is constantly scrolling, showing messages that people have posted for him. Today, there are twenty-three new ones, all wishing the sergeant a Merry Christmas. Most of the messages talk about how he died doing what God wanted him to, how the fact that he's with Jesus now makes everything that happened to him okay, and that he shouldn't worry about anyone because they're all doing fine even though they miss him every second of every day.

The messages are written directly to him, as if he were still here, even though they talk about him being dead. It makes me feel funny, but I start to think about what I would write to Dad on his page, and I understand why the sergeant's friends and family are doing it. It makes them feel like they're still connected somehow. Like they can reach out, even if he can't reach back.

Not everyone who died in the explosion has a memorial site, but since I first found the sergeant's page, more and more links have popped up, and now the pages of most of the people who died—most of the Americans, anyway—are linked to each other through the sergeant. I wonder who is maintaining his site. Is someone sitting at a computer right now, searching for Dad's site to link to, wondering if poor Alfonso Zarelli wasn't loved enough by his family to be immortalized forever on the web?

Dad's is one of the only names on the sergeant's page that isn't clickable.

I have to build Dad's site.

I don't know anything about domain names or servers that host sites or anything like that, but I can worry about that later. Right now, I just have to figure out how to design a page that he would like and that would be a tribute to him—a place where people could write him notes, or just see his picture if they want to. I have no idea who those people would be, but they might be out there.

My computer came with a program for building websites, and it has a tutorial. I open it and start following the step-by-step instructions. The first thing it suggests I do is pick a template from a bunch of premade ones. They have names like Retail and Invitation and Announcement. There is actually one called In Memoriam, and I click on it, despite the fact that it is, predictably, black with cheesy digital bunting. Hopefully I can change that later.

When the template opens, a page full of placeholder photos and text fills my screen. The photo is of an old woman who looks like she spends her days in an apron making cookies for her grandchildren. The title says "Nana Betsy." A second later, a pop-up box asks me for a new photo and title.

So much for easing into this—I've only been at it for two minutes and already, I'm stuck. Which picture should I use? How do I decide?

I click on my photo folder without thinking about the fact that I haven't looked at pictures of Dad since we planned the service for him over the summer. I'm not prepared to see so many photos of him at once. The icons in the folder are small, but I can make out important details like a beach or a cake on the kitchen table, and I know exactly which photo is which. Suddenly memories of Dad from different times in my life are crowding in on me simultaneously, and I feel like my brain is short-circuiting. There are too many photos, too many different memories. I close the folder and take deep breaths to ward off any attacks that might be lurking.

No attacks. After my minute of deep breathing is up, I decide it might be better to start with the title.

I put the cursor in the big box where it blinks expectantly. I type, "Alfonso Zarelli." Then I notice that there's a narrow box underneath it with smaller font. The sample text says, "Beloved Grandmother, Devoted Mother, Wonderful Sister." I type in a few different things—Great Dad, Word Lover, Funny Guy—and delete them all, feeling like there's nothing I could possibly say to sum him up the right way, nothing I could put in that narrow box that could be enough.

This is going to be way harder than I thought. I need a strategy.

I go back to the sergeant's home page and for once, I try to ignore the content—the graduation photo, the messages from people who still love him—and I look at the way the page is built. When I am able to stop focusing on his face, I start to notice some design things, like the home page now has only his photo, his name, and the box where people can leave comments. Then, across the bottom, there are names of other pages you can go to for more about him.

I go back to the template and keep going. I erase most of the boxes but leave one where I want to invite people to post comments. I leave another box on the other side of the photo for something else—I'm not sure what yet. Then I name the other pages that I'd like to build eventually: biography, information and articles, and photos. I spend another hour or so choosing colors and fonts, and playing with the special features that allow you to add borders and music and videos. In the end, I decide that I just want it to be as simple as possible, and I delete most of the things I added.

I give the message box a title, calling it, "Say Hello to Dad." That seems stupid and so wrong that I'm actually embarrassed, so I change it to "Talk to Alfonso." That's better, but it still doesn't seem right, somehow. Then I type, "Talk to my dad, Alfonso Zarelli." It makes it kind of obvious that a kid built the site, but I'm not sure that that's a bad thing, necessarily. I'll leave it for now.

The blank space under his name is a little too symbolic for me—I need to try choosing the photo again. I decide that the best way to do it is to randomly pick one as a placeholder. There's no reason to choose the final photo now. I open the folder, close my eyes, and slide my finger around on the track pad for a few seconds. Then I double-click and open my eyes.

My dad is in our kitchen, his crazy hair sticking straight up, wearing his favorite striped T-shirt and glaring at the photographer over the top of his coffee mug. If it weren't for a tiny smile on his mouth, he'd look mad, but I can tell he's just kidding. The photo makes me laugh a little, and I know it's totally wrong for the site, but it's the perfect place-holder for now.

I'm about to save the page and close out of the program when I remember the blank box I left on the other side of the photo frame. I click on the title box, waiting for some-thing to come to me. And after a minute, it does. "Word of the Day," I type. And then I add the first word that comes to mind.

Indispensable (*adjective*): absolutely necessary.

candid (*adjective*): blunt, honest
(*see also:* Angelo)

———

15

JANUARY SUCKED.

Mrs. Chen was both right and wrong—no one harassed me over break, but the homecoming thing definitely hadn't blown over by the time we were back at school. Regina spent the month leaving elaborate nail-polish artwork addressed to "911 Bitch" on all my desks and lockers. She didn't even expand her color palette, restricting herself to the hot-pink and fuchsia family. I guess it's her signature.

I still have no idea how she figures out which gym locker is mine, since it changes every time. If I had to guess, I'd say she's got spies. It's easy enough for her to find out where my assigned seats are—all she has to do is walk by my classes and look in—but that still takes a lot of time and effort. I imagine that she has color-coded charts and graphs to keep track of where I'll be and when, and I'm almost impressed.

But her January tactics now seem like nothing. She stepped up her game this month.

Last week, she got someone to hack into the school's website and post, on the home page, a Photoshopped picture of me in an EMT uniform, running to the scene of an accident. The headline above the picture read, "Worried you might have too much fun at a party? Never fear—Rose Zarelli is here!" She was smart enough not to use "911 Bitch" on the school's home page, which is too bad. I might have worked up the courage to turn her in if she had.

Peter thinks I should tell Mrs. Chen because, at this point, it really is harassment. But when I ask him if that's what he would do if he were in my place, he just says that it's different for guys. Meaning, of course, that he would just fight the guy and get it over with. I guess girls have the right to do that, too, but it's not my thing. Although I do like imagining grabbing fistfuls of Regina's hair and pulling really, really hard.

Peter also said that if I'm not going to tell Mrs. Chen, I have to at least talk to Jamie. But that would just make things worse for me in the long run. And what would I say? *Hey, Jamie, it was really fun kissing you and all, but your mean girlfriend is now threatening to kill me if I so much as look at you ever again. Could you talk to her, please?*

Yeah, right. Like she'd really listen. The more I get to know her, the less I understand what the appeal could possibly be for Jamie.

We haven't spoken since homecoming. I'm beginning to think I imagined the whole thing.

Now it's Valentine's Day, and I'm sitting by myself in study hall, trying to ignore the blight of red hearts taped on the tables, the chairs and every other surface in the cafeteria. Someone even managed to slap one on Mr. Cella's back without him noticing.

I see Angelo approaching, and I quickly look down at my French book, hoping that he won't talk to me but knowing that he will. He always does. I actually think that Angelo likes me. Not *likes* me likes me, but just likes me. And he's not that bad. He just, well, talks a lot. And I'm trying to cram for my French test. At this point I know that no one really gets any studying done in study hall, but still, I keep trying.

The PA system drones on with the Pledge of Allegiance, and everyone ignores it. Mr. Cella has stopped trying to get us to stand up for it—I think he gave up somewhere around mid-October, which was just fine with me. I'm never saying those words again.

"Hey, Sweater, how ya holdin' up?" Angelo asks, standing above me.

"I'm fine," I say without raising my head.

From the corner of my eye I see him notice one of Regina's special messages on his seat. "This graffiti shit is crazy."

"They'll stop eventually."

He snorts like I've said something hilariously stupid as he sits down, sprawling across several seats at once.

"Hey, Happy Valentine's Day," he says. I don't answer. "You doin' anything romantic tonight?"

"Not as far as I know." I slowly turn the page of my book.

"You're always readin', ya know that?"

"I like to pass my classes," I say.

"You wanna be a doctor or something?"

"A doctor?" I look up at him, confused.

"Yeah, doctors are always readin', aren't they?"

"Um, I don't know."

"Isn't your mom a doctor?"

"Sort of, I guess." I go back to reading, hoping he'll take the hint for once.

"Your pop was an engineer, right?"

Angelo has never mentioned my father before. I check to see if he's messing with me, but he just looks interested.

"Yeah, he was."

"You miss him?"

I nod.

"I have a cousin in the marines in Iraq."

I nod again. Angelo appears to be waiting for me to say something, but I can't. Weirdly, I have no idea what to say to someone who has a cousin who's fighting in Iraq. Now, if his cousin had died there, well, then I'd be qualified to say something deeply profound to Angelo.

"Sweater, how come you never ask me about me?"

Stumped again. It never even occurred to me that Angelo would want to talk to me about himself. But now that I think about it, that sounds suspiciously like a lame way to excuse extreme self-absorption.

"Um, I don't know, Angelo. What do you mean?"

"Well, like, we sit here at this table, just you and me, almost every day except the weekend and except when I cut, but, like, I'm always the one doin' the talkin' about, like, whatever. You never ask me questions like I ask you. You scared?"

"Scared? Like, scared you're going to hurt me or something?"

"No, like, scared your pals won't like you anymore if they think you and me are friends," he says, taking a swig from his milk carton. For some reason, he's opened all four corners and milk spills down the front of his shirt as he drinks. And then I notice something that completely blows my mind and changes everything I ever thought about Angelo.

Angelo, of all people, is wearing a Neko Case T-shirt.

I've seen Angelo in Nirvana and Metallica shirts—I thought he was a metal-grunge guy who was stuck in the glory days of Lars Ulrich and Kurt Cobain. But this…this is too much. Neko Case is a goddess and I didn't expect anyone in this stupid school—not a single person—to have any idea who she is, never mind wear a shirt with her name on it.

"Is that a...Neko Case shirt?"

He looks down at his shirt and then back up at me. "Yeah. That's what it says. N-E-K-O."

"Is it yours?"

"Well I'm wearing it, ain't I?"

"Yeah, but I mean, did somebody just randomly give it to you, or is it actually yours?"

"I got it at the concert," he says, like it's no big thing.

"You saw Neko Case *live?*" I practically shriek.

"Sweater, what's the big deal? You a Neko fan?"

"I *love* her. She's...she's...I just, I'm surprised because I didn't think that you...that she...that that was the kind of music you'd listen to."

"You think I'm too dumb to listen to a smart girl singer like her?"

"No! Nothing like that. But I've only ever seen you wear shirts for bands whose singers are dead, or who don't actually tour anymore."

"Metallica still tours!"

"They do?"

"Sweater, Metallica is one of the greatest bands that ever existed. They will never break up. Ever. Ain't you seen *Some Kind of Monster?*"

"What's that?"

"Oh, man. You gotta see that movie. It's old, but you can totally download it. It's all about, like, the psychology of being in Metallica, and how it almost killed 'em to create that shit together, you know?"

I can hardly believe my ears. "Are you a musician, Angelo?"

He chuckles a little and takes a final swig from his milk carton. "I don't know if anyone would call me that, but I play some guitar." He stands up and starts air-guitaring in the cafeteria, and no one even blinks. I have the weird sensation that Angelo, with his long hair and car grease under his fingernails, is invisible to most of the student body at this high school.

"Are you in a band?"

"Yeah. We're called Fuck This Shit, so we don't get hired a lot, but we're pretty good. We're gonna go on tour after graduation."

"That's awesome."

"There's a lot you don't know about me, Sweater. I can be a pretty cool, nice guy."

"I know."

"You think I'm nice?"

"Well, yeah, you've always been nice to me."

"Except for when I made you cry."

I blush, thinking of the day when Angelo wanted to know if Jamie and I were "doin' it." That was back when I would see Jamie on a regular basis. Due to Regina's campaign of terror, I've been avoiding him again. And he hasn't made an effort to talk to me, either. Not that I should be expecting him to. It's not like we're... I can't even finish that thought.

"You didn't mean to make me cry. I don't know what happened that day. I was just embarrassed or something."

He leans in conspiratorially. "I know Jamie kissed you. He told me."

I look over my shoulder to make sure that none of Regina's spies are around. Susan and Lena both have period-one study hall, although they're hardly ever here. I've never understood how people can so easily get away with cutting. My karma doesn't work that way. I always have to play by the rules, or I get caught. Almost instantly. Which is why I'm surprised that Regina doesn't already know that I kissed Jamie. If she's this crazy over the fact that she saw him follow me twice, I wonder what my life would be like if she knew what had really happened.

I lean across the table and whisper, "Angelo, we shouldn't talk about that. I mean, you know, Regina's scary and—"

"And you have a boyfriend?"

"Robert's not my boyfriend. He was just my date to homecoming. That's all."

"That ain't what Jamie thinks," Angelo says, tearing pieces off his milk carton and dropping them on the table, making a little mountain of soggy, waxy cardboard.

Why would Jamie think I lied to him about Robert?

Or maybe the more important question is, why is Jamie telling Angelo things about me? Is it possible that he's genuinely, truly interested in me? How could he be? We might as well be from different planets. Robert, as Tracy likes to remind me, is in our group of friends and a much more suitable boyfriend for me than Jamie.

But what does that mean? What is *suitable?* If you like someone and they like you back, shouldn't you just be able to go out with them?

Whenever I say that to Tracy, she sings this little song she wrote for me called "Rosie and Her Rose-Colored Glasses."

"Jamie told you that?"

"Jamie thinks the guy's your boyfriend. Want me to set him straight?"

As if on cue, Tracy arrives wearing her gold-and-black cheer uniform, her arms full of red carnations. The cheerleaders have sponsored a Valentine's Day flower sale in order to appear wholesome in the wake of the YouTube scandal and to raise money for the new outfits they want, which are so far from wholesome they should be illegal. She showed them to me online, and I tried to pretend that I thought they looked good. But they were so small, I could barely tell what they were, never mind whether they looked good or not. She told me to stop being such a prude. I gave her my speech about how I think women should be valued for more than how they look bouncing around in spandex, but she just said that feminism is out and kept showing me tacky uniforms that she knows the school will never let them buy.

"I've got a flower delivery for you," she says in a singsong voice. She hands me a carnation with a card attached to it and then stands there expecting me to read it while she waits, even though we both know it's from Robert.

"Thanks, Trace."

"Well, open it!"

"That's okay. I'll wait till later."

"Hey, Trace, you got one of those things for me?"

Tracy looks flabbergasted that Angelo addressed her by name. And she calls me a snob?

"Let me check," she says, looking at him as if he were something she scraped off the bottom of her shoe. And then something weird happens. Her face brightens, she giggles and she says, "As a matter of fact, 'Angelo Martinez, Study Hall Period 1,' I do have one of these things for you." She hands it to Angelo with a big grin, as if the fact that someone sent him a flower causes a complete metamorphosis and Angelo is no longer a vo-tech guy with dirt under his fingernails. He nods and accepts it, like he's been expecting it.

Looks like Angelo isn't quite as invisible to the student body as I thought.

"Thanks, Trace," he says. She's still standing there, waiting for both of us to open our cards, when Stephanie calls from their table across the cafeteria, "Come on, Trace, I want my flower!"

Tracy rolls her eyes and heads in Stephanie's direction.

Angelo watches her go, her short skirt swishing, swishing, swishing as she walks away. I can't really blame him. That's exactly what those skirts are designed for.

"Nice flower you got there," he says, grinning as he gets up, reaching into his pocket for a cigarette. "I'll tell Jame you say 'hey.'" He winks at me and walks away, his lighter in one hand, his flower in the other.

I want to tell him not to tell Jamie anything, but I know it's pointless. I look down at my flower and sigh. I might as well just get this over with.

I feel a tiny pang of guilt that Robert sent me a flower. I never officially accepted his apology, and he finally stopped trying last month. I don't know why I didn't just tell him it was okay—I don't even care about the condom thing anymore. A few days ago, he emailed me for the first time in a while to tell me that he's going to audition for the drama department's spring production of *Macbeth*. I hate amateur Shakespeare, but I should wish him luck anyway, as a kind of peace offering. I realize that, aside from the play, I have no idea what's going on with Robert for the first time since, well, since I've known him, I guess. It's a weird feeling.

I rip open the little white envelope and pull out the cheesy "Happy Valentine's Day!" florist's card illustrated with googly-eyed hearts that appear to be jumping up and down on pogo sticks. But when I look at the center of the card and see the message written in neat, blocky handwriting, my heart starts to do its own pogo-stick routine. Even though I've never seen the writing before, I know instantly who it belongs to. It says:

Meet me at the mall at 8. If you can.

transgression (*noun*): a bad deed
(*see also:* kissing someone else's boyfriend)

———

16

I'M STANDING NAKED IN FRONT OF MY CLOSET IN A HEAP of clothes that I've tried on and taken off. I can't even decide what underwear to put on, which doesn't make any sense because no one's going to be seeing it except me, when I go to bed later. I want to call Tracy for an emergency consultation, but if I do that, then I'll have to tell her where I'm going and why, and I want to keep this private. Not a secret, exactly, but private. Tracy already thinks this thing with Jamie is weird, and she doesn't even know what happened at homecoming.

Tracy is with Matt tonight. They're going to Susan's Valentine's Day party—which I am, of course, not invited to, since I am not a cheerleader—and then they're going back to his place. His parents are seeing a show in the city and, according to Tracy, she and Matt are finally going to do it. I don't believe Tracy when she says this anymore. Something always seems to prevent her from having sex with Matt, which has made me realize that she doesn't actually want to, no matter what she says.

She told me the other day that they'd had a huge talk about everything, and that she explained to him why condoms were so important to her, and that if he really loved her, he would want to be as safe as possible. According to Tracy, he said he did really love her and that he would use condoms. I felt like there might have been some embellishing going on, but I just said, "That's great, Tracy. I'm glad he finally came to his senses."

I wish I could ask Ms. Maso to help Tracy come to *her* senses.

I pick up my favorite pair of jeans from the pile on the floor, hating myself a little bit for choosing my go-to Levi's instead of putting some effort into creating an outfit. If Tracy were here, she'd whip together a look for me that I'd pretend to hate but that I'd secretly love, using one of the untouched issues of *Lucky* that live under my bed. I tried to read *Lucky* once, but it made me feel so far behind the curve that I couldn't deal. I didn't even understand half the outfits I saw in there, and there were pages and pages of jeans that all looked exactly the same.

I pull on a wool sweater I stole from Peter while he was packing to go back to school last month. The only fashionable touch I can manage is my boots. I have these cool Uggs that I bought last spring with my birthday money when Tracy, Stephanie and I went shopping together. I wasn't going to get them because they were stupid expensive, but Stephanie told me I'd love them and wear them nonstop, and she was right. At least the stripes on Peter's sweater match the color of my UGGs. Tracy would probably approve of that.

I start searching my room for some jewelry. Peeking out from underneath my PSAT study guide on my beanbag chair is the box with the necklace that Robert gave me, which I never thanked him for. I wonder if it's wrong to wear jewelry given to you by one guy on a date with a different guy. And then I wonder if tonight is a date. A Valentine's Day date.

I put the necklace on.

As I'm zipping my down coat—which Tracy has told me she now hates, ever since I wore it to homecoming—I decide that it's not a date. Jamie just wants to talk, that's all. About what, I'm not sure, but I can guess. He probably wants to tell me that he shouldn't have kissed me and that I can't ever tell anyone because Regina is a psycho.

But maybe he's not going to say that. I mean, he did send me a flower. And he did tell Angelo about the kiss. Maybe he's going to say that he ended things with Regina—why else would he be free on Valentine's Day?—and he wants to know if I'll go out with him. The thought makes my stomach flutter.

I try to picture us as a couple, walking down the halls holding hands and kissing at my locker. It's hard to do. For one, Jamie hardly ever seems to be in the halls at school anymore. I never know where he is. I don't even know what classes he takes, except for that remedial English class. Is it weird for someone in advanced English to go out with someone in remedial English? Is it weird for a freshman to go out with someone who is probably supposed to be a senior? Is it even legal?

I leave a note for my mom, who is in with a client, promising to honor my probation and be home by nine-thirty. The route to Cavallo's is the same route I take to and from school every day. It's a nice walk except for one creepy spot, right near the school, where there's an overpass. There are no houses on this stretch, and every once in a while, someone claims to have seen Mr. Nakey there. Mr. Nakey is a guy who likes to wear a raincoat and expose himself to kids—boys, girls, it doesn't matter. But he apparently has some standards, because no one under the age of fourteen has ever reported seeing him. In my imagination, he looks like a spy—trench coat, hat, dark glasses. I often wonder what I would do if I saw him.

I don't look anywhere but straight ahead as I walk under the overpass, though I'm guessing Mr. Nakey isn't interested in flashing his thing on a freezing night in February.

I don't exactly know where I'm going. I mean, "the mall" is kind of vague. So I start with Cavallo's, which is packed, as usual. Frankie is behind the counter, tossing pizza dough high in the air and talking to his guys, who are sitting at the counter. I always feel like I should say hi to Frankie when I see him, but he has absolutely no idea who I am. And then I see Michelle sitting in a booth in the corner, wearing a beautiful red, sparkly sweater. When she sees me, she waves. I manage not to look behind me to see if she's actually waving at somebody else, and I raise my hand and smile. And then I realize: Michelle's not supposed to be here. She's supposed to be at Susan's Valentine's Day party.

And so is Regina, who is sitting right next to her.

I put my head down and hurry past the booth just as Regina turns to see who Michelle is waving to. I quickly check the back for Jamie, but I'm guessing that if Regina's here, Jamie isn't. He wouldn't ask me to meet him here anyway—too many people would see us.

I try to sneak past Michelle's booth and head for the door, but I get caught in a crush of people who are trying to go the other way. My back is to the booth, but as I stand there, waiting for my escape, I hear Lena say, "He couldn't come out tonight because he's breaking up with Tracy. Things are going to be a little weird on the squad for a while."

"Lena, do you really have to steal Tracy's boyfriend?" Michelle asks.

"I'm not stealing her boyfriend!" Lena insists. "He started the whole thing."

"And you can't just say no?" asks Michelle.

"Oh, come on," says Susan. "He's a freshman on the swim team. What the hell do you want with a freshman?"

"I like him. He's cute. Tracy will get over it, I'm sure, even if it is Valentine's Day." Lena giggles mercilessly.

Would Matt really dump Tracy on Valentine's Day? Like I have to ask. Of course he would. Anything so he can go out with an older, more experienced cheer-witch than a virginal freshman.

I see an opening in the crowd and I push through it, out the door. This is one of those moments when I really wish I had a cell phone. If I did, I could call Tracy and warn her. Because what if Matt has sex with her and *then* breaks up with her? I remember what Ms. Maso said about having sex with someone who doesn't respect you, and the kind of humiliation that can cause. I wonder if Tracy is about to make a terrible mistake. Maybe I should find a pay phone.

Or maybe I should stop getting involved in other people's business. Do I really need a swim thug *and* a psychotic cheerleader after me?

As I stand there trying to figure out what to do, snow starts to fall. It looks pretty underneath the huge lights in the parking lot, swirling around and floating. I can still hear the noise from Cavallo's, but it's mostly quiet out here. Quiet and peaceful. I wish Tracy were here with me instead of getting her heart broken by Stupid Boy.

Headlights flashing on a parked car catch my attention. Jamie. My heart starts to pound as I cross the lot. I look over my shoulder to make sure that Regina isn't coming out of

Cavallo's with her claws bared, ready to rip my face off. Although I'm less nervous about that than I am about getting in the car with Jamie.

I open the passenger door and slide in.

"I woulda warned you but I don't have your cell."

"Oh, uh, I don't have one. Yet," I say, trying to seem like less of an idiot. "What happened to Susan's party?"

"Her parents' trip got messed up 'cause the airport's closed or something."

"Oh. So…where does Regina think you are right now?"

He shrugs. "I'm supposed to pick her up here later."

Well, that settles that. This is definitely not a Valentine's Day date.

"You got snow on your eyelashes."

I shake my head and brush the snow off my face. It lands on the seat of his car, and I start trying to brush it onto the floor.

"It's cool. It's vinyl," he says.

"Okay," I say, not really knowing how that's relevant. "The cheer-witches almost caught me in there."

"Who?" he asks, looking mystified.

"Regina and Lena and those girls."

"Yeah, but what did you call them?"

"Oh. Uh, cheer-witches."

Jamie throws back his head and laughs that beautiful laugh that I heard for the first time at homecoming. Except this time I'm not so green with envy over the thought of him being with Regina that I can't appreciate how nice it sounds. His laugh makes me laugh, and I feel warm inside. Too warm. Like I have to take off my coat and half my clothes immediately or I'll soon be soaked with sweat.

"Guess you got a thing about cheerleaders, huh?"

Before I can think about whether I should tell him the

truth or not, I say, "I think they're hideous. Like Lena? She's totally trying to steal Tracy's boyfriend, even though she and Tracy are supposed to be teammates. And cheerleading itself is quite possibly the dumbest excuse for a sport that there is on the planet. I'm as mortified that my best friend is a cheer-leader as she is that I'm *not* a cheerleader."

The words hang in the air. I realize that I just said way too much, and I used words that make me sound pretentious. When I get worked up about something, I forget to pay attention to how I sound, and "AP English words," as Robert calls them, come flying out of my mouth.

Oh, and also, I just totally insulted Jamie's girlfriend by going off on cheerleaders like they're one of the world's great evils or something. I mean, *I* think they are, but obviously not everyone does.

"You're a runner, right?" he asks.

"I don't know. Not really."

"I've seen you. You're pretty good."

I guess he watched me for longer than I thought at tryouts. Or longer than Robert wanted to tell me. The thought of him watching me completely bomb that day is almost more than I can bear. "Not good enough to make the team. I'm actually pretty terrible. Or at least I was that day."

"Something go wrong?"

I don't know how to answer that, so I just say, "I used to run with my dad."

Jamie nods like he understands exactly what I'm talk-ing about, and then he starts up the car and backs out of his space. I don't know where we're going, but wherever it is, I should probably just say I can't go because I told my mom I was going to Cavallo's and that I'd be home by nine-thirty. I've already made a fool of myself enough times in front of

Jamie, but I can't afford to get in any more trouble. I take a deep breath.

"Um, I know this is stupid and everything, but I have, uh, a curfew. And it's kind of early tonight."

"How come?" he asks as we pull out of the parking lot. He adjusts something on the dashboard and heat starts blasting into the car. "Sorry. I just gotta do this for a second because the defrost isn't working so great anymore. I gotta get Angelo to fix it."

"Angelo knows how to fix cars?"

"Yeah, he works at his dad's garage."

"Oh, cool," I say, hoping that he'll turn off the heat before I get any sweatier. I'm sure I've soaked right through Peter's sweater, although I know that would be impressive, even for me. "Angelo's a musician. Did you know that?"

I'm so dumb sometimes. Of course he knows that—they're friends.

"Lemme guess. Angelo talks your ear off in study hall."

I laugh a little. "Um, yeah, he likes to talk. He's nice. Although I liked study hall better when you were still there."

I can't believe I said that. I'm so nervous about whatever it is that he wants to talk to me about that I don't have any control over what I'm saying. But he changes the subject, which leaves me even more confused and nervous than I was before I said what I said.

"So what's up with your curfew?"

"Oh, um, I'm on probation. I was grounded over Christmas break. For the whole homecoming thing."

He looks at me, surprised. "You got grounded for that?"

"Yup. I did exactly what I was supposed to do, and I still got in trouble for it."

"You ever been grounded before?" he asks.

I wish I could say yes so I seem older. I mean, I could, but

Jamie would ask why and I'd have to lie, and I know he'd see right through that. I shake my head.

"What's with the 'probation'?" he asks with a slight smile.

"I guess two weeks of being grounded wasn't enough."

Jamie is now fully grinning, as if my story were funny to him. Well, of course it is. He's a junior. A junior who drives his own car and shows up at school when he feels like it. I wonder if he's ever had a curfew in his life.

"Hey, how come you weren't at the after-party at the hotel that night?" I ask.

"Didn't feel like it." I wait for more, hoping he'll say something about how Regina was driving him insane, but he just says, "I'll get you home on time. I wouldn't wanna make your mom mad."

I want to ask him what he meant that time when he said my mom helped him out once. But people only go see my mom if something is really, really wrong, and maybe he doesn't want to tell me about it.

After all, it's not like I'm his girlfriend.

We're driving on the main street in Union, which goes through what I like to call the ugly strip-mall section. Pretty much every fast-food joint and chain store in existence is in this part of town, and it's really lame. But once you get past the stores, it starts to get a little more woodsy, and there's a country-club golf course at the top of a hill with a nice view. I've heard that people sometimes have parties up there, or do other things. Like lose their virginity.

"Where are we going?" I ask, feeling my heart start to race.

"The golf course. It's nice up there. You ever been?" I look at him, and he apparently sees the panic on my face because he says, "I just want to talk about some shit that's happening."

Half of me wonders what he means while the other half

is thinking about how sexy it is when he swears. It's weird, the things that I think are sexy about Jamie: swearing, the fact that he doesn't talk much, that he's more practical-smart than school-smart, that he's just who he is and nothing else. I guess they're things that make us different from each other. Maybe opposites do attract.

We're both quiet until we get to the golf course. He drives past the entrance to the parking lot and takes the service road all the way to the top of the hill, pulling into what seems like an alcove, hidden behind some trees. He turns off the headlights but leaves the car running so we don't freeze to death. The moon is really bright, which I didn't notice until now. I smell that same clean car and rain smell that I remember from the first time I was in this car. I have a feeling Jamie takes better care of this car than some people do their kids.

"Regina's asking questions about you," he says. "She can get crazy jealous."

I nod, hating how it sounds like he knows her so well.

"Do you know why she's doing that?"

I'm confused. All this time, I pictured Regina screaming at Jamie about following me at Halloween and again at homecoming. But suddenly, I realize that Regina would never dare—because Jamie wouldn't put up with it. If she treated him like that, he'd disappear so fast, she wouldn't know what hit her. So she's never said a word about Halloween or homecoming.

She's smarter than I thought.

"Yeah, I know why she's been asking about me."

Jamie waits for me to continue. I'd rather just sit in silence inhaling his clean-laundry scent than say another word. But this is an opportunity that I shouldn't pass up. I stare straight ahead and focus on the snow that is piling up on the branches of the trees that line the golf course, waiting for enough courage to make words come out of my mouth.

"She's upset because she thinks I somehow made you follow me at the Halloween party, and at homecoming," I say in a rush.

"How do you know that?" he asks, sounding slightly suspicious.

"She cornered me in the locker room before Christmas. She told me that if I ever looked at you again, she'd beat me up. And get Tracy thrown off the team." I take a deep breath. "She's the one writing '911 Bitch' everywhere."

Jamie's brow furrows like I've just said something that is incomprehensible to him. "It's her? She's doing that?" I nod. "Why didn't you tell me?"

"I don't know. I figured it was better if I didn't. It's not like you can do anything anyway. If you do, it'll make her think that…it'll make her more jealous."

He leans back against the headrest. "Fuckin' crazy," he says, shaking his head.

The unasked question that has been lurking in my mind for months is now on the tip of my tongue, but it still takes a few seconds for me to work up to asking it. "I don't get it, Jamie. Are you…with her?"

He shrugs. "Sorta. We grew up together."

"What do you mean? Like, you were neighbors or something?"

"Yeah. And I lived with her family for a while."

My brain scrambles to process this information. Jealousy takes over, trying to get me to say things that I shouldn't. I clear my throat.

"Why did you have to live with her?"

Jamie turns on the wipers to get rid of the snow that has

built up on the windshield. He adjusts the heat again and traces the grooves on his steering wheel before answering me.

"My mom died and my dad went bat-shit crazy. The Deladdos said I could stay with them until he got it together. He kinda never did, but I moved back home anyway." He looks directly at me. "That's why I know your mom. I got booted off the hockey team after my mom died. The school sent me to see her."

How is it that I could hear every piece of gossip about Jamie Forta—everything about how stupid he is and how he's been held back a million times and all of that—and not know that his mother is dead, and that she died not that long ago, probably right before Jamie's sophomore year?

"But I never heard—"

"She didn't live with us. Nobody around here knew about her. The funeral was in Boston." He looks so uncomfortable talking about her that I almost tell him he doesn't have to, but I can't—I crave every scrap of information he's willing to share. "I missed a lotta school last year. That's why I gotta take that English class."

"Was it cancer?"

"No." He turns on the headlights and the golf course in front of us is suddenly illuminated in a bright wash of light. "She was in an institution."

He watches me as if trying to gauge my reaction. For a split second, there's so much sorrow in his eyes that I want to reach out and touch his hair, his face—find a way to make him feel okay. Then it's gone.

Peter must have known about Jamie's mom. That's why he asked Jamie to look out for me this year. Because Jamie knows exactly what it feels like to lose someone. He knows how the entire world suddenly turns into an alien planet, and people—all people, even the people who know you better than anyone else—can seem like insensitive, clueless losers when they get tired of you being sad after a while. Jamie knows all about this.

"Why didn't you ever tell me?"

"You have your own shit to deal with."

"Why was she... I mean, she was in the institution because she was sick?"

"I'll tell you about it someday," he says, turning in his seat to look over his shoulder as he backs the car out. "Forget Regina. She don't get to say who you can talk to. You and me are friends. You can talk to me whenever you want."

The combination of the quick change of subject and his declaration that we're "friends" is like a punch to the stomach. I know he means "friends" in a positive way, but I'm sitting in a car with him on Valentine's Day in the most romantic spot in our stupid town, and he just told me one of his deepest, darkest secrets and we're just...friends.

So many questions are competing to get out of my head that they all clog the exit and none of them make it. I'm disappointed. Confused. A tiny bit relieved. Then disappointed again.

Jamie keeps his eyes on the road. The snow is falling hard, and I wonder if his car can make it down the hill without sliding, but he takes it slowly and we make it just fine. We listen to static on the radio till we get to my house. As we sit there on the street, I imagine that he reaches over and touches my face like he did that night in Robert's car. In reality, he doesn't move.

"Thanks for the carnation. It's pretty."

"You're welcome," he says with that slight smile that makes the back of my neck tingle with warmth.

I don't want to be just friends with Jamie Forta.

What would happen if *I* leaned over and kissed *him?* Do I have it in me to do that? Would he stop me?

"Are you going back to Cavallo's?" I ask.

He nods.

"To pick up Regina?"

He turns, studying me like he's looking for information. I picture Regina sitting where I'm sitting right now, holding Jamie's hand while they drive somewhere, or talking to him about something only the two of them know about from when he lived with her family. It occurs to me that Regina probably helped Jamie get through his mother's death, and then, before I know what I'm doing, I lean over and kiss him on the mouth, too hard.

It's not the sexy, grand gesture I had in mind, and I start to pull away before I mess it up any further, but Jamie catches my arm and stops me. I look down as his hand begins to slide up my arm, over my shoulder, stopping at my collarbone to touch the necklace Robert gave me. For a second, I feel guilty. But the guilt vanishes as Jamie takes the "R" pendant in his hand and gently pulls me toward him, pressing his lips to mine. I feel his tongue on my bottom lip, sliding back and forth before finding its way inside my mouth. My tongue meets his, and his kiss becomes a little more forceful as he wraps his other arm around my waist and pulls me closer. His mouth shifts to my neck, planting kisses in a row up and down. And then the kisses turn into little bites, and I make a weird sound. The sound startles me, and I try to pull away again, embarrassed, but he tightens his hold on me and says in my ear, "It just means you like it."

And he's right. I do like it. I could stay here all night with Jamie's arms around me and his mouth on my neck. I want more. I want his hands on me, everywhere at once. I suddenly wish that he would touch me under my shirt, and I realize that I'm moving closer, pressing my body against him, willing him to slide his hand under there.

And then he stops. "Shit. Sorry," he says, his arms still around me.

I suddenly hear myself breathing too hard and too loud. I start to feel stupid, dumb, needy. Fifteen minutes ago, Jamie Forta said we were just friends, and so what do I do? I kiss him. And I get so into it that, for the first time in my life, I'm wishing that a boy would take off my shirt. And then he swears and apologizes, and now here I am, so close that I can feel his heart beating, but it's all wrong. The way he's holding me now has nothing to do with the way he was kissing me five seconds ago.

It's crazy. This whole thing is crazy. I'm crazy.

I force myself to pull back, disentangling from him. I'm hot all over—I know my face is flaming red. I still can't catch my breath, and I have a very strange ache between my legs that I've never felt before but that is pretty easily identified. He looks weird and closed-off.

"Sorry," he says again, leaning against the door, putting distance between us. "I shouldn'ta done that."

"Why?" I ask, my breathless voice giving too much away.

He puts his hands on the steering wheel and tightens his grip for a second as he takes a deep breath. Finally, he says, "A lotta reasons."

Heat floods my face, as if I could be any redder. So there are multiple reasons that Jamie shouldn't kiss me, not just the one big one named Regina. Great. What are the other reasons?

One of them is probably that I'm the world's worst kisser. Actually, maybe that has replaced Regina as the number-one reason.

I'm horrified. I just want to get out of his car before I do something else that's stupid. I grab the handle and shove the door open.

As I flee, Jamie's voice follows me out the open door and up the front walk.

"You okay?" he asks, surprise and confusion in his voice. "Hey—Rose?"

If I were a normal person, I would stop and tell him that I'm fine, and I'm sorry for the misunderstanding. Maybe even wish him a Happy Valentine's Day.

Instead, I pretend I can't hear him and I run up my front walk like my life depends on getting away from him, cursing myself for ever thinking that I could possibly kiss a guy like Jamie Forta and get it right.

SPRING

mortifying (*adjective*): incredibly, painfully embarrassing
(*see also:* stirrups)

─────────

17

TODAY IS DAD'S BIRTHDAY. AND WHAT AM I DOING TO remember him on this day? Sitting in a free clinic, waiting to talk to a gynecologist about birth control.

Dad would be so proud.

Not.

It's been a completely surreal day, partly because I'm sleep deprived. I was up half the night studying the websites of the people who died with dad, trying to figure out what I should say on the site about the explosion. Should I just post links to the articles? That would make the most sense, but all these people have basically written essays about that day, with details they learned from reading this report or talking to that person in the military. They did research in order to put together the whole story, digging for information like there was a mystery to be solved and posting the pieces as they found them, whereas I just read one article and figured there was nothing else to know.

What a lame daughter I am.

I was really hoping to have the whole thing finished by Dad's birthday so I could show it to Mom and ask to use her credit card to register the domain name. But the site's not ready yet. Though I've posted a bunch of family photos on the picture page—including some of Peter—I still haven't chosen the main photo.

Again. Lame daughter.

The first surreal thing that happened this morning was I went down to breakfast and saw a picture of myself on the cover of the *Union Chronicle,* the local paper. My mom had left it for me, right next to my orange juice, before she started seeing her morning clients. In honor of Dad's birthday, the paper ran a nice photo of him next to a terrible photo of me, crying at his funeral in June. The caption under this terrible photo?

Daddy's Little Girl.

As if having a photo of myself with snot running out of my nose on the cover of a newspaper weren't bad enough, I also have to be called Daddy's Little Girl? Luckily, the readership of the *Union Chronicle* is probably, oh, around twenty or thirty people, all over the age of eighty, most of whom can never find their reading glasses. I think. I hope.

The next surreal thing that happened was that I lied to my mom after having just finished months of "probation"… for lying. So much for punishment being a deterrent. I left Mom a note saying that Tracy and I were going to the mall, when really, we were planning to get on a bus and go see a gynecologist at the free clinic downtown. Why I agreed to do this with her, I have no idea. I don't need birth control, so there's no reason for me to see a doctor. But Tracy convinced me that a really good friend would go through the experience with her and not just sit in the waiting room.

And the final surreal twist to the day? Tracy telling me

on the bus ride how she and Matt are happier together than they've ever been, and that they finally said "I love you" to each other last night. I'm betting Matt said "I love you" in response to Tracy saying "I'm going on birth control."

Call me a cynic.

Matt didn't break up with Tracy on Valentine's Day. I wonder if he ever intended to, or if that was just the lie he told Lena to explain why he couldn't see her that night. Now I'm wondering if Matt is actually going out with Tracy *and* sleeping with Lena simultaneously. If Stupid Boy is smart enough to pull that off, I'll have to upgrade his nickname. To Sleaze Boy.

When I talked to Tracy the day after Valentine's Day, she said everything was great—although once again, they hadn't had sex. She said Matt was worried that his parents were going to come home and they'd get caught. I wonder if Matt would tell the same story.

But now, Tracy has decided that after everything that has—and hasn't—happened, it's time to go on the pill. I practically have whiplash from all the times she's changed her mind about this. She says that he has waited long enough and things are really good now. She also says that compromise is the heart of any relationship—I'd bet money she read that in her mother's *Cosmo*—and since he compromised by agreeing to use condoms, she can compromise by agreeing to go on the pill.

Logic isn't really Tracy's strong suit.

Condoms, pill, pill, condoms—I'm sick of the whole thing. I never want to have another conversation about birth control again, as long as I live.

I flip through the pages of *Parent* magazine, which seems to be the only option in this waiting room, aside from a copy of the *Union Chronicle*, which I've turned over so no one can see my snotty picture. Tracy is going on about the fact that there are all kinds of different pills now, and there are these plastic rings, too, that you put in once a month. I don't bother reminding her about STDs. I'm too nervous to pay close attention to what she's saying anyway. I'm about to have my first gynecologist's appointment. And from everything I've heard, it's awful and humiliating.

Just what I need. More humiliation. Maybe Regina will show up and paint *First Gynecologist's Appointment* in nail polish on my forehead while the doctor has her hand inside me. Although I shouldn't complain—except for the occasional scowl, Regina has basically left me alone since I talked to Jamie on Valentine's Day. I don't know how Jamie did it. Maybe he just told her he doesn't care about me one way or the other.

I still can't believe Jamie's mom is dead and I didn't know.

I've been thinking about every moment of the Valentine's Day kiss at least thirty times a day since then, and I can't figure out exactly what went wrong. Did he stop kissing me back because a) he has a girlfriend, b) I'm a terrible kisser, or c) he finds me repulsive?

B and C may sound similar, but there are differences. C is much worse than B.

Occasionally I think, who *am* I, kissing someone else's boyfriend, even if that someone else is Regina? Am I the kind of person who helps a guy cheat on his girlfriend? It's so far from my idea of who I am that it almost seems like it didn't happen. My first lesson in denial.

I look back down at my magazine. The articles in *Parent* have nothing to do with my life, and I'm finding some weird comfort in that. Tracy is flipping through her *Lucky,* oohing and aahing over things I wouldn't know how to wear if

I tried. Then she leans forward, picks up the *Chronicle* and looks at the headline, *Remember Local Hero on His Birthday.*

"You know," she says, "your birthday is right around the corner. So's Matt's."

I know what she's about to suggest, in order to avoid recreating last year's fiasco, when she blew off our long-standing tradition of pizza, ice cream and a movie on my birthday in order to spend it with her brand-new boyfriend, Matt. To her credit, she still feels bad that I stayed home that night with my mom. Mom made my favorite chocolate cake with espresso frosting, but it didn't make up for the fact that my best friend was with her boyfriend while I was home watching TV with my mother on my birthday.

Funny. What I wouldn't give to be home watching TV with my dad on my birthday this year.

"What do you think about having a double birthday party?"

What I want to say is, *I'd rather stick needles under my fingernails than have a party with that jerk.*

"Why?" I say instead.

"It would be fun, don't you think? We could, like, take over Cavallo's. Ooh, or maybe even have it during the day at the park! We could get a band to play, and have a keg—"

"Trace, you don't have to include me in Matt's birthday celebration. I'm over what happened last year."

She knows that isn't really true because every once in a while I can't help but make a "joke" about how my best friend spent my fourteenth birthday with her boyfriend.

"It's not that, Rosie. I just think it would be great to get all our friends together, and maybe you and Matt could figure out how to get along a little better."

"I can tell you right now that he is not going to want his name on an invitation with mine."

"What makes you say that?" she asks, sounding hurt.

"Face it, Trace. Matt and I do not like each other anymore, and we probably never will again."

"That's not true. He likes you. He just thinks you're a little...possessive of me."

I practically do a spit take, although I'm not drinking anything.

"Did he tell you that?" I say, my voice rising to Alvin-the-Chipmunk pitch as the door to the mysterious inner sanctum of the doctor's office opens. "Does he know that I'm 'possessive' of you because he's a total jerk who treats you—"

"Tracy Gerren?" the nurse calls.

Tracy is so excited by the prospect of getting the pill or the ring or the whatever that she doesn't hear the last part of what I say. She pops out of her seat like she's on springs.

"Don't even think about going anywhere," she says to me. "We made these appointments together, and we are going to keep them. You'll make me look bad if you freak out and leave."

I love how Tracy is able to make everything about her.

"I'm not going anywhere. I'm actually really looking forward to trying out those stirrups for the first time. I hear they're lots of fun."

"Come on, Rosie, this is important for your health," she says, taking *Parent* out of my hands and giving me her *Lucky,* as if I'm supposed to be studying up on clothes. "And you like to do things that are good for your health. It makes you feel...virtuous, or something."

The nurse calls her name again, and Tracy disappears down a long hall with her, looking as confident as if she were about to buy a new dress at Forever 21. I'm relieved that she's gone—I can still run out of here if I want to.

Should I? I mean, what am I doing here? I don't need this appointment. I'm still learning how to kiss.

I look around the waiting room and notice a display of pamphlets with titles like, Which Birth Control is Right for You? and Coping With HPV, and Thinking of Getting Pregnant? What You Should Do NOW. I was sort of hoping there'd be one that said, What to Expect During Your First Appointment, or at least, What We're Doing When You're Lying There on Your Back With Your Legs in the Air.

No such luck.

I can't really read now anyway. I'm so agitated that I can't focus on anything.

The door opens again. "Rose Zarelli?"

I consider saying nothing, pretending that I'm somebody else, waiting for the nurse to assume that Rose Zarelli isn't here today. But the nurse looks right at me and asks, "Rose?"

Tracy must have tipped her off that I might run. After all, what are friends for?

I stand up on shaky legs.

"Right this way," the nurse says, smiling sympathetically. I follow her down the hall as the door closes behind me with a thud and a click. There's no turning back now.

"I'm Betty," she says over her shoulder as we walk. "I'm the nurse practitioner, and I'm going to be performing your exam today. Is this your first time?"

"Yes," I say, sounding as scared as I feel. She leads me into an exam room, and I see them instantly. The stirrups. They're sticking up from the table like some sort of torture device. Betty follows my gaze. She crosses to the stirrups and gives each one a shove. They fold back slowly against the table like the legs of some creepy insect.

"I know they look intimidating, but they're not that bad,

I promise," she says kindly. "Now hop on up here and I'll tell you what we're going to do."

I approach the exam table cautiously, worried that the stirrups might spring back up and grab me. They don't. I step on the little black platform attached to the table near the floor and vault myself up backward, white paper crinkling loudly underneath me as I position myself on the edge, facing Betty.

"Tell me a little about yourself. You're in high school?"

"I'm a freshman."

"What do you like to do?"

"Um, I'm a runner—well, sort of. I'm going out for the track team next week."

"Ah," says Betty, making a note on the chart. "So you're an athlete. Well, that's good." I want to ask her what being an athlete has to do with my gynecological health, but I can't seem to make the question come out. "Do you have a boyfriend?"

"I...well, I don't...um..."

"Let me rephrase that. Are you sexually active?

I don't know how to answer that, either. "There's a guy who, um, I kissed a few times. Is that sexually active?"

I expect Betty to laugh at me for not knowing the technical definition of "sexually active," but she doesn't.

"I was asking if you are having sexual intercourse, but sexually active can mean any kind of sexual activity, and kissing fits into that category. Has anything else happened with this friend?"

"No."

Betty hesitates for just a second, then says, "Do you think it will?"

I shake my head, unsure whether I'm lying. "We might kiss again, but I'm not...I don't want to do anything else right now."

Betty smiles and surprises me again. "That's great, Rose. It's good to know where you stand, to know what you do and don't want. Don't do anything until you're absolutely ready."

I wish I had a tape recorder so I could play Betty's words for Tracy. I envision getting Betty and Ms. Maso together for a sex intervention where they gang up on Tracy and tell her she's making a terrible mistake.

But then it occurs to me that maybe Tracy really *is* ready for all this stuff. Maybe the problem isn't Tracy.

Maybe the problem is actually me.

"So what brings you here today, Rose?"

Sometimes I think my life is just one long string of questions that I have no idea how to answer.

"Um, I just thought… I figured I should make an appointment, I guess," I say, not wanting to admit that my best friend is so skilled at getting me to do what she wants that I'm here even though I have no real reason to be.

"Okay. Let's go through a few basic questions. Are your periods normal?"

"What's normal?"

"Regular. You get them on a regular basis?"

"Yes."

"And do you have any pain?"

"Sometimes. Sometimes I have really bad cramps." This is, in fact, a lie. I hardly ever have cramps. But I'm suddenly feeling the need to justify being at this completely needless exam.

"Okay. So here's what we're going to do. I'm going to perform a pelvic exam. What that means is, I'll be checking inside you with my eyes and my hands to make sure that everything is okay. Since you're young and you haven't started having intercourse yet, there's no reason for me to do a Pap test—that involves me collecting some cells off your cervix with something that looks like a long Q-tip, and sending the cells to the lab for testing. But you don't need that right now, because you're not having sex. Right?" she says, looking at me very carefully, as if she thinks I might be lying about why I'm here.

"Right," I respond with as much confidence as I can muster as my eyes dart back to the stirrups.

"Okay. Now, I'm going to give you a paper gown. Take everything off and put the gown on, open to the front. I'll come back and knock on the door to see if you're ready in a few minutes."

Betty leaves me in the room, and it takes me a full minute just to take off my jeans. It's not like I've never been to the doctor before, but I've never had anyone check me inside. I take off my underwear, but I don't know where I'm supposed to put them. Should I hang them up on the peg, like I did with my jeans? Then she'd see them up there, and they might gross her out. Should I put them in my bag? That grosses *me* out. After another minute of contemplation, Betty knocks on the door.

"All set?" she asks.

I crumple my underwear into a wad and hide it—in my fist.

"Yes," I answer.

"Okay!" she says, coming into the room with the enthusiasm of someone about to spend an afternoon at an amusement park. "Here's what's going to happen. I'm going to put the stirrups up and you're going to put your feet in them, okay?" She turns around for a second and puts some supplies on a tall tray on wheels. Then she pulls the tray over and sits on a low stool in front of me. "Here we go."

She pulls up the torture devices and instructs me to lie

back on the table. "One foot up," she says as she snaps on a pair of plastic gloves.

I can't make my leg move.

"Rose, I'm going to pick up your foot and put it in the stirrup, okay?" I feel her hand on my foot, lifting it into the air. I expect the metal to feel cold on my skin, but I realize I've left my socks on. It seems I've left my shirt on, too. I wonder if this was wrong—was I supposed to take these things off? I can't remember.

I feel her hand on my other foot, placing it in the stirrup. Then I notice a strange silence in the room, as if she's waiting for something to happen.

"I need you to open your knees a bit now," says Betty quietly, like she's afraid I'll freak out if she talks too loud. I realize that my knees hurt because they're pressed together tightly even though my feet are spread wide in the stirrups.

I really don't want to spread my legs.

"You said you're going to try out for the track team, right?" I can't imagine why she's suddenly talking about track until her hands are on my knees, gently pressing them open. She's trying to distract me.

Cold air hits my crotch, and I have to fight the urge to snap my knees back together. "Yes," I say, trying to sound normal. "Tryouts are next week."

"You're going to feel a little pressure and some coldness as I put the speculum in now." She holds up something that looks even more like a torture device than the stirrups. "So what do you have to do at a track tryout?"

I can barely answer her because the sensation of having what looks like a giant eyelash curler pushed into me is too weird for words. It doesn't hurt, but she should have said a lot of pressure instead of a little. I sort of feel like I have to pee.

"Um, I have to run some sprints— Ow—"

"Sorry, I'm opening the speculum inside you now, so I can take a look at your cervix. What were you saying?"

"I, uh, I just have to run some timed sprints, I think," I say breathlessly.

"I see. And the people with the fastest times make the team, is that right?"

"Uh-huh," I say, wondering just how long I have to have this thing inside me.

Betty doesn't ask me anything else. In fact, she's quiet for a good twenty seconds. I'm just starting to get freaked out when she says, "Rose, are you sure you haven't had sex yet?"

If I weren't so terrified about whatever it is that's making her ask that question, I would laugh. Because yes, I'm positive I haven't had sex yet. Is there any way to not be positive about that?

"Um, yeah, I've only done kissing—kissed—however you say it."

She looks up at me from between my legs—it's a really strange view—with a serious expression on her face. "Has anyone ever touched you down here, inside? Anyone at all?"

"No. I swear," I add. I don't know why, but it seems really important to convince her that I'm telling the truth. "Why? Is something wrong?"

"No, no, nothing's wrong. Do you know what a hymen is, Rose?"

"Uh-huh," I answer, thinking of the chart of female reproductive organs Ms. Maso showed us in health class one day, when someone asked where the expression "popping her cherry" comes from. Ms. Maso will answer any question, as long as she's sure it's genuine.

"Well, girls who haven't had sex usually have a hymen, but you don't."

"Is that...bad?" I ask, not sure whether I should be upset

about this or not. I mean, I know I'm supposed to have one, but I'm not sure if it matters that I don't.

"No, not necessarily. Some girls lose theirs if they're very active playing sports," she says as she reaches behind her to the tray and picks up the giant Q-tip. "That's probably the case with you, since you're an athlete. But I'd like to do that Pap test after all, okay?" Before I can say anything, the creepy Q-tip disappears between my legs.

"Now I'm taking some samples of the cells on your cervix with this swab, and we'll send it off to the lab to make sure everything is normal, which I'm sure it will be." I feel her moving the Q-tip around in there, and then she takes it out, sticks the swab in a container and writes something on it.

"The next step is the pelvic exam," she says as she finally takes out the giant eyelash curler. I'm relieved until she grabs a tube, squeezing some clear gel on her gloved hand. "I'm going to put my fingers inside you while I press on your abdomen. I want you to tell me if anything hurts." She slides her fingers in and starts pushing on my stomach.

I wonder if this is what it would feel like to have a guy touch me inside. Then I try to stop thinking about it because it's probably a bad thing to think about when your gynecologist is examining you. I look up at the walls and try to concentrate on the framed black-and-white poster of the bottom half of the Eiffel Tower that is hanging there. There's a layer of dust on top of the black plastic frame. In the picture, there are pigeons on the ground, looking for crumbs. There are people walking arm in arm, and a couple is kissing. Just when I think I've successfully transported myself to Paris, I find myself twisting away from her and sitting halfway up. "This feels really weird," I say, suddenly wanting her to stop touching me.

"Weird bad, or just weird?"

"I guess just weird."

"That's okay," says Betty, putting one hand on my shoulder and gently urging me to lie back down while her other hand is still inside me. "It feels weird because what I'm doing is checking your uterus and your ovaries just to make sure—"

"Are you finished yet?" I interrupt loudly. I'm so done with this.

"Almost. Are you all right?"

"I have to…pee," I lie, saying the only thing I can think of that might convince her to stop.

"Okay," she says, pulling her hand out of me and snapping off her rubber gloves. "That's it. We're done." Her eyes land on my shirt, which I remember now I was supposed to take off. "Usually I perform a breast exam at an annual appointment, but I think we'll just do that next time. I want you to come back and see me if you become sexually active—if you and your friend advance beyond kissing, okay? We can talk about what you should be doing to protect each other. Also, feel free to call me if there's anything you decide you want to tell me, something that maybe you didn't want to tell me today. Here's my card."

Betty thinks I'm lying about something. Is she wondering if I was sexually abused, and that's why my hymen is already broken or gone or whatever?

This whole thing is making me totally paranoid. I have to get out of here.

Betty, who has been staring at me while I've been trying to figure out what it is she thinks I'm not telling her, realizes that I'm not going to say anything. "You can sit up and put your clothes back on, and when you're ready, you can meet your friend back in the waiting room. It was nice to meet you, Rose. I'll call if there are any problems, which there won't be." She looks down at the chart. "Is this your cell phone number?"

I shake my head. She looks back down again.

"Oh, I see. It's your friend's number. But I can leave a message for you there?"

I nod, practically catatonic.

"You did really well," she says and starts to go out the door.

"Um—"

She stops sharply. "Yes, Rose?"

"I'm still a virgin, right? I mean, even though I don't have a…" I can't finish the sentence.

Betty nods slowly. "Yes, Rose, if you haven't had sex, you're still a virgin." She waits another second, then smiles at me and leaves, closing the door behind her.

After I manage to extract my underwear from the death-grip of my fist, I get dressed. I don't know what I'm supposed to do with the paper gown and the sheet she used to cover me, so I throw them in the trash can. I find my way back to the waiting room where Tracy is pacing and texting like a crazy woman.

"Trace, let's go," I say. "I don't want to miss the bus and have to wait an hour for the next one."

"Would you believe that doctor wouldn't give me birth control?" she hisses. "I'm texting Lena right now."

"Lena?" My mind spins at the implications.

"Yes! She told me that they don't ask any questions here, and they just give you what you want. But the doctor said she wouldn't give me anything unless I came back with my 'partner.' She wants to talk to us both," she says, rolling her eyes.

All right, it's time. I can't ignore this any longer. If Lena is pulling stupid crap like this, Tracy deserves to know why.

"Tracy," I say, taking a deep breath, "there's something I need to tell you about Lena."

Tracy looks up from her phone. "What?"

"Can we get out of here first?" I plead. "I really don't want to be here anymore." I grab her arm and pull her out of the clinic.

"Tell me," she says, scowling up at the rainy sky as we start walking to the bus stop.

"Well, on Valentine's Day, I was actually at Cavallo's for a minute—"

Her head snaps in my direction. "I thought you stayed home on Valentine's Day."

"It's a long story. But the important part is that when I was there, I heard Michelle, Susan and Regina talking to Lena about Matt. Lena said that Matt was going to break up with you that night. For her."

I wait for the volcanic eruption, the crying fit, the major freak-out. But Tracy stays calm. Deadly calm.

"Lena has a crush on Matt," she says. "He thinks it's funny. But he doesn't like her."

I want to grab her shoulders and give her a good shake to rattle her brain into reality. "Tracy, he's probably been seeing Lena since you saw them in your parents' bedroom on Halloween. Why can't you admit that?"

She throws out a hand to stop me from walking. "Is that what you really think?"

"Yes! She's been after him since your party and she doesn't care if you get hurt. She's a total...bitch."

"If that's what you think, why didn't you say anything before now? Friends tell each other that kind of stuff, Rose. They also don't lie to each other about what they were doing on Valentine's Day."

I was really hoping she was going to let that one go, but there's no way I would ever get that lucky.

"Jamie sent me that flower on Valentine's Day. Not Robert."

Tracy stares, not saying a word.

"And he asked me to meet him," I finish.

"Before he went out with Regina."

"I guess so, yeah."

"Were you ever going to tell me?"

"I don't know." I look up at the rain and wish I were anywhere but here. The memory of all the things I felt while Jamie and I were kissing—and the embarrassment of him stopping and apologizing, of saying that he shouldn't have kissed me back—makes me blush. I try to push it out of my mind, but it's too late.

"You kissed him."

I hate that she knows me so well that she can tell from the look on my face what happened to me a few weeks ago.

"If what you say about Lena is true," she says, "then you're just as bad as she is. Jamie is someone else's boyfriend, Rose." The bus pulls up to the stop and the door swishes open. "You're a hypocrite."

If I could open my mouth and tell Tracy everything about Regina—about the graffiti and the threats, about how crazy she is, about how she doesn't deserve Jamie—I could make her understand that I'm not like Lena at all. But I can't do it. Because if I tell Tracy about Regina, she'll have to choose between her best friend and her beloved squad—and I'm pretty sure I know which she'd choose.

Tracy gets on the bus and pays, taking a seat without looking at me. The driver waits, but all I can do is stare at Tracy through the window. The door closes and the bus pulls away.

nemesis (*noun*): archenemy
(*see also:* take a wild guess...)

———

18

I HAVE AN AUDIENCE AT TRACK TRYOUTS, AND IT'S MAKING me more nervous than I already was. Jamie and Angelo are in the parking lot right next to the track, working on Jamie's car. Every once in a while, Angelo stops what he's doing, looks up from his work on the engine and waves at me or gives me a thumbs-up sign.

Jamie does not.

I've decided that's because the cheerleaders are practicing on the field on the other side of the track. It's pretty far away, but I wouldn't put it past Regina to have supernatural vision. Jamie probably doesn't want to do anything that will start up trouble with the Blond Witch again.

Or else he's just worried that if he so much as looks at me, I'll kiss him again.

Robert is leaning on the fence with a few people I don't know who are also watching the tryouts. Except he's watching Jamie and Angelo more than he's watching the tryouts.

Robert and I have stopped talking. Maybe he's finally realized that I'm kind of mean to him and he can do better, even as far as friendship goes.

Speaking of which, I'm totally friendless this week. Tracy and I are still in a fight, and when Tracy and I aren't talking, Stephanie feels weird around me. She'll say hi, but that's about it. So that brings my friend count down to...zero. I'd like to say Jamie's my friend, but we don't talk in front of other people, so I don't think he really counts. Plus, there's the fact that we've kissed twice. Which means he's not a friend, he's...something else.

If I make track—and that's a big "if," given what happened to me at cross-country tryouts—I'll make new friends, I've decided. Track is going to be different. A fresh start.

Whatever the hell that means.

I stomp the ground to get my feet all the way forward in my track shoes. As I bend down to lace up, I realize I'm Angry today, with a capital A—I can feel it. Good. Maybe it'll make me run faster.

Coach Morley blows her whistle. "Zarelli! Stop daydreaming and get over here! Line up for the four hundred. Lane three."

Fantastic. I'm already making a great impression.

I find my lane, and out of the corner of my eye I can see that Jamie and Angelo have stopped working and they're watching. Robert has separated himself from his group a little bit, still watching Jamie. I can hear the cheerleaders practicing a new chant, and I wish they would just shut up. The sound grates on my ears, now more than ever.

I have so many butterflies in my stomach, I wonder if I'm going to fly when I try to run.

I need to stop worrying about Jamie and Robert and the squad and focus on what I'm doing, or I'm never going to make the team. And if I don't make the team, I'm going to have to accept the fact that I'm a loser. With zero friends.

I get into starting position and wait for the whistle. When it sounds, I take off as best as I can. Soon calm washes over me—everything falls away, and my brain stops going a mile a minute. The butterflies are gone, and I'm actually running the way Dad taught me to. Long strides, smooth arm motion, still torso. I didn't realize how convinced I was that I would never be able to run like this again until I feel relief over the evidence that I can.

The quarter mile is going to be my event, I can feel it. I might win this one if I have just a little extra left for the final one hundred. As I get close to the last turn, I suddenly see pom-poms in my peripheral vision. A few of the girls are lined up on the side of the track, like they're cheering someone on. I'm tempted to look back to see who it is, but I'll lose my stride if I do. I keep going. I get closer and closer to them, and I realize too late that it's Lena, Susan and Regina. Just as I'm about to pass them, they chant, "How did Daddy's Little Girl like the gynecologist?"

Not only do I lose my stride, I lose my balance. I go sailing onto the track at full speed. I manage to stay in my lane so that I don't trip everyone else as they run past me. I slide and bounce on the red rubber, feeling skin burning off my arms and legs. But that's not all I feel. Rage fires up inside, and I can tell by the way it's taking over my entire body that I won't be able to control it this time. I hear Coach Morley's whistle blowing, signaling the end of the race, and I stand up. My legs start to bleed, and I seem to have no skin left on my forearms at all.

And then, before I know what I'm doing, I'm running across the lanes that separate me and the cheer bitches. It doesn't matter that it's three against one. After everything

Regina has done to me, I want the satisfaction of hurting her. I run faster. I start screaming.

Lena and Susan look like deer caught in the headlights of an oncoming car—I must seem like a complete maniac, flying at them, covered in blood, screaming like a madwoman— but Regina stands her ground with a surprised half smile on her face, as if she didn't think I had it in me but she's glad to find out I do.

"I warned you!" she yells as I get closer. "I told you to stay away from him!"

Tracy. Tracy told her I kissed Jamie.

I slam into Regina with every ounce of strength I have, knocking her to the ground. Her pom-poms go flying into the air, and I hear a gasp from her minions as her skirt flaps up. I'm blind with fury now, and I pin Regina down with my body weight and one arm. The fingers of my other hand form a fist. I can hear Coach Morley frantically blowing her whistle—the sound is getting louder, which probably means she's running toward me. A tiny part of my brain tells me not to hit Regina because if I do, an all-out war will start that will probably end with me having to transfer to a different school.

I don't care.

As I pull my arm back to get a good wind up before letting my fist fly, someone grabs me by the waist and lifts me into the air, off Regina. I can tell by the look of rage on her face that it's Jamie. You'd think she'd be happy that he just saved her from getting punched in the face, but really, she's pissed that he took away her excuse to pummel me. He pivots and puts me down, holding me back with one arm, stretching out the other to keep Regina, who's now on her feet, at bay. Angelo grabs hold of Regina's shoulders and gets in her face, talking fast, though I can't hear what he's saying. I seem to have gone deaf—all I can hear is the whooshing of blood in my ears. I shift my attention to Jamie, who is staring at my bleeding legs and arms, and I suppose I should thank him for saving me from getting suspended or expelled, but I'm beside myself. I wanted to hit her. I don't think I've ever wanted anything more in my entire life.

"Are you all right?" he asks, his voice cutting through the pounding of my pulse. "Rose?"

Regina looks at him in disbelief, like she can't possibly process why he's asking me that and not her.

Am I all right? No, I am not all right. None of this is all right. Nothing has been all right since June. Tears scald my cheeks. I still feel ready to kill. Jamie senses this somehow and moves directly in front of me, blocking my view of Regina, forcing me to look in his eyes.

Coach Morley arrives, furious until she sees all the blood. She looks at Regina. Angelo is still holding her back, his hands wrapped around her wrists. She is struggling and clawing her fingers at me as if she wants to scratch my face off. I see Morley notice Regina's bright-fuchsia nail polish, and I watch her face as she puts two and two together, solving the graffiti mystery. She gently puts her arm around my shoulder, leading me away from Jamie, across the football field in the center of the track, toward the locker room.

"Next time, Zarelli, tell an adult before it gets to this point," she says. "Bullying is a serious offense."

I almost laugh. First of all, bullying happens to kids on the playground in elementary school. What Regina did is called harassment. Second of all, telling an adult would have made things worse. If Morley would just take the time to think back to high school, she would remember that if you tell on someone, that person just finds a way to get you back ten-fold when no one is looking.

I don't bother to ask Morley if I made the team because I already know the answer. Granted, there were unusual circumstances, but it doesn't matter—if you don't finish your race, you get disqualified. I'm 0-for-2 this year. Guess I won't be making new friends after all.

As we get close to the school, I hear someone running behind us. I hope Regina has escaped from Angelo because I'm ready to finish this thing. I whirl around, my heart instantly racing again, but it's not her. It's Tracy, super freaked-out and on the verge of tears.

"Tracy," Morley says, "will you take Zarelli to the locker room for me? Help her get cleaned up, okay?"

Tracy nods. When we're out of earshot of the coach, Tracy says, "Rose, I'm so sorry. I didn't know what Regina was going to—"

I raise my hand to shut her up.

We walk the rest of the way to the locker room in silence.

I'm standing at the sink, picking pieces of dirt and rubberized track out of my forearm. I can see Tracy in the mirror, hovering behind me, wanting to help but not wanting to get too close to the gore. I can also see the first locker that Regina painted on back in December. The nail polish is gone but whatever they used to remove it lightened the metal so you can still read, "Suck it, Stupid 911 Bitch." I'm pondering the irony of the fact that the school's cleanup effort made the graffiti permanent when Tracy says the thing that begins the end of our friendship as we know it.

"I had to tell her, Rose. She needed to know the truth about you and Jamie."

There are so many things wrong with those two statements that I hardly know where to begin. I look at her in the mirror. She looks unsure of herself. Tracy doesn't know what to do when the tables are turned, and I have power, which only happens when I get really, really mad. The storm roils in my brain and I know that I'm about to say everything I haven't been saying all year.

"*You* don't even know the truth about me and Jamie."

"I know that you kissed him," Tracy says.

"That's all you know."

My mouth hurts, and I lean over and spit blood into the sink, realizing that I bit the inside of my cheek when I fell.

"What did Regina mean, 'I warned you'?" Tracy asks.

"She saw Jamie follow me at your party and at homecoming. She told me if she saw me near him again, she'd kick my ass and throw you off the squad. That's when she started with the graffiti."

"*Regina* was doing that?" She actually looks surprised, like she couldn't possibly imagine dear, sweet Regina doing something that horrible.

I turn the water on and watch the blood rinse away. "I kept my mouth shut for you, Tracy."

This isn't exactly the truth. I kept my mouth shut out of fear—fear of Regina, fear of Tracy choosing the cheerleaders over me, fear of being labeled a tattletale who can't fight her own battles—but I want her to believe I did it all for her so that she'll feel as bad as possible.

"I kept my mouth shut so you could stay on that stupid team that you love so much, with those pathetic, messed-up girls. Did you hear what they said to me? They brought my dad into it, Tracy. My dad! What kind of person does something like that?" I rasp, humiliation knocking the wind out of my lungs.

She has no answer.

"They're not your friends. Not one of them. Lena is sleeping with your boyfriend and they've all known about it for months. When are you going to realize that?" Suddenly I'm dizzy. I grab on to the sink and start wheezing like I have asthma. The color begins to drain from the edges of the world.

Tracy's eyes fill with tears, but she grabs my shoulder and spins me around so that we are no longer arguing through the mirror. I lose my balance and reach out for the wall to steady myself. Everything in the locker room starts to blur.

"And when are *you* going to realize that if you would just stay away from Jamie, everything would be fine? I don't even know why you want him anyway! He's not even smart. And he's kind of a freak and a loser. But maybe you are, too, Rose. Maybe that's why you like him."

And there it is. It's finally on the table. My best friend from forever thinks I'm a freak and a loser, and she's choosing the pom-poms over me because they're cooler.

Welcome to high school, Rose Zarelli. It's survival of the coolest here. And you, with your running shoes and your French horn and your fear of sex and your missing hymen and your weird attacks and your dead father, you are definitely not part of the posse.

Well, fine. So be it.

Fuck cool.

"You think I'm the loser? You're a cheerleader! You spend all your time cheering for people instead of actually *doing* something yourself. What's the point of it, other than to wear short skirts and feel like you're better than everyone?"

I might as well have slapped her, she looks so stunned. Apparently everybody is learning what I'm made of today—including me.

"I cheer because I like to encourage people," she says, ice in her voice. "*That's* actually the point of cheering." She looks in the mirror and wipes a finger under each eye to catch the mascara running down her face. She straightens, throws her shoulders back and turns to me. "You might try being supportive sometime, Rose. It'll help you make some new friends, which you're going to need, especially if you keep making out with other people's boyfriends."

She grabs her pom-poms off a bench and heads out the door just as black-and-white patterns swim before my eyes and my throat closes off. I sink to the floor and pass out.

enlightenment (*noun*): insight
(*see also:* turning 15)

————

19

I NOW HAVE A REPUTATION AT SCHOOL AS A BADASS, thanks to the YouTube stalker, who caught the whole fight with Regina on camera and posted it online.

Or at least, Robert tells me I'm now considered a badass. I have no idea if it's really true. I'm home in bed with mono, where I've been for the past week. And today is my birthday.

Needless to say, I'm not having a party with Matt. But that was a no-brainer from the get-go. It's my second lame birthday in a row. But, hey, at least I'm not in the hospital anymore.

After my fight with Tracy, Coach Morley found me passed out cold on the locker room floor and called 911. Bobby Passeo, my old pal, came to collect me in the very same ambulance that broke up all the fun at homecoming, and I spent the afternoon in the emergency room, being stuck with needles and having gunk picked out of my arms and legs with tweezers. Bobby stayed until my mom got there, which happened just as the doctor was asking me how long my glands had been so swollen that I could hardly turn my head. "I could see those Frankenstein bolts the second I walked in the room," he said to my mom, who looked so ashamed that I sort of felt bad for her.

The doctor was surprised that my blood test showed the mono was mild. After Bobby told him I'd been passed out for more than five minutes, he thought I might have to be admitted. I opted not to tell him what had happened in the ten minutes before I passed out, which might have had something to do with my desire to remain blissfully unconscious for a while.

My mom is thrilled—she feels that my having mono explains my uncharacteristically violent attack on a fellow student. At least, that's what she told Mrs. Chen, who called to "check" on me, or rather, to tell my mom what had been happening in school. While they talked, I imagined Mrs. Chen on the other end of the phone, wearing her Christmas headband with the antlers.

Mrs. Chen said everyone missed me at school and was looking forward to my return, which I thought was pretty funny. I'm sure people couldn't care less where I am, but there *is* a part of me that wouldn't mind walking the halls of good old Union High, enjoying my temporary YouTube celebrity. By now, though, people have probably moved on to something else. I bet the video isn't even posted anymore—Mrs. Chen's cyberspies monitor all activity that takes place on the computers, so if students are sending a specific link to their friends using their Union High email addresses, Mrs. Chen finds out about it fast.

The doorbell rings. It's Robert. He's stopped by every day this week with my homework, which is really nice and convenient, seeing as how he's my only friend right now. We've talked more this week than in the past few months—I even told him about Regina—but he still hasn't brought up Jamie. And neither have I.

My mom calls to me, saying that Robert's coming up, and I attempt to make myself more presentable, which is hard to do when you're propped up in bed sporting sweats, greasy hair and giant, oozing scabs on your arms and legs.

"Come in," I say when he knocks.

"Hey. How's it going?" He takes his usual spot in my old beanbag chair as he digs through his backpack to find my homework.

"Hey, guess what? I think I'm back on Monday."

"You're lucky. When I had mono, I was out forever. Stop picking," he says, looking at my left fingers working away at my right forearm.

"You were out with mono? I thought that was juvie."

"Ha-ha," Robert says dryly. "May I remind you that I never did time for my minor infractions?"

"Ooh, 'infractions.' That sounds like an AP English word, Robert."

He rolls his eyes and hands me a bunch of disorganized folders with paper sticking out of them every which way. I start to look through them and then think better of it, dropping the mess on the floor. "I thought you had rehearsal today."

"Dress rehearsal tonight. Seriously, stop picking."

"It itches."

"So put some stuff on it. Do you have it? Where is it?"

I point to my desk, and he grabs the ointment off my laptop. "So how're final rehearsals going?"

"Ordinarily, high school students should stay the hell away from Shakespeare," he says, handing me the tube. It occurs to me as I start to put the stuff on that Robert is one of only a few people I would do this in front of. "But I have to admit, things are going okay. Meg Bennett is pretty brilliant as Lady Macbeth. She even makes sense when she talks."

"And who are you playing again?" I ask, pretending I don't know as I slather the stuff on my scabs.

He grins, takes a theatrical sip from an imaginary flask and says in a gravelly, old-man voice, "The porter." The porter is a really small part in *Macbeth*, but he's the comic relief in the middle of endless tragedy, and all the upperclassmen in the drama department were super pissed off when Robert got the role. But he deserved the part—people talked about how awesome his audition was for at least a week, and Robert was sort of an underclassman hero for a while there, having scored a victory for all freshmen.

"Are you going to come see it?"

"If Mom lets me out of my bed this weekend. And if you can guarantee me that I won't have to see Tracy, or anyone else we know."

Robert shifts around, uncomfortable in the chair. When he finally gets settled, he puffs up his cheeks and lets the air release slowly in a giant sigh. He's buying time.

"What?" I ask.

"Nothing."

"Something."

"Yeah, okay, something." He reaches into his pocket and takes his pack of cigarettes halfway out before he realizes what he's doing. He shoves it back in, sighs and leans forward as much as he can in the beanbag chair. "There's a rumor. I don't know if it's true."

"About me?" I brace myself for the worst.

"Actually, it's the first one this week that isn't about you. It's about Tracy. Word is she finally did the deed."

If there's one thing that drives home the point that your

best friend is no longer your best friend, it's hearing from someone else that she lost her virginity.

"Seriously?"

Robert shrugs. "That's what they say. Sorry you had to hear it from me."

I can't believe she did it. Even though she knows about Lena. She probably did it *because* she knows about Lena. And what are the chances that they used condoms? Not as good as the chances that she just went ahead and had unprotected sex out of desperation.

"The other rumor is that he dumped her and is now with Lena."

I feel sick to my stomach and it's not the mono. Tracy is now just a notch on Stupid Boy's swim-team-issued thong, which is probably what he was after all along. "Do you think it's true?"

Robert cocks his head and pauses for dramatic effect. "Maybe you should call her and find out," he says with fake innocence.

No. Uh-uh. I am not calling Tracy. Not after what she did to me. How can we even be friends anymore anyway? She's still on the squad, probably kissing up to Regina, even after I told her what Regina did. Everything is too different now. We're not even in the same universe at this point. I shake my head.

"What else is going on?" I ask.

"That's all you have to say about Tracy?" he says, looking disappointed in me. I shrug. "She's still the same person, Rosie. It's not like doing it with Matt turned her into someone new."

"We're not talking to each other right now, Robert."

"Because she told Regina that you kissed Forta?"

So he *does* know. We stare at each other for a few seconds in a sort of standoff. Then I nod slowly.

Robert extracts himself from the beanbag and closes my door. Then he sits in my desk chair, rolling it over to my bed. He leans back, his arms crossed.

"Tell me what's going on with Jamie—the truth."

"I don't know. Honestly. It's…confusing."

"He ran across the track the other day like you were on fire or something."

There's a look in Robert's eyes that I've never seen before. It's like he's closing down, or shutting off. A knot forms in my stomach—I sense something bad is coming, something that I now realize I've been expecting for a while. Something that I deserve, if I'm honest with myself.

"People say he's a player. But you like him. I mean, you kissed him. At least once."

"People say he's a player?"

"Yeah, well, he's been seeing you *and* Regina, hasn't he?" Robert says, annoyed by my response. "People think that that's what the fight was really about."

"That fight was not about Jamie. It was about Regina saying something about my dad and doing everything she could to make my life miserable this year."

"All of which she did because you're after Jamie."

I start picking again, not able to confirm or deny. This time he doesn't tell me to stop.

"It's time for me to go, Rose."

"Okay. Thanks for bringing my homework."

He shakes his head. "No, I mean, I'm not hanging around for this anymore."

I'm still not getting it. "What?"

"It's just, I really thought that this year, you'd be with me.

But you met him. And then homecoming happened, and, so, I just think that…I'll be your friend, but from afar. Unless…"

"Unless what?"

"Unless you do want to go out with me."

I look away from him before I can stop myself.

Robert stands up.

"Wait—"

"Look, if you're going out with Forta, be careful, okay? I don't think he's the great guy you think he is." Robert takes his cigarettes out of his pocket and smacks the package against his hand a few times. "And I really am sorry about homecoming. If I'd known… It doesn't matter now." He leans over and kisses me on the cheek. "Happy Birthday, Rosie the Rose."

"I'll come see your show this weekend," I say, surprising myself by sounding a little desperate.

Robert puts an unlit cigarette in his mouth. "It's cool. You don't need to," he answers without looking back as he walks out of my room.

I listen to him going down the stairs, wishing I could go after him but knowing I shouldn't. Robert is smart to do this—to move on or let go or whatever he's doing—because he thinks I don't appreciate him.

I look at the velvet jewelry box on my dresser where the "R" pendant lives—which somehow I could never thank him for, and which I only wore once—and I know that he's right.

First Tracy, now Robert. How does someone lose her two closest friends in one week?

"Rose," my mother calls from the bottom of the stairs. "Dinner's ready."

The last thing I want to do is try to make conversation with my mom. Once again, it's just us on my birthday, for the second year in a row. I guess this is how I spend my birthdays now. I drag myself out of bed and make my way downstairs.

All the lights are off in the kitchen, and my mom is standing at the table with a giant chocolate cake covered in candles. Fifteen, to be exact. I can tell just by looking at them that they're trick candles, the kind that relight after you blow them out. My father loved to put them on our cakes and act surprised when they'd burst into flame again, as if he had no idea how they'd gotten on the cake in the first place.

I expect to feel angry at her for using Dad's candles. I wait for it, but it doesn't come. Turns out I think it's kind of nice that she did that. Surprise, surprise.

"Birthday cake for dinner?" I ask.

"If ever there was a year to do it, this would be the one. Happy birthday, honey," she says. "Make a wish."

I usually get stressed out about birthday wishes—choosing the right thing is so much pressure. Too many wishes come into my head at once, and I try to prioritize them and decide which would be the smartest thing to ask for, and then I become totally paralyzed. But this year is different. I close my eyes, and nothing comes into my head aside from the obvious. But since I'm not a three-year-old, I don't bother wishing that my dad weren't dead. Instead, I just pretend I wished for something good, and I blow out the candles. Mom turns on the lights and hands me the knife to make the first cut, which, in Zarelli family tradition, ensures that my birthday wish will come true.

"I asked Robert to stay, but I don't think he heard me," she says apologetically, as if she knows I'm bummed I don't have anyone else to spend my birthday with but her.

"It's okay. He's mad at me, along with everyone else in the universe."

I give her back the knife, and she cuts two big, dinner-size pieces for us. We sit at the kitchen table together and each take our first bite at the same time.

"Yum, Mom, this is awesome," I say with my mouth full. My mother makes the world's best chocolate birthday cake.

"I'm glad." She smiles, pleased, and I realize that I haven't said a single nice thing to her since dad died. Not a single one. "So why is Robert mad?" she asks delicately, as if preparing to hear that it's none of her business.

"He got tired of waiting for me to go out with him," I answer.

"He's just not for you, huh?" I shake my head. "Is there someone else?" she asks.

I can tell by the way she isn't looking at me that she already knows the answer. I decide to just tell the truth and make it official by finally saying it out loud. It suddenly seems weird to me that I've gone this long without doing that.

"I like Jamie."

"Are you together?"

"No. He's with that cheerleader, Regina."

"The one you knocked down?"

There's something funny about hearing my mom say this, and I grin a little. "Yup. That's the one."

"Rose, you know it's not funny, right? Physically attacking another person is not a funny thing," she says. If she were talking in her therapy voice, I'd get up and leave the room right now. But she's not. She just sounds like my mom. "What happened, honey?"

I don't know if I can explain it to her in a way that she'll understand, but I'm willing to try, for once.

"Well, Regina made fun of that picture of me at the funeral, and she stares me down all the time, and...I didn't want to ignore her anymore, I wanted to hurt her. When I fell, something kind of snapped and I had to hit her. I just had to." I look at my mom, expecting to see anger or disappointment on her face, but she just looks sad, like she feels sorry for me. "Jamie's the one who saved me from punching her in the face. If he hadn't been there, I'd probably be suspended right now."

My mother nods. "That's what Mrs. Chen said. But she also said that your extenuating circumstance would have been taken into consideration."

I wonder how much longer my dad's death will be considered my "extenuating circumstance." It occurs to me that he would be a fan of the word *extenuating. File that one away,* he'd say to me. *Good PSAT word.*

"Honey, I want to talk to you about your anger." She watches closely to see my reaction. "I want to talk about Dad. Is that okay?"

My eyes start to tear up, but I nod anyway.

"You're so mad all the time," she says, "and I just wonder if you understand why." She waits for me to respond, but I take another bite of cake instead. "I think you're mad for the same reason I'm mad. Because Dad is gone."

It doesn't seem right to be mad at Dad for getting killed, especially after I went off on Peter for being mad. But it sure would explain a lot of things.

"And I think you're also angry at me."

She's right about that, too.

"When Mrs. Chen told me about the fight with Regina, and about the graffiti that someone has been writing about you, I realized that I've been absent. I thought that I was giving you space to deal with your grief, but the truth is, I was taking space to deal with mine. I left you all alone. And I'm so very sorry about that."

Now the tears start to spill. Mom reaches across the table and wipes them away with a sad smile.

"The other thing I need to tell you is why that happened. The truth is, I feel guilty about Dad's death. If I hadn't had such huge concerns about money after he lost his job, he never would have taken that contractor position. And I think I owe you an apology for that, too."

Now I'm really crying hard. She gets up, comes to stand behind my chair and puts her arms around me.

"I know that's probably hard for you to hear. And we don't have to discuss it anymore today. But I'm going to start talking to someone about it—to a therapist—and I'd like it if you'd come with me. Will you think about that?"

I hate the idea of going to therapy like I'm one of those crazy kids that my mom sees every day.

But what if I *am* one of those crazy kids?

"Yes," I say.

"Good. Thank you."

The phone on the wall rings. My mom looks behind her at the caller ID, her arms still around me. "It's Peter, honey, probably calling to wish you a happy birthday. Do you want to talk to him?"

"Later." I sniffle.

I sit there, listening to the quiet ring of the phone, feeling my mother's arms around me for the first time in a long time. I can tell that something has shifted, and it's both good and bad. We're moving forward, my mom and I, but in order to move forward, we have to leave Dad behind in a way. And I hate that. I want to dig my heels in and refuse, but I can't. I'm just too tired to fight it.

When my mom and dad were first dating, he took her to see *La Bohéme* at the Metropolitan Opera, and she thought it was the most romantic thing anyone had ever done for her. It's still her favorite opera, and she wanted me to see it, so

she got tickets for my birthday. To be honest, I don't really
love opera—when she and Dad used to listen to it at home,
I'd leave the room because it always seemed to me like the
sopranos were screeching—but I've never seen an opera live
before, so it could be cool.

On Saturday afternoon, we get in the car and head toward the city. I have some guilt as we pass Union High—I
should be seeing Robert in *Macbeth* tonight if I ever hope to
talk to him again. But I'm just as happy to have an excuse
to stay away from school until Monday. And I have no idea
what I would say to him right now anyway.

An hour and a half later, we're driving through the Upper
West Side toward Lincoln Center and the Met. I look at all
the huge apartment buildings and wonder what it's like to
live in New York City. I see every kind of person I could
ever imagine in just a few blocks—all ages, all colors, all
styles. I see two guys holding hands and talking to an old
lady who is walking a poodle. I see some little kids cruis-
ing down the sidewalk on scooters while their parents carry
groceries and try to keep them out of the way of a group of
teenagers who are shoving each other around in front of a
shoe store. I see cops on corners, crowds of people coming
above ground and pouring onto the sidewalk from the sub-
way, run-down delis selling hundreds of gorgeous flowers
in giant white buckets, a black plastic bag blowing off the
top of a trash can and getting caught in the corner of a bus
stop where a guy stands, nearly missing the bus he's waiting
for because he's texting like crazy on his phone, looking like
his life depends on getting his message out.

Something in my chest eases a little for the first time
since last summer. Life is moving forward outside of Union.
There's a world out here.

We pull into a parking garage and cross an insanely busy

intersection where a whole bunch of streets seem to collide
and taxis are flying through yellow lights at what seems like
ninety miles an hour. And then, there it is: Lincoln Center. It's a collection of a few huge buildings with a beautiful fountain in a courtyard in the middle of them. Behind
the fountain is the Met, with crystal chandeliers hanging in
massive glass windows that look like they're ten stories high.
I can see the audience going up a grand, red-velvet staircase
to find their seats, and the unfamiliar sensation of genuine
excitement catches me off guard. My mom smiles as we pick
up the pace past the fountain—which is shooting water impossibly high in a sort of choreographed dance—and hurry
to get to our seats before the opera starts.

"This way, this way," the usher calls as hundreds of people press forward. We hand him our tickets, which he reads
with something that looks like a ray gun, and then we're
swept up the open staircase along with everyone else. I clutch
the shiny brass banister as we pass a restaurant on one level
where people are finishing dessert and drinking coffee as if
they have all the time in the world, even though the bell is
ringing to announce that the show is starting soon. Some
people are dressed in incredibly fancy clothes, like tuxedos
and ball gowns; others are wearing jeans. Mom and I are
somewhere in the middle.

A lady helps us find our seats in the front row of the balcony that's called the Grand Tier, and we have to climb over
a woman draped in a fur coat who gives us an annoyed look
and doesn't stand up to let us pass. I try to figure out what
her problem is, but just as we sit, the lights start to go down,
and the crystal chandeliers that are hanging throughout the
room rise slowly to the ceiling like beautiful snowflakes in
reverse. One goes right past my seat—I could reach out and
touch it if I felt like getting thrown out or, more likely, ar-

rested. The massive gold velvet curtain parts as the orchestra begins to play, and there, on the stage, is an entire apartment with two guys in it—one painting, the other, writing. I can hardly believe my eyes.

It's not like I've never been to the theater before. In fact, I grew up seeing all kinds of plays with my family. But this is the biggest stage I've ever seen in my life—it looks like it could fit an entire town. And in fact, it does. The second act takes place on the streets of Paris, and there are markets and crowds of people and cafés and even horses—there are *real horses* on the stage, pulling carts while the people around them are singing their hearts out.

The singing is beautiful—it sounds very different to me in person than it does on the radio or through speakers at home. And at the Met, there are little screens in front of each seat that tell you, in English, what the singers are saying in Italian, so you know exactly what's going on. So from what I understand, there are these artist guys who live in an apartment at the top of a building, and they can't pay the rent. It's Christmas Eve and they're cold, but they have no firewood, so in order to stay warm, they start burning the pages of something that the writer, Rodolfo, has written. He doesn't seem to be too upset about it, which makes the audience laugh.

When the painter goes to a café to drink with some friends, leaving Rodolfo behind to finish his work, a beautiful girl named Mimi knocks on the door. There's something wrong with Mimi—she's sick and constantly coughing, and she faints. But Rodolfo quickly falls in love with her. And then Mimi sings this incredibly beautiful song—I guess it's called an aria—about how her name is Mimi and she embroiders flowers for a living and she's sorry to bother him.

While I'm watching the opera, time goes by like it's nothing. During the second intermission—after Act III, where it literally snows on the stage—my mom takes me to the bar in the lobby and orders a glass of champagne for us to share. She asks me if I'm enjoying the opera, but I can't even find the words to tell her what I'm feeling as I watch those singers perform. Their voices are all so different, but each one is so strong, so powerful. And they're acting, too—it's not like they're just standing there singing at the audience, which is what it always looked like to me whenever I saw opera on TV.

The bell rings for the final act. The curtain comes up on the apartment again, and for some reason, I can tell right away that things are not going to go well—the artist guys are having so much fun that something bad is bound to happen. Just as the guys are running around the apartment pretending to fight each other with swords, Mimi's friend shows up and says that Mimi is too sick to make it up the stairs. They help her into the apartment and bring out a bed for her to lie on. They go out to the street and sell their prized belongings so that they can afford a doctor and medicine for her. But I know that none of that is going to matter, and I'm right—Mimi dies right there on stage.

No one is watching when she dies—her arm just slides off the bed to the floor, and that's how the audience knows she's dead before the people in the apartment know. The whole audience is sniffling and wiping tears off their cheeks, including both my mom and me. Poor Mimi—she was too poor and too sick, and even love couldn't save her. When Rodolfo discovers she's dead, he lets out this long, loud cry, and he falls over her body, taking her in his arms and sobbing as if he couldn't bear to live another minute. I can't take my eyes off him, and when the curtain starts to come down, I want to stand up and protest that I need to know what happens next. How does Rodolfo go on without Mimi? What will he do? Will he keep writing? Will he write of nothing but Mimi for the rest of his life, or will he never be able to write her name again?

As we drive home, I try to puzzle out what the opera means. I guess there are two ways to look at it, depending on your outlook on life. If you're cynical and you think that life sucks, then the message is that love and friendship are not enough, timing is everything, and nothing can save you. If you're a positive person and you think that life is basically good, then the message is that Mimi was very lucky to find love before she died, because love and friendship and taking care of each other is all we have in the end.

I can see it both ways. And I can see how both things could be true simultaneously. Which, I think, means that *La Bohéme* is kind of brilliant.

Images from the opera are stuck in my head—the dingy but happy apartment, the friends running through the streets together laughing, the snow falling on Paris, the way Mimi's arm silently slid off the bed to the floor to show that she was gone. I can still hear her singing that aria, and tears fill my eyes. I sneak a glance at my mother to see if she's noticed, but her eyes are fixed on the road and she's a million miles away, maybe back on her first date at the opera with my dad.

As I turn my head to hide the fact that I'm wiping tears off my cheeks, I have a very strange thought: could I perform? Could I sing or act and make people feel? What would it be like to create someone else? To *be* someone else for a time? Is it a way to learn who you really are, or a way to leave yourself behind?

My first thought is to call Robert and tell him that I think I'm starting to understand why he does plays. My second thought is that Robert isn't my friend in the same way he used to be, and I should probably just leave him alone.

We get home really late, and I go up to my room and climb into bed, but I can't sleep. The opera is still ringing in my ears, like I've got the stereo on. I give up trying to sleep, get up and open my laptop to go online and find out when the next auditions are at Union. When the screen wakes up, my dad's memorial page is there—I must have forgotten to close out of it the last time I was working on it.

The page isn't live yet because I still haven't asked my mom if she'd buy the domain name for me. Well, that's not really true—the page isn't live yet because I haven't asked my mom because I still haven't chosen the photo. My cursor travels over to the photo folder, hovering for a second, and then I click on it. The folder springs open, and I choose "slideshow." My father appears, grinning, his eyes hidden by aviator sunglasses that are way too cool for him to pull off. That photo disappears, replaced by one of him in the backyard, sweaty, digging a hole for a sapling that sits next to him in a bucket. That one disappears, replaced by another and then another.

The last photo in the slideshow is one I don't remember ever really looking at before, though I remember taking it. It's from the day he left. He's standing by a car waiting to take him to the airport with his bags at his feet, and he's leaning forward, reaching for my mom to hug her. I can't see her face, but I can see his, and he's not smiling.

No wonder my mom feels guilty. Underneath the brave face dad is putting on is sadness and worry. And fear.

I drag the photo into the template box, replacing the funny image of him scowling over the coffee mug, and I enlarge it. Now that it's bigger, I can see that my mom is running to him, running into his embrace. The way her arms are stretching forward makes me think that she intends to not just hug him but hold on to him forever, to stop the plan that's been set in motion and pull him back into the house so he can plant more trees in the yard and drink more coffee in the morning.

For the first time since Dad left, I wonder why Peter and I never told them we thought the plan was a bad one.

Does that make us responsible for what happened?

Just to see how it feels, I type *Sending Dad to Iraq* in the empty caption box underneath the photo.

I delete it the moment I finish writing it.

The cursor keeps blinking, waiting for me to come up with another caption. But the truth is, there is no other caption for that photo.

I shut down my laptop and climb into bed, exhaustion taking over as I tell myself there's time, there's no rush to launch the site, I don't have to finish it right now. Later, I dream of a beautiful apartment in Paris where my mother, my brother and I laugh and eat perfect food and sip champagne out of crystal glasses as my father lies on a bed in the corner, his eyes closing, his arm silently slipping to the floor.

release (verb): to let go
(see also: breaking up)

———

20

COACH MORLEY KEEPS TRYING TO GET ME TO ADMIT THAT Regina is the nail-polish stalker, but I won't do it. If I tell Coach Morley, then she'll tell Mrs. Chen. And I figured out that the information is more useful to me if I keep it to myself. Regina knows I'm not afraid of her anymore, and now I can get her in big trouble any time I want.

While I was home sick in bed, *Gossip Girl* reruns taught me a thing or two about how to hold something over a person's head. Information is power, and I want to hang on to it as long as I can.

Three things have been keeping me going since I came back to school: my little advantage over Regina, the music from *La Bohéme* on a continuous loop in my head and art club. I had wanted to take art as my second-semester elective, but so did everyone else in the universe, and I didn't get in. So when I came back to school, I decided to try the after-school art club.

I thought about trying out for a singing club, but auditions for chorus and the a cappella group happened a few weeks ago. It's fine—I'm not quite ready yet to discover whether I can sing. It might crush me to learn that I can't, so for now, I'd rather just imagine that I can, occasionally picturing myself singing the role of Mimi, feeling silly but also excited, like I have something to look forward to.

Taking anything that ends in "club" and meets after school is guaranteed to get you labeled as lame, but fortunately, nobody cares what I'm labeled anymore. I was sort of cool for a while because of the YouTube thing, but when the rumor hit that Richie Hamilton got busted at a club in the city and might have lost his football scholarship to Ohio State, I sank back into obscurity.

There's some comfort in obscurity. It's a nice relief from trying to squeeze into a world I have no business trying to squeeze into.

I'm terrible at art. I can't draw, I can't paint, I can't sculpt. But I like it. And I love the art room. It reminds me of elementary school, with student work hanging all over the walls. Ms. Botero, the teacher, puts people's work up next to art by famous artists. If someone's drawing reminds her of a certain Picasso, she'll find a poster of the painting and put it up next to the drawing. And nine times out of ten, I can see exactly why she thought the two pieces should be side by side.

Being around all the art, and around her, quiets my brain. Until the door to the art room opens and Jamie walks in.

Ms. Botero looks up and greets Jamie as if she sees him in here every day, which can't be true because I had no idea he belonged to the art club. But I do remember that day in study hall at the beginning of the year when he was drawing that house. Jamie's a really good artist, unlike me. Which is why, when he grabs his stuff off the shelf in the back of the room and sits right next to me, I feel a little intimidated, along with everything else I feel when I'm around Jamie.

Like, hot. Literally. Not in the sense that people mean it when they're talking about passion. It's like someone just turned the heat up to a thousand degrees and I'm about to melt, my face on fire. But, come to think of it, maybe that's exactly what people mean when they talk about feeling "hot" in that way.

Ms. Botero comes to our table with an armful of books. "Jamie, I'm glad you're back. I got these for you from the library." She puts the books down on the table with a thud. "This is the book about Frank Gehry, and this is the Zaha Hadid. The Calatrava book was out, but I told the librarian to let me know when it's in."

"Thanks," Jamie says. He looks a little overwhelmed by the number of books in front of him. Ms. Botero smiles and I realize that, aside from my own mother, I've never seen an adult be nice to Jamie, not like this. Ms. Botero treats him like he's a real person, a person with ambitions and a future.

She peeks at my paper. I've been drawing the same flower over and over again, like I'm creating wallpaper or something. But really, I'm just trying to get it right.

"Nice, Rose. I love repeating motifs. Are you interested in textile design?"

I nod, having no idea what textile design is. She turns to help the person at the next table. It's quiet—no one really talks while they're working—but I have some things I have to say to Jamie Forta.

"You saved me from getting expelled," I whisper. "Thanks."

"So you're a brawler, huh?" Jamie says.

"I'm not. I'm really not. I was just mad." I don't know how much Jamie already knows about what went down, and

I wonder if maybe I should just leave well enough alone. But predictably, I can't. "Tracy and I had a fight. I didn't tell her that you…that we…um, about those two times, but she figured out that something happened between us. And she wanted to get back at me because I said I thought Matt was sleeping with Lena. So she said something to Regina. Sorry. I hope you didn't get in trouble."

He looks at my arms, at the giant scabs that are finally starting to heal after I wiped out on the track that day. "She deserved to get knocked on her ass," he says.

Relief floods through me. "I'm not really a violent person by nature. At least, I don't think I am."

"I heard you passed out and went to the hospital."

"Mono," I say. "I'm better now."

Jamie nods and takes the first book off the stack Ms. Botero gave him. I can smell his clean-laundry smell. Sunlight from the art-room windows falls across his neck and face, and I want to trace its path with my finger. Then I remember that he's not interested in me. That he said he was sorry for kissing me.

I turn back to my paper.

"You like architecture?" he asks without looking at me.

"I don't know much about it. You like it?" I say, sounding more surprised than I mean to.

He shrugs. "Ms. Botero wants me to check it out."

He flips through the book, which is filled with crazy, shiny metal structures that don't look like buildings and have names like Dancing House. Ms. Botero turns on some jazz to inspire us while we work. She turns it up a little louder than she should, which makes me like her even more.

"Look at that one," I say, pointing to a building that seems like it could fly off the page. He stares at it for a while and then looks at my paper. I can't stop myself from covering it with my scabby arm.

"It's just the same flower, over and over again. It's not good."

"I saw it before. It's good."

"It's not."

"You put yourself down a lot, you know that?"

When he says things like that to me, about me, it makes me feel naked. His ability to see right through everything actually makes me a little mad right now, given our weird circumstances. He doesn't want to be with me, so he shouldn't get to say stuff like that. I change the subject. "What are you working on?"

Jamie hesitates, and I wonder if he feels shy about his artwork. But then he opens his sketchpad and starts to show me his houses. They're not all like the one that I saw that day a million years ago. Some of them are modern, like the stuff we were looking at in the book. They're beautiful and wild. I feel strange looking at them, until I realize that what I'm feeling is pride. I'm proud that Jamie can do this.

"Jamie, these are all really beautiful."

He keeps his gaze on the page, not acknowledging that I spoke. But I need him to—I need to make sure he heard me.

"You can create beauty. Not everybody can, you know."

My words don't have the desired effect. He looks at me as if I've suddenly started speaking in a foreign language and I'm making him uncomfortable. I'm guessing Jamie doesn't get compliments on a regular basis because he obviously has no idea how to handle them. He puts his pencil down. "What do you want?" he says, sounding almost angry.

"What do I—what do you mean?" I stammer, even though I know exactly what he means.

"From me," he clarifies, looking hard at me, like he doesn't trust me.

This is my chance to tell him how much I think about both times we kissed, and how I want to kiss him again. But I'm guessing there's a right answer to his question, and telling him I want to kiss him again isn't it. My mouth dries out and I swallow. "Well, I…I'm not sure," I say, just to be safe.

He watches me for a second more and then picks up his pencil again. I look down at my stupid drawing of the same flower over and over, cursing myself, wishing I could just, for once, say the right thing in the right way.

I wait for him to start drawing, but he stares at his blank page. My brain is in knots and I'm sweating rivers down my back. My shirt is sticking to me.

"I like you," he says. "You're smart. Pretty." My breath catches in my throat. I've never been called pretty by anyone except my dad, and that doesn't really count, as much as I would like it to. "I'm not right for you, Rose" is what finally comes out of Jamie's mouth. "I'm different. And you're… young," he adds.

The way he says it is not mean or condescending, but it embarrasses me. And I'm dangerous when I get embarrassed—I lash out and say things I don't mean. Which, of course, is exactly what happens.

"Too young for you to *do it* with, you mean?"

After a second during which we're both in shock, Jamie stands, leaving his sketchpad and books on the table, and walks out the door before I understand what's happening. Ms. Botero looks at the door, confused, and then her gaze travels to me. I'm paralyzed for a second, and then my brain untwists and commands me to get off my ass. I run into the hall. He's already at the other end, heading down the stairs. "Jamie, wait!" He doesn't. I sprint, finally catching up with him at his locker. I struggle for air. "I'm sorry," I manage to say.

His eyes are dark as he looks down at me. "You think that's what I meant? You think I'm like that?"

"I don't. I don't think that. I'm just... I don't get any of this."

He turns from me and opens his locker. There's nothing on the inside of the door—no pictures, no notes, nothing. He grabs his army jacket.

I lower my voice. "You kissed me at homecoming," I start. Then I stop. Then I start again. "Then I kissed you on Valentine's Day, but you told me that I shouldn't have—"

"That's not what I said."

"It is."

"No. I said I shouldn'ta kissed you."

"What's the difference?"

"It's on me—it's my fault."

"Why, Jamie?"

"I told you—a lotta reasons. I was with somebody. I got problems. And you're fourteen—"

"Fifteen," says a voice behind us. I look over his shoulder and see Regina in her uniform. I wonder how long she's been there, how much she heard, and how the heck she knows it was my birthday. "She just turned fifteen."

Jamie turns around and stands in front of me. I step to the side so I can see her—as far as I'm concerned, I don't need protection from Regina Deladdo anymore—but she doesn't even look at me. Her eyes are glued to him.

"I've been waiting for you at Cavallo's," she says.

"I told you I wouldn't be there."

"I didn't believe you."

"I bet you do now," he says. I'm surprised by how harsh he sounds—I've never heard him talk like that before. Her eyes flicker over me, taking me in. I wait for a bitchy comment, but she just looks back at Jamie.

"I'm sorry," she says. It seems like it costs her a lot.

"Tell Rose that, not me," Jamie responds.

I know there's no way she can do what he's asking—it's probably physically impossible for her.

"What about prom?" Her voice shakes.

"What about it?"

She clenches her jaw. If I didn't know any better, I'd think she was about to cry.

"Are we going?" she asks, emphasizing each word through gritted teeth, trying to keep it together.

"What do you think?"

Her breath escapes in a giant exhale as if she's been punched in the stomach. "Are you going with her?"

"I don't know. You wanna go to prom with me, Rose?" he says without taking his angry eyes off Regina.

This is it—this is the payback I've been dreaming of for months now, for everything Regina has done to me. But I can't enjoy it, no matter how much I wish I could. First of all, he's just asking me to piss her off—it probably never would have occurred to him to do it if she hadn't brought it up. But also, Jamie is crushing Regina, breaking her twisted little heart right in front of *me,* the person she hates more than anyone in the world these days. It's got to suck. As Regina turns away and starts up the stairs without waiting to hear my answer, I realize that I feel sorry for her.

I practically kick myself. How dumb can I be? I'm never going to survive high school if I can't even be happy when my enemies get what they deserve.

Regina stops at the top of the landing and looks down on us, hatred blazing in her eyes again, and the pity vanishes as if I'd never felt it in the first place. So does the rush of courage I had when I first saw her standing there.

"After everything my family and me did for you, Forta, you're gonna regret this," she says.

Regina disappears into the dark of the stairwell as a little chill creeps up my spine—I know firsthand what kind of revenge she's capable of when she puts her mind to it. Jamie slams his locker shut with a bang so loud that it reverberates through the empty halls. He stalks away without so much as another word to me.

I have no idea what just happened, but I think it's very possible that a) Jamie and Regina are officially broken up and b) I might be going to the prom.

retribution (*adjective*): payback
(*see also*: Regina's revenge)

———

21

"HIYA, ROSE, I'M SHERRI. ARE WE WEARIN' IT UP OR DOWN for tonight?" asks my stylist as she plays with sections of my hair, probably wondering how the heck she's going to do anything with all the limp, lame stuff on my head.

I've never been one of those girls who fantasize about the prom—I think those are the same girls who dream about their weddings—but I'll admit that I'm excited for tonight. I got a beautiful dress, and I'm having my hair and makeup done at a salon. Basically, I'm not making any of the dumb grooming mistakes I made with homecoming.

"I think I'd like to wear it up in a twist or something. Will my hair do that?"

"Of course it will! We can get your gorgeous hair to do whatever we want. That's the beauty of product." She grabs a spray bottle. "This is just water. I'm gonna wet your hair down so we can put some serious gunk in it, okay?"

I nod and she sprays, making me look like a drowned rat.

"You a senior?"

"Freshman."

"Wow! A freshman and you're goin' to prom with all the juniors and seniors? That's huge! Congratulations! Who's the lucky guy?"

"Um, he's a friend...I think," I say.

"Ooh, I love that. I love when you don't exactly know. It's so exciting, isn't it?"

I like Sherri's positive spin on things. But the truth is, I have no idea what I am to Jamie other than a great way to piss off Regina.

Sherri sprays a huge amount of mousse into her hand and starts rubbing it in my hair. Now I look like a drowned water rat with shaving cream on its head. "You know, my baby sister is a senior at Union now. Michelle Vicenza. You know her?" Sherri asks.

"Michelle's your sister?"

She nods, smiling. "Yup. I can't believe she's graduating."

If Sherri is Michelle's sister, Michelle is getting her hair done here. And if Michelle is getting her hair done here, the rest of the squad probably is, too. Low-grade panic sets in as I scan the salon for emergency exits, replaying Regina's threat in my head. I remind myself that I can handle her—I did knock her down with the intention of punching her, after all.

"So you know Michelle?" Sherri asks again.

"She was friends with my brother before he graduated, and my best friend—well, the girl who used to be my best friend—is on the cheerleading team with her," I say, noticing that Sherri actually looks a lot like Michelle, just with big, blond hair.

"Sounds like there's a story there," Sherri says, turning on the blow-dryer and saving me from having to say anything else. She combs my hair straight up while she dries it. I watch my flat hair get impossibly huge in the mirror and wonder if I'm going to end up with a giant bird's nest on my head. Maybe it's not such a good idea to have the head cheerleader's sister doing my hair for prom.

The salon door opens, and the inevitable happens. My palms get all sweaty as Michelle, Regina and Susan come in. Michelle comes over and kisses her sister on the cheek. She waves at me in the mirror, but she doesn't look like her usual cheerful self. She stands there, looking back and forth between me and Sherri, like she's waiting for Sherri to turn the dryer off so she can say something, but Susan pulls her away. I keep an eye on Regina in case she decides to come after me, but she doesn't even look my way. The cheerleaders sit down in the reception area and start flipping through hairstyle magazines, looking for up-dos they like.

I heard Regina is going with Anthony Parrina tonight. He's the hockey player from West Union who Jamie high-sticked in the neck, which got him kicked off the team. I guess she's trying to make Jamie jealous. Or maybe she's hoping Anthony will try and beat the crap out of Jamie.

Sherri turns the dryer off, takes a pick and starts teasing my hair into a giant mass. I have no idea why she's doing this. A stylist comes and leads Susan and Michelle to the back to get their hair washed, but not Regina. She continues to flip through her magazine.

"I'm gonna put a little spray on now, okay?" Apparently "a little spray" does not mean the same thing to Sherri that it means to most other people. She practically uses an entire can on my head.

Then, miraculously, she takes the giant mass of sticky, matted hair and transforms it into a beautiful French twist in about thirty seconds. Suddenly I'm a totally different person. She opens a drawer in the little table next to me and pulls out a piece of white cardboard with tiny rhinestones on it. "Let's put some bling in your hair. I love these," she says as she applies them. I turn my head and the light catches the glass at various points. It's pretty. *I'm* pretty. I barely recognize myself.

Regina's phone rings, and I look at her before I can stop myself. She meets my eyes for a second before she takes her phone out of her bag and goes outside to answer it.

"What do you think, Rose?" Sherri asks, turning me around in the chair and handing me a mirror so I can check out the twist on the back of my head.

"It looks beautiful. I really didn't think my hair would do that," I say. "Thank you so much."

"You are so welcome! You have a great time tonight, okay?" She smiles the famous Vicenza smile and goes to check in with Michelle and Susan. Regina comes back inside and sits down near reception, a strange expression on her face that I can't read but which makes me nervous anyway.

I dig into my pockets and pull out my money, leaving a tip on Sherri's table. The next thing I have to do is pay, which means going to reception. I glue my eyes to the desk and head straight there, not looking at anything else. I see Regina look up out of the corner of my eye, but I turn my back on her. I'm hoping that she'll get called into the salon before I have to turn around, but it doesn't happen.

"Nice hair," she says.

She's being sarcastic, of course. I hand the receptionist my cash, turn and walk past her to the door.

"It's a waste, though."

Michelle suddenly appears at the desk with one of those

black plastic salon drapes on, her hair wet and long. I have no idea what Regina means or why Michelle is standing here.

"Regina. Don't."

Regina turns to Michelle with that strange look on her face. It's like she's sort of freaked out but really happy about it.

"Leave Rose alone," Michelle says.

"I was just going to tell her—"

"Just stop!"

"Tell me what?" I ask, a creeping sensation of panic starting across my skull.

"Call Jamie, okay, Rose?"

"What happened?" I ask. "Is he okay?"

"Just call him," Michelle says as she takes Regina by the arm.

"You won't get him," says Regina, "but don't worry. You can always sell your dress on eBay. Although, if it's as ugly as the one you wore to homecoming..." Regina spits the words out with a harsh laugh as Michelle yanks her backward into the salon.

"I'm sorry, Rose," says Michelle. "I didn't know. I swear."

Jamie's phone goes straight to voice mail each time I call.

Is he ignoring me? Is he mad at me? Is he hurt? In the hospital? Dead?

I'm trying as hard as I can to stay calm, to breathe and not let my brain go to the worst-case scenario. It isn't easy—my life has been all about worst-case scenarios for the past year.

I can hear my mom rummaging around in the closet outside my room, looking for the digital camera so she can take pictures while she's lecturing me about how I'm supposed to come straight home after this dance or I'll never be allowed out of the house again.

I know that she doesn't need the camera or the lecture.

It's 6:45. Jamie is supposed to pick me up at 7:00. My hair and makeup are done, but I'm in cutoffs and one of my dad's shirts. My blue sheath dress is laid out on the bed and my super-high heels are still in the box. I can't make myself put any of it on because I know there's no point.

When I hear someone pull up outside at 6:55, half of me wants to run down the stairs and the other half wants to hide under the bed. I decide to go to the front door like a normal human being. My mother announces from somewhere on the second floor that she's still looking for the camera, she'll be down in a minute and I'm not to go anywhere until she gets there. I open the door to see Angelo getting out of his car.

His lifts his hand to wave, but he doesn't smile and that's when I know for sure that something bad happened. Angelo always smiles, even when he shouldn't, which is probably why he gets into trouble all the time. I'm suddenly sick to my stomach.

I meet him on the sidewalk in front of my house and realize that he's wearing a tuxedo that's a little too small on him.

"You look really nice, Angelo," I say, putting off asking what I know I have to ask.

"Thanks, Sweater. You know, you look pretty nice yourself. You clean up good."

I look down at my cutoffs and the shirt I wore to the salon. Tracy taught me that trick—wear a button-down shirt to the salon so you don't have to pull anything off over your head and risk messing up your hair when you put on your nice clothes later.

I'm still staring down at my shirt. I can't make myself look at Angelo.

"Jamie ain't comin', Rose."

I nod, willing myself not to cry. Angelo hates it when girls cry.

"What happened?" I ask. "He changed his mind?"

"No, nothin' like that. He'd be here if he could. But he's in jail."

I can't process what Angelo is telling me. "He's in jail," I repeat like a parrot.

"Regina got him busted for buyin' with his fake ID." I just stare at Angelo dumbly. "I guess, uh, Regina asked Michelle to ask Jamie to buy for the party tonight, and he said yes because it was Michelle askin', not Regina. And then the bitch called the cops and told them to bust him at the store."

"And they put him in jail?"

"Yeah. Fake ID and buyin' for minors. His dad told his cop buddies not to go easy on him, and he ain't gonna bail Jamie out till tomorrow, either. He's the kinda asshole who would let his kid sit in jail all night just to prove somethin'."

Regina is a genius. An evil genius.

"I went to see him and he asked me to take you tonight."

I can't believe it. Jamie is worrying that I'm going to be bummed about missing the prom while he's sitting in jail.

Angelo pulls at the lapel of his tux. "He rented this for himself so it don't fit me so great, but I'm ready to hit that hotel ballroom if you are."

I actually manage to laugh a little. Angelo pretends to look offended.

"What? Dontcha think I look good?"

"You do. But aren't you already going with someone?"

"Nah. Fuck This Shit is going to play at one of the after-parties, but I don't wanna go to no—" He stops. "Uh, sorry, I didn't mean that. I mean, I wanna go if you wanna go, but…"

"Thanks, Angelo, but I don't want to go without Jamie."

"Yeah. I told him you'd say that. He made me promise to

come over anyway." Angelo tugs at his bow tie, which seems to be strangling him. "Fuckin' Regina. I wish Jamie woulda let you punch her when you had the chance."

This time I really laugh, knowing he's only half joking.

Angelo pokes gently at one of the sparkly things in my hair. "I can tell he likes you, Rose. And he's really, really sorry." He reaches into the bulging pocket of his tuxedo jacket and pulls out a wadded-up T-shirt and a crinkled piece of paper folded a bunch of times. "The T-shirt's clean, I swear. I can't say about the note one way or the other."

He winks, turns and heads back to his car, pulling off the bow tie and throwing it through the window before he gets in. Then he starts up the engine and guns it a few times before he drives down my street, his long hair blowing out the window, vintage Nine Inch Nails blaring. He honks the horn once as he turns the corner.

I hold up his gift and see that it's the Neko Case concert shirt he was wearing on Valentine's Day. I look at the note, almost afraid to open it.

The writing isn't as neat as it was on the card that came with the carnation. It's ragged, like it was written in a car— maybe the back of a cop car. Maybe they didn't cuff him because of his dad.

Rose. Like I said. I am not right for you. I'm different. Believe me. Be good.

Why do I feel like he's breaking up with me when I'm not even sure we're together? And what is it that makes him so sure he's different from me?

I want to call Tracy. But how can I, after weeks have gone by and I still haven't talked to her to see if she's okay after what happened with Matt?

I suddenly hate myself for being scared of things this year.

I was scared of people knowing I like a guy who has to take remedial English. I was scared of standing up for myself when Regina was doing her psychotic graffiti. I was scared of losing Tracy to the cheerleaders and to sex, and I thought if I just buried my head in the sand, nothing bad would happen. And yet, bad is exactly what did happen.

Bad things happen whether you're scared or not, so you might as well not bother being scared. It's a waste of time.

I look back at the house and see my mother standing at the front door, uncertain, camera in one hand and phone in the other. She holds up the phone to tell me I have a call. I sprint up the walk into the house and grab it from her before she can even tell me who it is.

"Jamie?" I gasp, sounding as desperate as I feel.

"It's Tracy." For a second, I'm not sure my ears are working right. "I heard. Are you okay, Rosie?"

The sound of my ex-best friend calling me "Rosie" floods me with such relief that my legs go wobbly. I can't believe she's calling me—she knew I'd want to talk to her, no matter what happened between us before. I stagger up the stairs to my bedroom, sink onto my bed and stare up at the ceiling, no longer concerned about messing up my hair.

"Rosie?" she says again.

"Yeah, I'm okay. Are you?"

"I'll be fine."

Silence.

"I should have called, Trace."

"It's okay. I know why you didn't."

"I'm really sorry." My voice comes out in a whisper.

"Me, too. I didn't know Regina would do that," Tracy says.

"I'm kind of glad she did. I never would have gone after her if she hadn't."

"That was totally crazy, Rose. You were scary. I've never seen you do anything like that." I've never seen me do anything like that, either. I wish I could say that nothing like that will ever happen again, but if I've learned anything this year, it's that I can't make any promises as far as my behavior goes.

"Is Jamie really in jail?" she asks.

"His dad's going to leave him there overnight to make a point." I try to imagine what jail is like. Union is a small town, so I'm going to guess that Jamie's not in danger—I can forget the prison images embedded in my head from HBO shows. Probably the worst that will happen is he might have to share a cell with somebody who had too much to drink at Morton's and puked down the front of his shirt after grabbing at a cocktail waitress or something. But I'm still scared for him.

I turn my head and see the blue flower I drew on the wall way back in October while I was on the phone with Peter, the day after Tracy's Halloween party. It seems like a million years ago that Peter said he had asked Jamie to look out for me. I bet Jamie never thought that saying yes would land him in jail.

"So, um, you did it, huh? How was it?" I ask, trying not to sound judgmental or ask if they used a condom. I know that if I want to keep talking to Tracy, I should put off that question until later. Much later.

"Terrible," she says in her matter-of-fact voice. "Ms. Maso was right. And you were right, too. He's a total jerk and I should have saved it for someone else. If you feel like it, you can say 'I told you so.'"

"Yeah, well, so can you, so let's pretend we both already said it and forget about it."

"Okay. So, did you get your hair done?"

There are a million things we should be talking about,

like what happened between us this year and how it got so ugly, but really, she'd much rather talk about my hair. And for once, so would I.

I tell her about Sherri and the bling, and my shoes and my blue dress. I tell her about how Jamie sent Angelo over in his tux in case I still wanted to go to the prom. I tell her about what happened at the salon with Regina and Michelle. It feels so good to tell her things after keeping everything to myself for so long, I can't believe I survived without doing it.

"So, is Jamie your boyfriend?"

I look down at the note that is still in my hand. Does Jamie really think that he can get rid of me by saying "I'm different"? It just makes me want to kiss him again.

"He's not my boyfriend. We kissed twice, and he said we shouldn't have."

"But he asked you to the prom."

"Not really. He did it just to piss off Regina, I think."

"Rosie, Jamie doesn't seem like the kind of guy who would bother with the prom just to piss someone off."

"All I know, Trace, is that I like him." I hesitate. "I want to be with him."

"Then you have to do something. If I were you…" she starts.

"If you were me, what?" I ask.

"If I were you, I'd tell Mrs. Chen everything, from the first time Regina threatened you and wrote graffiti on your locker, to what she did to Jamie today."

"But what if she makes good on her threat, Trace? I mean, what if she takes it out on you and figures out a way to get you thrown off the team?"

"Then I guess I'm off the team. It's not like I want to be around Lena anyway," she says.

"But—"

"It doesn't matter anymore, Rose," she says. She sounds really sad, and I wonder if she means that it doesn't matter because she doesn't care about cheerleading anymore, or it doesn't matter because she's not with Matt. "Turn the bitch in."

"What if getting her in trouble just makes her crazier next year?" I ask.

"You can't worry about that now. Regina deserves some serious payback. Especially after what she just did—I mean, Jamie is sitting in a jail cell right now, and you're both missing the prom because of her. Morley's been trying to get you to tell Mrs. Chen, right? Well, here's your chance. If you email now, I bet she'll get it just in time to stop Regina when she's trying to pick up her tickets at the hotel ballroom, in front of everyone. It'll be totally perfect."

I've been keeping the secret about Regina for so long that the idea of releasing it into the wild is mildly terrifying. I look at my laptop sitting on my desk, waiting for me to take action.

"Will you help me?" I ask, feeling sick to my stomach.

"I'll be there in five. I want to see this 'bling' in your hair anyway," she says, hanging up before I can say another word. I imagine her yelling to her mom that she's coming to my house as she runs out her red front door, just like she's been doing ever since we were allowed to cross the street by ourselves. My best friend is coming over to help me. I feel calmer than I have in weeks.

I look out the window over the back garden, where the dogwoods are in bloom and my mother's flowers are starting to come up. I don't like getting people in trouble. But Regina Deladdo deserves this. I have no idea what the fallout is going to be, but Tracy's right—I can't worry about that now. I was saving this information for the perfect moment, and the perfect moment is here.

No fear.

I go to the desk and open the laptop. The screen springs back to life.

★ ★ ★ ★ ★

escalate (*verb*): to increase in intensity, often in reference to a conflict or war; to get worse
(*see also:* Rose Zarelli's sophomore year)

CONFESSIONS OF AN ALMOST GIRLFRIEND
Coming in 2013 from Harlequin TEEN.

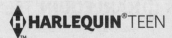

The Clann

Available Now

Coming October 2012!

The powerful magic users of the Clann have always feared and mistrusted vampires. But when Clann golden boy Tristan Coleman falls for Savannah Colbert—the banished half Clann, half vampire girl who is just coming into her powers—a fuse is lit that may explode into war. Forbidden love, dangerous secrets and bloodlust combine in a deadly hurricane that some will not survive.